WARCRAFT

Also available from Titan Books and Christie Golden

WARCRAFT: DUROTAN
THE OFFICIAL MOVIE PREQUEL

THE OFFICIAL MOVIE NOVELIZATION

WARCRAFT

by CHRISTIE GOLDEN

LEGENDARY
TITAN BOOKS

Warcraft: The Official Movie Novelization
Print edition ISBN: 9781783295593
E-book edition ISBN: 9781783295616

Published by Titan Books
A division of Titan Publishing Group Ltd
144 Southwark St, London SE1 0UP

First edition: June 2016
10 9 8 7 6 5 4 3 2 1

A CIP catalogue record for this title is available from the British Library.

Printed and bound in the USA.

LEGENDARY

LEGENDARY.COM   TITANBOOKS.COM

WARCRAFT

PROLOGUE

Moonlight bathed the throne room of Stormwind, causing the the white stone of the empty royal chair to glow as if with its own deep radiance, and transforming the golden lions crouched at its base to silver beasts with hollowed eyes. Cool, milky light caught the clean lines of weapons on display, and turned the shadows in the corners, where its pale fingers could not reach, into pools of infinite darkness. In the fey glow, someone with a keen imagination might think the decorative suits of armor standing sentry were not so empty after all.

The moon's illumination was challenged by the light of a single lamp, which shone its warm, ruddy glow on the intent face of a boy. He held two carved toys in his hands. One was a soldier, wearing a painted version of the armor that loomed in various places of the quiet room. The other was a hunched beast—green, with tusks and an axe that was fully half again the size of its wooden adversary.

On the floor were other soldiers and beasts. Most of the toy monsters were still standing.

Most of the toy soldiers had been toppled.

The room brightened as the door was opened. The boy turned, displeased at having been interrupted, and glowered momentarily at the figure who entered before turning back to his playtime.

"So," the man said, his voice youthful, "this is where you've been hiding."

A prince does not hide, the boy thought. *He goes where he wants to when he wants to be alone. That's not hiding.*

The man moved beside him. In the faint lamp light, his hair did not look quite so gray, nor was the scar that ran from chin to eye quite as ugly as it appeared in the daylight. He gazed down at the scene the boy was reenacting. "How goes the battle?"

As if he can't see it. As if he doesn't remember.

The boy said nothing at first, staring at the small green toys, and then he said in an angry voice, "Every orc deserves to die. When I'm king, I'll be like Lothar, and kill them *all*!"

"Lothar is a soldier," the man said, not unkindly. "He fights because it is his duty. *You* will be a king. *Your* duty will be to find a just peace. Don't you think we've had enough of war?"

The boy did not answer. A just peace. Enough of war.

Impossible.

"I *hate* them!" he shouted. His voice rang, too loud in the stillness. Tears suddenly burned in his eyes.

"I know," the man said quietly, and his lack of judgment of the boy's outburst calmed the youth somewhat. "But war is not always the answer. You need to understand that not all orcs are evil, even if it seems that way."

The boy frowned and threw the man a skeptical glance. Khadgar was very wise, but what he was saying seemed unbelievable to the boy.

"You know," Khadgar continued, "the orcs came from another world, far away from ours." He lifted his hand and moved his fingers. A reddish-orange ball appeared in his hand. The boy watched, interested now. He loved to see Khadgar work his magic. The orb spun, green energy crackling around it. "It was dying," Khadgar continued. "It was consumed by a dark magic called the fel." The prince's eyes grew wide as the strange green glow seemed to eat away at the brown, dusty-looking world. "The orcs had to escape. If they didn't…they would die with it."

The prince had no sympathy to spare for orcs or their dying world. His fingers tightened around the toy orc he clutched in his hand. "So, those green monsters invaded *our* world!"

"They weren't all green when they came to Azeroth. Bet you didn't know that."

The prince stayed silent rather than admit his ignorance, but he was curious now.

"Only the ones poisoned by the fel magic,"

Khadgar continued. "It changed them. But we once met an orc who resisted it. One who almost stopped this war from ever happening. His name... was Durotan."

No windows were needed in the Chamber of Air. It was as its name stated, a chamber of air; in it, and of it.

Strangers to this place might marvel at the sight, might gasp in beauty and fear both, and wonder how it was the Council of Six could stand here and not have concerns for their safety. But there would be no strangers, not ever, not here in the Violet Citadel of the Kirin Tor.

Like magic, the Chamber was not for anyone but mages.

The blue sky and white clouds that served for walls and ceiling set off the colors of gold and purple that decorated the stone floor. The floor was also inlaid with a symbol—a stylized, watchful eye, and the boy who stepped inside and stood in the center of that room thought it particularly appropriate today.

He was eleven, of fair to middling height, with brown hair and eyes that changed from blue to green depending on the light. He was dressed in a white tunic, and he was the sole focus of attention of the entire Council of the Kirin Tor.

They stood high above him on a ringed platform, clad in violet robes embroidered with the same Eye that gazed up from the floor. They and the Eyes they wore stared down at the boy as he himself might have peered at an insect. He was unconcerned about their regard, more curious than anything, and peered at them boldly, arching a brow.

One of the figures, a tall, thin man with a beard as white as the magic that flowed along the tower's walls, met the boy's gaze and nodded almost imperceptibly. He began to speak, and his sonorous voice echoed impressively in the vast chamber.

"There is a theory that every star in the sky is a world," Archmage Antonidas said. "And that each of these worlds is alive with beings of its own. What says our Novice to this concept?"

The Novice answered promptly. "No world can equal Azeroth," he replied. "The beauty of Azeroth, its vitality and abundance, are unique."

"Who can be trusted to care for such a treasure?"

"One who can marshal the forces of magic to keep our world safe. The Guardian."

"I see." There was the barest hint of a smile on Antonidas's thin lips. The Novice wondered if he should modulate his voice. Sound a bit more humble. But honestly, he'd memorized all this *ages* ago.

"*All* the forces?" Antonidas continued.

"No," the Novice replied promptly. "The dark forces are forbidden. The dark forces are the mirror of corruption." He realized he was starting to sound sing-songy and bit his lip hard. It wouldn't do for them to think he didn't take this seriously.

"The dark forces," he said, solemnly this time, "turn the user back against his own intentions."

"And what do we learn from this?"

"That magic is dangerous and must be kept from those without instruction. No race of men, no dwarf, gnome, or elf—none but the Kirin Tor must use magic."

This is all just for us, the Novice thought, watching the flow of the silvery-white liquid chase itself around the walls and ceiling of the Chamber of Air. *Not because we're greedy, but because we know how to handle it.*

He watched Antonidas carefully and saw the archmage's shoulders relax. They were done with the first part, and he hadn't messed up. Good.

The elderly mage smiled a little, his eyes kind. "We sense your power, Medivh," he told the Novice. "We admire your focus, your appetite for knowledge. We probe and test it as best we can, but sadly, the most important question is one that cannot be answered until it is too late."

Medivh stiffened. Too late? What did Antonidas mean?

"The life of a Guardian demands sacrifice that you cannot begin to understand. Yet we ask you now, as a boy, to bind yourself forever to the wheel of this vocation."

Antonidas's eyes narrowed and his voice grew harder. *Here we go,* Medivh thought. "Are you willing to prepare yourself, in all ways, for the day you will become the master of the Tower of Karazhan?"

Medivh didn't hesitate. "I am."

"Then *prove yourself!*"

The creature was born of the shadows the light-magic could not reach. It went from a sliver of darkness into a fully formed, ink-black, distorted *thing* that towered over the boy. Medivh instinctively dropped into combat stance, the response drilled into him so rigorously he reacted even though he was taken utterly by surprise. It opened a mouth crowded with teeth as long as his arm and emitted a series of sounds that made Medivh's gut clench. As it towered over him, he saw that it had no natural depth or contours, which only made it more terrifying. It was a thing of nightmares, its shadow-hands ending in claws that looked razor sharp—

No *natural depth* or *contours*.

It wasn't real. Of course it wasn't real! Medivh spared a quick glance around the room and—there, the mage Finden mumbling into his thick, bushy white beard. The boy struggled to suppress a grin.

He lifted his hand. A small orb of glowing white energy formed in his palm and Medivh hurled it— directly at Finden. The white ball flattened into a small rectangle that wrapped itself around Finden's jaw with so much force that the elder sorceror stumbled. His fellows caught him; the only injury was to the mage's perhaps overly inflated ego.

The shadow-thing disappeared. Medivh looked up at Antonidas, allowing the smallest of smiles to quirk his mouth. Antonidas's eyes danced as their gazes met.

"Not what I had expected," the archmage allowed, "but... effective."

The surface beneath Medivh's feet began to

move. Startled, he hopped backward, watching as the inlaid pupil of the Eye of the Kirin Tor started to open like an iris. Medivh stood, mesmerized, as a pool of bubbling water began to rise up from the opening, and gasped sharply when he realized what he had taken to be churning water was in fact a white flame, burning, impossibly, in the watery depths.

Above him, Antonidas murmured an incantation and floated gently down from the ring above to stand beside his pupil. He smiled, with what looked to the boy like pride.

"Give me your hand, Medivh," Antonidas said. Wordlessly, the boy obeyed, placing his small, pale hand in the papery skin of his master's. The archmage turned the hand over so Medivh's palm faced upward. "The day will come when you are called to serve."

Medivh's gaze flickered from Antonidas's seamed, serious visage to the white flame, then back. "The oath you pledge is forged in light," the mage went on. One of his hands continued to clasp Medivh's, the other, with a deftness perhaps surprising in hands so aged, rolled back the boy's white sleeve to his elbow. Gently, Antonidas turned Medivh so that he faced the fire which burned in the depths of the pool. The boy winced: the unnatural, but beautiful, white fire was hotter than he had expected. His eyes fell on his extended arm and he felt a knot of unease in the pit of his stomach, a cold lump in the face of the impossible heat.

"No mage shall be your peer; none, your master.

Your responsibility will be absolute."

Antonidas released Medivh's hand and began to push him forward. The boy's eyes widened and his breath came quickly. Whatever happened, he knew it wouldn't kill him. The Council wouldn't kill him.

Would they?

Would they let him die if he was found somehow wanting? The thought had never occurred to him until now, and the coldness inside him increased, spread through him with every beat of his rapidly pounding heart, chilling him even as he wanted to avert his face from the heat of the magical fire. Instinct screamed at him to yank his hand back, but the pressure on his back pushed him inexorably forward. Mouth dry, Medivh tried to swallow as his arm came closer to the flicking white tongue of flame.

Suddenly the flame snaked outward, wrapping itself around Medivh's extended arm in an agonizing embrace. Tears formed in his eyes as the flame seared a pattern on his skin. He bit back a cry and pulled back his arm. The smell of his own burned flesh filled his nostrils as he stared down at the once-unblemished skin.

The Eye of the Kirin Tor, still smoking, gazed back at him. He had been accepted. Branded.

The pain still ripped at him, but awe chased it away. Slowly, Medivh lifted his gaze to the men and women who had stood in judgment upon him mere moments before. All six of them now stood with their heads bowed in a gesture of acceptance... and respect.

No mage shall be your peer; none, your master.

"Guardian," said Antonidas, and his voice trembled with pride.

1

The journey had been long and brutal, harder than Durotan, son of Garad, son of Durkosh, had ever anticipated.

The Frostwolf orc clan had been among the last to answer the call of the warlock Gul'dan. Although ancient stories told that the Frostwolf clan had once been nomads, long ago one chieftain, almost as loyal to Frostfire Ridge as he was to his clan, had begged the Spirits for permission to stay. His plea had been granted, and for a time nearly as long as their guardian, Greatfather Mountain, had existed, the clan had stayed in the north; separate, proud, strong in the face of challenges.

But Greatfather Mountain had cracked open, bleeding liquid fire upon their village, and the Frostwolf clan had been forced to become nomads once again. From place to place they had wandered. Even though the clan faced great hardship, the warlock Gul'dan—a stooped and ominous figure whose skin was an unnatural shade of green—had been forced to ask them twice to join his Horde before Durotan had finally, seeing no other choice, accepted.

Gul'dan had come to the beleaguered Frostwolves with promises that Durotan was determined the warlock would honor. Draenor, their home and that of the Spirits of Earth, Air, Water, Fire, and Life, was dying. But Gul'dan claimed he knew of another world, where the proud race of orcs could hunt fat prey, drink their fill of cool, clean water, and live as they were meant to—with passion and pride. Not groveling in the dust, emaciated victims of despair, while their whole world withered and died about them.

Yet it was dusty and emaciated Frostwolves who now trudged the last few miles of their exhausting journey. For over a full course of the moon, his clan had been on the march from the north to this desiccated, scorching place. They had known little of water, less of food. Some had died, unable to endure the physical demands of walking so many leagues. Durotan wondered if the ordeal would be worth it. He prayed to the Spirits, so weak they could barely hear, that it was.

As he marched, Durotan carried with him two weapons that he had inherited upon his father's death. One was Thunderstrike, a spear carved with runes and adorned with leather wrapping. Notches had been carved into its wooden surface, each representing a kill. A horizontal slash stood for a beast's life; a vertical one, that of an orc. While horizontal notches all but covered the shaft, there were several vertical ones as well.

The other weapon once used by his father, and his father Durkosh before him, was the axe Sever. Durotan made sure it was always as sharp as when it had been forged, and it more than lived up to its name.

Durotan went on foot, allowing others who were weaker or ill to ride the great white frost wolves that served the clan as both mounts and lifetime companions. Beside him strode his second-in-command, Orgrim Doomhammer, the massive weapon for which his line was named slung over his broad, brown back. Orgrim was one of a small handful who knew Durotan bone-deep, and whom he trusted not only with his own life, but with those of his mate and future child.

Draka, warrior, mate, and mother-to-be, rode her wolf Ice beside Durotan. For most of the journey, as was fitting, she had marched beside her mate. But eventually Durotan asked her to ride. "If not for your sake or the child's, for mine," he had said. "It is exhausting, wondering if you will drop in the dust."

She had grinned at him, her lips curving over her small tusks, her dark eyes sparkling with the humor that he loved so well. "Huh," she said. "I will ride, if only because I fear you will topple over trying to pick me up."

In the beginning, spirits had been high. The clan had faced and defeated a terrible foe, the Red

Walkers, but they had also learned that they could no longer expect aid from the weakened Spirits.

Durotan had assured his clan that they would always stay Frostwolves, even if they joined together with other orcs in the Horde. The thought of meat, fruit, water, clean air—things the clan badly needed—was heartening. The trouble, Durotan realized, was that the clan—and, truth be told, he himself—had departed thinking that their troubles would be over soon. The journey's hardships had beaten that out of them.

He looked over his shoulder at his clan. They shuffled, they did not stride; and there was a bone-weariness about them that made his heart ache to see.

The light touch of his mate's hand on his shoulder drew his attention back to her. He gave her a forced, weary smile.

"You look like you should be riding, not me," she said, gently.

"There will be time enough for all of us to ride," he said, "when we have enough meat that our wolves stretch out with bulging bellies beside us."

Her gaze flickered from her own stomach back to his and her eyes narrowed teasingly. He laughed, surprised by the mirth, almost convinced he had forgotten how to. Draka always knew how to calm him, whether with laughter, love, or the occasional punch to help him get his head back on his shoulders. And their child—

The real reason, he knew, why he had left Frostfire Ridge. Draka was the only Frostwolf who was pregnant. And in the end, Durotan could not find a way to justify bringing his child—*any* orc child—into a world that could not nourish it.

Durotan reached to touch the belly he had teased her about, laying his enormous brown hand on it and the small life within. The words he had told his clan, on the eve of their departure, flitted through his mind: *Whatever the lore says about what was done in the past, whatever the rituals stipulate we do, whatever rules or laws or traditions there are—there is one law, one tradition, which must not be violated. And that is that a chieftain must do whatever is truly best for the clan.*

He felt a strong, rapid pressure against his palm and grinned in delight as his child seemed to agree that his decision had been the right one. "This one would march beside you already," Draka said.

Before Durotan could respond, someone shouted for him. "Chieftain! They they are!!"

With a final caress, Durotan turned his attention to Kurvorsh, one of the scouts he had sent on ahead. Most Frostwolves kept their hair; it was only prudent in the frigid north. But Kurvorsh, like many others, had opted to shave his skull once they had traveled south, leaving only a single long lock he tied off. His wolf halted in front of Durotan, her tongue lolling from the heat.

Durotan tossed Kurvorsh a water skin. "Drink first, then report." Kurvorsh swallowed a few thirsty gulps, then handed the skin back to his chieftain.

"I saw a line of structures along the horizon,"

he said, panting a little as he caught his breath. "Tents, like ours. So many of them! I saw smoke from dozens… no, hundreds of cook fires, and watchtowers positioned to see us coming." He shook her head in wonder. "Gul'dan did not lie when he said he would gather all the orcs in Draenor."

A weight that he'd never even acknowledged lifted from Durotan's chest. He had not let himself dwell on the possibility that they had been too late, or even that the entire gathering had been an exaggeration. Kurvorsh's words were more of a comfort to the weary chieftain than he could know.

"How far?" he asked.

"About half a sun's walk. We should reach there with enough time to make camp for the evening."

"Maybe they will have food," Orgrim said. "Something freshly killed, roasting on a spit. Clefthooves do not come this far south, do they? What do these southlanders eat, anyway?"

"Whatever it is, if it is freshly killed, roasting on a spit, I do not doubt you will eat it, Orgrim," Durotan said. "Nor," he added, "would anyone in this camp refuse. But we should not expect it. We should not expect anything."

"We were asked to join the Horde, and we did." The voice was Draka's, and it was at his side rather than above him. She had dismounted. "We bring our weapons, from spears to arrows to hammers, and our hunting and survival skills. We come to serve the Horde, to help all grow strong, and eat. We are Frostwolves. They will be glad we have come."

Her eyes flashed and her chin lifted slightly. Draka had once been Exiled, when she was young and frail. She had returned one of the fiercest warriors Durotan had ever seen, and had brought the Frostwolves knowledge of other cultures, other ways, that would now, no doubt, be all the more valuable.

"My mate is right," Durotan said. He made as if to lift her back onto Ice's back, but she put out a hand, *no*.

"She *is* right," Draka agreed, smiling a little, "and she will walk beside her chieftain and mate into this gathering of the Horde."

Durotan looked toward the south. For so long, the sky had been mercilessly clear, with no chance of rain in the offing. But now, he saw the smudge of a gray cloud. As he regarded it, the billowing mist was abruptly lit from within by lightning that glowed an ominous shade of green.

Kurvorsh had calculated their travel speed well. The sun was low on the horizon when they arrived at the encampment, but there would still be plenty of light for the clan to prepare the evening meal and erect their tents.

The sound of so many voices talking was foreign to Durotan, and there were so many unfamiliar sights to behold it was exhausting. His gaze swept over the large, circular tents, similar to the one he and Draka shared, and came to rest on the field that had been roped off so that children from different clans could play together. He took in all the scents and sounds—conversation, laughter, the rough music of a lok'vadnod being sung, the pounding of drums, so many that Durotan could feel the earth tremble beneath his feet. Smells: of fires, and grain cakes cooking and flames roasting meats, stews bubbling, and the strong but not unpleasant musk of wolf fur and orc teased his nostrils.

Kurvorsh had not exaggerated; if anything, he had minimized the absolute vastness of this seemingly endless stretch of leather and wood structures. The Frostwolves were among the smallest of the clans, Durotan knew. But for a moment, he was so overwhelmed he couldn't speak. Finally, words came.

"So many clans in one place, Orgrim. Laughing Skull, Blackrock, Warsong… all have been summoned."

"It will be a mighty warband," his second-in-command said. "I just wonder who's left to fight."

"Frostwolves."

The voice was flat, almost bored, and Durotan and Orgrim turned to see two tall, burly male orcs marching up to them. They were unusually large and well muscled, given that the land was dying and many orcs had too little food. Unlike the Frostwolves, who had only a few pieces of mail or plate armor, relying mostly on spike-studded leather to protect them, these orcs wore undented pieces of shiny plate on their shoulders and even on their chests. They carried spears and moved with a united sense of purpose.

But it was not their healthy, muscle-laden forms, nor their shiny new armor, that drew Durotan's eye.

These orcs were *green*.

It was a subtle shade, much less obvious than the nearly leaf-colored hue of Gul'dan, the leader of the Horde, who had ventured to the north with his equally green-skinned slave, Garona. This was darker, more like the typical brown color of orc skin. But the tint, that strange, unnatural tint, was still there.

"Who among you is the chieftain?" one of them demanded.

"I have the honor of leading the Frostwolves," Durotan rumbled, stepping forward. The orcs looked him up and down, then glanced appraisingly at Orgrim. "You two. Follow me. Blackhand wishes to see you."

"Who is Blackhand?" Durotan demanded.

One of them stopped in mid-stride and turned around. He grinned. It was an ugly sight.

"Why, Frostwolf pup," he said, "Blackhand is the leader of the Horde."

"You lie," snapped Durotan. "Gul'dan is the leader of the Horde!"

"It is Gul'dan who brought us all here," the second orc said. "He is the one who knows how to take us to a new land. He has chosen Blackhand to lead the Horde in battle, so that we will triumph over our enemies."

Orgrim and Durotan exchanged glances. There had been no mention of a battle for this "new land" when Gul'dan had spoken to his father, Garad, or to him. He was an orc; and more than an orc, he was a Frostwolf chieftain. He would fight whomever he had to in order to ensure a future for his people. For his unborn child. But that Gul'dan had not seen fit to mention it disturbed him.

He and Orgrim had been friends since childhood, and could all but read one another's thoughts. Both orcs held their tongues.

"It is Blackhand who left instructions for when you arrived," the first orc said, adding with a sneer, "if you had the courage to leave Frostfire Ridge."

"Our home is no more," Durotan said bluntly. "Just as yours is no more, whatever your clan."

"We are Blackrocks," the second orc said, chest swelling with pride. "Blackhand was our chieftain before Gul'dan saw fit to give him the glory of leading the Horde. Come with us, Frostwolf. Leave your female behind. Where we go, only warriors will follow."

Durotan's brows drew together and he was about to make a scathing retort when Draka's voice came, deceptively mild. "You and your second-in-command go and meet with Blackhand, my heart," she said. "The clan will await your return." And she smiled.

She knew when to pick the battle. She was every bit the warrior he was, but realized that, in her present condition, she would be dismissed by those who seemed to crave conflict more than food for their people.

"Find us a place to camp, then," he said. "I will meet with this Blackhand, of the Blackrock clan."

The guards led him and Orgrim through the encampment. Families with children, surrounded by cooking tools and sleeping furs, gave way to orcs with scars and hard eyes cleaning, mending, and forging weapons and armor. The ring of hammer on metal came from a blacksmith's tent. Other orcs chiseled stones into wheels. Still others fletched arrows and sharpened knives. All spared a glance for the two Frostwolves, and their gazes flickered over Durotan like something physical.

The sound of steel on steel and the cry of "Lok'tar ogar!" reached Durotan's ears. *Victory, or death.* What was going on here? Heedless of his escorts, he moved toward the source of the sound, shoving his way through to behold a vast ringed area where orcs were fighting one another.

Even as he watched, a lithe female armed only with two wicked-looking knives darted beneath the arm of a male orc swinging a morning star, her blades drawing a twin line of reddish-black across his ribs. She had the chance for a clean kill, but did not take it. Durotan's gaze traveled to another cluster of orcs—four-on-one here, another one-on-one pairing there.

"Training," he said to Orgrim, and his body relaxed slightly. He frowned. A full third of the orcs practicing before him had that same dull green tinge to their brown skin.

"Frostwolves, eh?" came a booming, deep voice behind him. "Not quite the monsters I expected."

The two turned to see one of the largest orcs Durotan had ever beheld. Neither he nor Orgrim were small specimens—indeed, Orgrim was the burliest Frostwolf for several generations—but this one forced Durotan to look up. His skin, a dark, true brown with no hint of green, glistened with either sweat or oil and was adorned with tattoos. His massive hands were completely black with ink, and his eyes gleamed with amused appraisment as he regarded them.

"You will see we live up to our reputation," Durotan said quietly. "You will have no finer hunters in your new Horde, Blackhand of the Blackrock clan."

Blackhand threw his head back and laughed. "We will not need hunters," he said, "we will need warriors. Are you equal to those who came before you, Durotan, son of Garad?"

Durotan glanced over at the still-bleeding orc, who had been caught off guard. "Better," he said, and it was true. "When Gul'dan came to ask the Frostwolves to join the Horde... *twice*... he made no mention of fighting for this promised land."

"Ah," Blackhand said, "but what is to savor in simply walking onto a field? We are orcs. We are now a *Horde* of orcs! And we will conquer this new world. At least," he added, "those of us who are brave enough to fight for it. You are not afraid, are you?"

Durotan allowed himself the barest of smiles, his lips curving around his lower tusks. "The only things I fear are empty promises."

"Bold," Blackhand approved. "Blunt. Good. There is no place for bootlickers in my army. You have come just in time, Frostwolf. Another sun, and you would have been too late. You would have been left behind with the old and the frail."

Durotan frowned. "You would leave some behind?"

"At first, yes—Gul'dan has ordered so," Blackhand said.

Durotan thought of his mother, the Lorekeeper Geyah, the clan's elderly shaman, Drek'Thar, the children... and his wife, heavy with child. "I never agreed to this!"

"If you protest, it would give me great pleasure to fight a mak'gora."

The mak'gora was an ancient tradition, one known and practiced by all orcs. It was an honor battle, one on one, a challenge issued, and accepted. And it was to the death. A few months ago, Durotan, mindful of how the numbers of his clan were dwindling, had refused to slay a fellow Frostwolf he had defeated in a mak'gora. Blackhand obviously had no such reservations.

"Gul'dan will lead the way to the new homeland tomorrow at sunrise," Blackhand said. "This first wave, which will wash over our enemies, will be made up only of warriors. The best the Horde has to offer. You may bring those among your clan who are young, healthy, quick, fierce—who are your best warriors."

Durotan and Orgrim exchanged glances. If indeed this land had dangers that could threaten those most vulnerable, it was a sound strategy. It was what the strong should do.

"You speak sense, Blackhand," he said reluctantly. "The Frostwolves will obey."

"Good," Blackhand said. "Your Frostwolves may not look like monsters, but I would hate to have to kill you without at least being able to watch you all fight first. Come, I will show you the might the orcs will bring when we descend upon this unsuspecting land."

2

Darkness had fallen by the time Orgrim and Durotan returned. Under Draka's direction, the clan had been busy erecting their makeshift traveling tents. Frostwolf banners, depicting the clan's symbol of a white wolf on a blue background, hung limp in the still, dry air outside each one. Durotan looked around at the veritable sea of structures; not just theirs, but those of other clans as well. They, too, had banners that looked as worn out as Durotan felt.

Abruptly the banners stirred and the faint breeze carried the welcome scent of roasting meat to Durotan's nostrils. He clapped Orgrim on the back. "Whatever betides us on the morrow, we have food tonight!"

"My belly will be grateful," Orgrim replied.

"When was the last time we ate something larger than a hare?"

"I cannot remember," Durotan said, sobering almost at once. Game had been almost scarcer on the journey than it had been in the frozen north. Most of their meat sources were small rodents. He thought about talbuks, the delicate but fierce gazelle-like creatures, and the huge clefthooves, which were more than a challenge to kill, but once fed the clan well. He wondered what sort of beasts Gul'dan had found here, in the desert, and decided he did not wish to know.

They were greeted with the welcome sound of laughter as they approached 'the Frostwolf camp. Durotan strode forward to find Draka, Geyah, and Drek'Thar sitting around one of the fires. Together with Orgrim Doomhammer, these three comprised Durotan's council of advisors. They had always given him sound advice, and Durotan felt resentment stir as he recalled Blackhand's orders. If the tattooed orc commander had his way, everyone except Orgrim would be forced to remain behind. Other families clustered over similar small fires. Children drowsed nearby, exhausted. But Durotan saw that their bellies were rounded with food for the first time in months, and he was glad.

In the center of the fire were several spits of smaller animals. He gave Orgrim a rueful look. It would seem that they were still to feed on animals no larger than the size of their fists. But it was meat, and it was fresh, and Durotan would not complain.

Draka handed him a spit from the fire and

Durotan tore into it. It was still hot and his mouth burned, but he didn't care. He hadn't realized just how long it had been since he had eaten fresh meat. When the first edge of his hunger had been blunted, Durotan told them what he and Orgrim had witnessed, and what Blackhand had told them. For a moment, there was silence.

"Who will you take?" Drek'Thar asked quietly. Orgrim looked away at the question. His expression told Durotan that his friend was relieved that he was not chieftain and thus not forced to deliver the bad news.

Durotan spoke the list he had been composing in his mind since he and Orgrim had left their meeting with Blackhand. Draka, Geyah, and Drek'Thar were not on it. There was a lengthy silence. Finally, Geyah spoke.

"I will not argue your decision, my chieftain," she said. "For my part, I will stay behind. When Drek'Thar and I were visited by the Spirit of Life, it told me that I would need to stay with the clan. Now, I understand what it meant. I am a shaman, and I fight well, but there are others who are younger, stronger, and faster than I. And I am the Lorekeeper. Spirits guard you, but if this vanguard should fall, at least the history of our people will be kept alive."

He smiled at her gratefully. She sounded resigned, but he knew how badly she wanted to fight at her son's side. "Thank you. You know I will come for all of you as soon as it is safe."

"I understand as well," Drek'Thar said, sorrow

tinging his voice. He gestured to the cloth he always wore to hide his ruined eyes. "I am blind, and old. I would be a liability."

"No," said Draka, her voice hard. "My heart, reconsider taking Drek'Thar. He is a shaman, and the Spirits told us they would be there, in this world we are about to enter. As long as there is earth, air, fire, water, and life, you will need a shaman. Drek'Thar is the best we have. He is a healer, and," she added, "you may need his visions."

A chill ran along Durotan's skin, lifting the hairs on his arm. More than once, Drek'Thar's visions had saved lives. Once, a warning from the Spirit of Fire had spared the entire clan. How could he not bring Drek'Thar? "You will not fight with us," he said. "Only heal, and advise. Have I your word?"

"Always, my chieftain. It will be honor enough to go."

Durotan looked at Draka. "I know, my heart, that you can fight, but—" He broke off, rising to his feet, one hand going to Sever's hilt.

The visitor was almost as large as Blackhand. The firelight cast shadows on a physique as sculpted as if it had been chiseled from stone. Blackhand had impressed him, but this orc was, if not as large, more muscled, more powerful looking. Like Blackhand, he too wore tattoos, but whereas the commander's hands had been inked solid black, it was this orc's jaw that was dark as midnight. His long black hair was pulled back in a topknot, and his eyes glittered in the fire's glow.

"I am Grom Hellscream, Chieftain of the Warsong," the orc announced, his eyes sweeping the newcomers. "Blackhand told me that at long last, the Frostwolves had come." He grunted in amusement and dropped a sack of something at Durotan's feet. "Food," he said.

The bag twitched and moved, bulging out here and there. "Insects," Grom said. "Best eaten live, and raw." He grinned. "Or dried and ground into flour. The taste is not bad."

"I am Durotan, son of Garad, son of Durkosh," Durotan said, "and Grom Hellscream, Chieftain of the Warsong, is welcome at our fire."

Durotan decided not to introduce the other members of the clan assembled around the fire, as he did not want to draw undue attention to them— not if he planned to take Drek'Thar with him at sunrise. He caught Draka's eye and she nodded. She rose, quietly touching Drek'Thar and Geyah on the shoulders and taking them to another fire.

Durotan indicated the vacant seats, and Grom dropped down beside him and Orgrim. He accepted a spit from the embers and bit into the dripping meat with gusto.

"Though you and I have never met," Durotan said, "some members of your clan once hunted alongside mine, years past."

"I remember our clan members said the Frostwolves were good hunters, and fair," Grom acknowledged. "If perhaps a bit too..." He groped for the word. "Reserved."

Durotan refrained from telling Grom what the Frostwolves had thought of the Warsong. The words *impulsive, loud, fierce* and *crazy* had been used. Sometimes, admittedly, with admiration, but not always. Instead, he said, "It seems as though Gul'dan has managed to unite all the clans, now."

Grom nodded. "You were the last to join," he said. "There was one other, but they are gone, now. So Gul'dan says."

The Frostwolves shifted uneasily. Durotan wondered if Grom spoke of the Red Walkers. If, in truth, the clan was dead down to the last member, it was a good thing, and he would not mourn.

"We," Grom said with pride, "were among the first. When Gul'dan came to us and told us he knew of a way to travel to another land, one rich in game and clean water and enemies to battle, we agreed right away." He laughed. "What more could an orc want?"

"My second-in-command, Orgrim, and I met with Blackhand upon our arrival," Durotan said. "He told me of his plans to take a wave of warriors to this land first. We spoke of weapons and those who wield them, but I am curious as to Gul'dan's preparations."

Grom took another bite, finishing off the meat. He tossed the stick into the fire. "Gul'dan has found a way for us to enter another land," Grom said. "An ancient artifact, long hidden in the earth. His magicks led him to it, and when we arrived here, we began to dig. We have unearthed it at last, and tomorrow, we will use it."

Durotan's brows rose. "A hole in the ground?"

"You'll see it soon enough," Grom assured him.

The more Durotan learned of these plans, the less he liked them. "It sounds like a grave."

"No," Grom assured him. "If anything, it is a rebirth for our people. It's the path to a new world!"

"You believe this?" Orgrim asked. He sounded more skeptical than hopeful.

Grom eyed Orgrim for a moment. Then he lifted one powerful arm and leaned forward, extending it closer to the fire. In the firelight, Durotan saw what the shadows had obscured earlier. Like many of those he and Orgrim had seen training, Grom Hellscream's skin was tinged with green. And when he spoke, his words were addressed to Orgrim, not Durotan.

"I believe in Gul'dan. I believe in the fel. His death magic has made me powerful." He flexed his arm, and his bicep, large as a melon, bulged. "You'll see. You'll feel the strength of five."

"Blackhand seems strong enough without it," Durotan said bluntly.

Grom's bright eyes darted to the Frostwolf chieftain. "Why be strong enough when there is stronger still?" His lips curled away from his tusks in a grin that was as sinister as it was savage, and Durotan could not but wonder if "stronger still" would ever become "strong enough" to appease the Warsong.

By the time Durotan retired to his tent, Draka was stretched out, asleep on the furs they had brought from the north.

Once, she would have rested on a pile of thick, warm clefthoof skins, and her hut would have been the chieftain's hut—a solid, stable construct of timber and stone. She would have had plenty of good, healthy food to nourish the body housing not only her warrior's spirit, but the small life that now curved her belly; the only soft part of her strong, hard physique. Now, all that separated her flesh from the hard rock was rabbit fur, and the clan had walked the last several leagues with no food at all.

Geyah had insisted Durotan and Draka take what they could from Frostfire Ridge to remind them of the clan's heritage. So this makeshift shelter, a bit more solid than most, contained the Frostwolf crest and decorative wards constructed and blessed by the shaman to augment battle prowess and ward off dangers. Inside, a variety of weapons lay within easy reach: spears, axes, hammers, maces, bows and arrows, swords. And, of course, Thunderstrike. Durotan unfastened Sever and placed it beside the furs as he sat and regarded his mate.

A wave of tenderness washed over him as his gaze roved her body, from her fierce, strong face and long black hair, to the swell of her belly as she lay on her side, breathing evenly. Her lids still closed, she reached out a hand to him.

"I can feel your eyes." Draka's voice was low and throaty, warm with affection and amusement.

"I thought you were asleep."

"I was." She shifted her swollen body to lie on her back, searching unsuccessfully for a comfortable position. Her husband's hand moved to her belly, his massive fingers and palm almost completely covering it, silently connecting with his child. "Dreaming of a hunt through the snow."

Durotan closed his eyes and sighed. It was almost painful to recall the sharp, familiar bite of the winter, the cold challenging their bodies as they attacked prey that fought to survive. The shouts, the smell of fresh blood, the taste of nourishing flesh. Those years had been good ones. Durotan stretched beside her on the furs, recalling the first night Draka had returned from her Exile. He had pushed her for stories of her travels, and they had lain beside one another as they did now, on their backs, but not touching. Looking up at the stars, watching the smoke rise up.

And he had been content. "I've thought of a name," Draka continued.

Durotan grunted. He was angry with himself for his nostalgia. Where Draka's dream was just that—a true, honest dream, not wistful, deliberate recollection—the time he yearned for was gone, never to return.

He took her hand in his as he teased, "Well, keep it to yourself, wife. I'll choose the name when I've met him... or her."

"Oh?" There was amusement in her voice. "And how will the great Durotan name his son, if I do not travel with him?"

"A *son*?" He propped himself on an elbow, regarding her, his mouth slightly open. Always before, he had accepted that he might have a daughter or a son. The gender was less important to him than ensuring that the baby was healthy. Frostwolf females were fierce warriors—Draka was a perfect example of that. Tradition, though, held that the chieftainship could only pass to a male. He blinked at her. "Are you having visions like Drek'Thar now?"

She smiled and shrugged. "I just... feel it."

He thought again of that first night, and all the others they had shared with one another since. He did not want to think of a long stretch of nights when they would be without each other; did not want to think of his son being born without his father present.

"Can you hide your fat belly?" he said, grinning in anticipation of her retort.

Draka, who knew him all the way to his bones, punched him in the shoulder—lovingly, but quite firmly. "Better than you can hide your fat head."

Hearty laughter burst from him, a balm to his spirit, and his wife laughed with him. Again they lay back together, Durotan's hand once more protectively over their son. They would face this new world together.

Whatever happened.

3

The next morning, as Draka strategically strapped a small, circular shield adorned with tusks over her stomach, she caught Durotan's eye and he nodded slightly, somewhat reassured that she was able to hide her swollen belly and protect their unborn son at the same time. The last several years had been so difficult that Draka had not been able to gain any weight that had not gone directly to the developing child. No softening of her muscles, no roundness to her face revealed her pregnancy once her belly had been covered. It was useful now, but he felt a stab of regret that she had been so deprived.

Drek'Thar wore a hooded cloak pulled low to hide his white hair and the cloth that covered his disfigured face. Another shaman, Palkar, who had tended him for years, would be guiding him. Durotan walked over to them both as they assembled, awaiting the call to march toward the "hole in the ground."

"I cannot promise you will not be discovered," Durotan told them. "If this is a risk you choose not to take, no one would blame you."

"We understand," Drek'Thar said. "All is as the Spirits will it."

Durotan nodded. Draka had already said her farewells to Geyah and now stepped aside. Durotan placed his hands on his mother's shoulders. "You will be in charge of the clan while Orgrim and I are gone," he told her. "I can think of no finer hands in which to leave the Frostwolves than those of their Lorekeeper."

Her eyes were dry, and she stood tall and strong. "I will protect them with my life, my son. And *when* you return, we will gladly come join you in this verdant new land."

Everyone knew that there might not be a return. So much was unknown about this promised place. They were getting there by magic, with no idea what awaited them save what Gul'dan had told them. What if he was wrong? What if he'd lied? What if there were dangers so great that not even an orc could face them? In the end, it didn't matter. What was here could not be borne.

"I am certain we will conquer swiftly," he said, and hoped his voice was as solid as he wished it to be.

Horns blew, summoning them. Durotan embraced Geyah. She clung to him for a moment, then released him and stepped back. Durotan looked over his clan, at the children, the orcs, male and female, who were artisans and shaman, not warriors. He had done everything he could for them.

Now, it was time to discover if Gul'dan's word could be trusted.

Blackhand's orcs directed them, funneling the clans into a single channel of brown and green skin, glinting steel, and dull white bone that trudged downward through the dust. Yet again, Durotan marveled at seeing so many orcs marching shoulder to shoulder, united in a single purpose. Hope swelled inside him. They were orcs! What could they *not* do? Whatever creatures awaited them, they would fall beneath racing feet, swinging weapons, and the bellowed cries of "Lok'tar ogar!"

He glanced at Draka, who grinned at him. She clasped his hand once, quickly, then let it go. No one gave her a second glance. Durotan strode forward carrying Thunderstrike, Sever strapped to his back.

One of Blackhand's orcs jogged along the line, calling out instructions. "Veer to the right!" Durotan and Draka obeyed.

And there it was.

"Hellscream was right," Durotan murmured. "It is not just a hole in the ground."

Durotan's entire clan would have taken up only the smallest fraction of the expanse that had been unearthed, and all could have run shoulder to shoulder through the large stone structure that had lain hidden by sand. It towered up, huge and imposing, a great, winged serpent coiled atop it and two carved, hooded figures, each the height of a hundred orcs, standing to either side. The right figure and the pillar from which it was carved stood freely. The left side of the gate was still connected to the earth. Scaffolding cluttered parts of it, and lift mechanisms ferried orcs who looked no larger than a flea as they scurried about their business, working on the great gate even now. There had not been much of a semblance of order to begin with, and as more warriors beheld the sight of this gargantuan carved edifice, what little there was began to dissolve. Everyone started talking. Durotan saw Blackhand's orcs with angry, frazzled looks on their faces as they repeatedly shouted out orders that went unheeded. Orcs were fierce, wild, and strong. They obeyed their clan leaders, but clearly, the commander was going to have his black-inked hands full trying to manage this many individuals.

"Durotan!" Draka called. "Look!" She pointed up at the topmost step of the portal. It was Gul'dan, his green skin unmistakable. Seeing him, Durotan felt as if no time at all had passed since Gul'dan had first come to Frostfire Ridge. He looked as he had then, leaning on a staff decorated with small skulls and bits of bone. His cloak's cowl partially obscured his lined face, but even at this distance Durotan could see Gul'dan's white beard and unmistakable eyes, glowing that sickly, luminous green shade. Spikes had been affixed to his cloak, and impaled on them were more tiny skulls. Then, as now, Durotan shivered with a sense of intense dislike. He recalled Drek'Thar's words upon first encountering the warlock: *Shadows cling to this orc. Death follows him.*

Walking behind the stooped warlock, an exaggeratedly heavy chain attached to her slender neck, was his slave, the half-breed Garona. Durotan remembered her as well. She had been with her master the two times Gul'dan had made the arduous trek north to speak with the Frostwolves. The second time, she had managed to give Durotan's clan a warning: *My master is dark and dangerous.* For a slave, the way she carried herself was not obsequious. Indeed, if it were not for the contemptuous glances thrown her way when any orc deigned regard her at all, Durotan might have thought that it was she who was the master, not the warlock.

It was then that he realized that the two were walking past cages constructed from twisted, dead tree branches. They were crowded to overflowing with blue-skinned forms.

Draenei prisoners.

One of them, a female, reached out an imploring hand and seized Garona's hand. She looked like she was begging the strange half-orc for something, but Garona detached herself and spoke to Gul'dan.

"What did they do?" Draka wondered. Her voice was shot through with pain and horror. Unlike most orcs, who usually scorned the blue-skinned, goat-legged draenei, she had actually traveled with a group of them for a time. She had told Durotan they were not cowardly; they simply avoided confrontation. Durotan himself knew that the draenei had courage—they had selflessly rescued, and returned, three Frostwolf children.

Now, Gul'dan had imprisoned them.

"Does it matter?" Durotan hated the scathing tone of his own voice. "Gul'dan is sending us through this portal, to attack whatever lies on the other side and take their land for our own. We need this land—and we need him. Right now, he can do what he pleases."

Draka gave him a searching look, but then closed her eyes. There was no arguing with the ugly truth. Doubtless, the draenei had done nothing at all. He knew some other orc clans killed them for sport. Perhaps there was to be a display of some sort before Gul'dan permitted the orcs to enter this much-vaunted new land.

A snatch of the draenei's shouting came to him, just one word. Durotan did not know much of their language, but he knew this.

"*Detish!*" the female sobbed, still reaching imploringly after Garona.

Detish.

Child.

Durotan and Draka exchanged horrified looks.

There came a rumble of thunder. The very hue of the sky had shifted, to the yellow-green of a fading bruise. A line of bright emerald now limned the interior of the portal, and green lightning flickered in the sky. "What is that?" Draka asked.

"Gul'dan's magic," Durotan replied, grimly. And as he uttered the words, the warlock spread his arms wide as he surveyed his army.

"Death. Life. Death. Life. Do you hear it?" He

lifted a hand to his ear and his lips curved in a smile around his tusks. "The beat of a living heart. The fuel for my magic is life. We may only have enough prisoners to send through our strongest warriors, but that will be enough. The enemy is weak. When we arrive, we will take *them* as fuel! We will build a new portal, and when it is complete, we will bring through *all* of the Horde!"

Durotan again looked at the imprisoned draenei. His father, Garad, had spoken of a time in his youth when the Frostwolves had sacrificed the life of an animal to thank the Spirits for a good hunt. Gul'dan had said that his death magic was similar. *You are fed with the creature's flesh, clothed with its hide. I am fed with strength and knowledge, and clothed... in green.*

Gul'dan turned to face the gate. Holding his skull-crowned staff aloft in one gnarled hand, he spread his arms and arched his back. From everywhere and from nowhere, a voice arose. But it was like no voice that Durotan had ever heard. It was deep, thrumming along the bones, rasping and harsh and piercing, and everything in Durotan wanted him to cover his ears and cease listening to it. He tensed against the desire and took deep breaths to steady himself, although his heart was racing. With fear? Anger?

Anticipation?

The draenei prisoners on either side of the gate arched in agony, their bodies taut. Durotan watched, stunned, as blue-white, curling tendrils of mist extended from the prisoners, racing toward Gul'dan. He opened his mouth, drinking in the misty spirals, letting them bathe and caress him.

The green-skinned orcs in the forefront seemed to go mad. They roared, pelting up the steps to the portal. The draenei spasmed. Their skin grew paler, their bodies weaker, frailer—older. When they were little more than husks, the glowing blue radiance of their eyes winked out. The rush of life energy ceased flowing from them, and the green outlining the portal crackled and flared with fire, as if in anticipation. An enormous sound shattered Durotan's ears as a glowing orb shot from Gul'dan's hands toward the portal and exploded. Where once one could see through the portal to the stone and earth on the other side, now the interior of the entire rectangular gateway was a pulsating, sickly emerald hue. Then the green swirl's color became tinted with others; the blue of a sky, the rich browns and natural colors of trees.

A vista bought with so many lives. Was it worth it, even if it meant the survival of his clan?

The painful answer was… yes.

"For the Horde!" Someone had shouted it, and others were now taking up the cry. "For the Horde! For the Horde! *For the Horde!*"

Orgrim flashed Durotan a grin and raced past his chieftain. The chant pounded on Durotan's ears like the pounding of his heart, but he did not break into a frenzied run as so many others did. He turned around to regard his mate. At her questioning look, he told her, "Let me go first." If he were to die going through, he would at least have his death serve to warn his mate.

"For the Horde! For the Horde!"

Draka slowed, obeying her chieftain. Durotan lowered his head, gripped Thunderstrike, and muttered beneath his breath, "For the Frostwolves," and ran through.

Draka frowned and set her jaw as her beloved disappeared, vanishing into the shimmering, sky-blue-tree-green entrance to... what? What had Durotan thought to do? Others ran through, but no one returned. She could not wait for him to tell her all was well. She had to join him.

She clenched her hands into fists, and, growling low in her throat, strode forward with the rest of the shouting, sweaty mass of bloodlust-fueled warriors. Her eyes straight ahead, Draka, daughter of Kelkar, son of Rhakish, entered the portal.

The earth fell away from beneath her feet.

She floated in dim green light as if in a lake, disoriented, her breath coming quickly. Behind her was the light from the portal; ahead, increasing darkness. Other orcs swam-fell past as thin ribbons of light reached out before her. She could still hear the strange thunder from the Draenor side of the gate, but it was muffled. Now and then a blast of illumination would sear her eyes. She pushed aside the threat of debilitating fear and focused on the one thing she could see—a needle-prick of light, of hope, in the enveloping darkness. Draka started trying to move toward it. She felt as though she did not weigh anything. How then to reach this light?

Reaching out with her arms, she pulled them back—and floated forward. She smiled to herself and kept going. This new land was on the other side of this strange tunnel. Her mate awaited her there. The child within her kicked, as if in protest.

Be calm, little one, Draka thought. *We will soon—*

Pain stabbed her as her stomach contracted, hard, like a fist clenching before delivering a blow. Startled, Draka gasped. She had never been with child before, but she had spoken with the other females. She knew what to expect. The orc life was one of unceasing vigilance, and babies therefore came swiftly and with little pain so that their mothers would be prepared to move or fight if necessary.

But this—

It was too soon. The agony that ripped through her abdomen was a warning, not a herald. The babe needed at least another moon in his mother's sheltering body. Panting, sweat popping out over her dark skin, Draka struggled to remove the camouflaging shield, tossing it away into the darkness. The light was closer now; she could see other orc shapes around her, all struggling toward the light, and for a moment, Draka felt a sudden kinship with her child. In a way, they were both being born.

Another orc, wheeling weightlessly, floated past her. Durotan! He reached out to her, seeing that she was in torment, trying to catch her, but he tumbled past, inexorably swept along by the strange current.

Another object tumbled slowly toward her—an uprooted tree. Draka curled in on herself despite the horrible, dagger-sharp pains, doing what she could to protect her child. The tree's branches scraped her skin as it passed.

She reached out as the light intensified, almost blinding after the darkness of this journey. Her questing fingers brushed against something solid— earth! Draka growled in frustration, digging her sharp-nailed fingers into the soil and pulling herself up and out of the portal.

Feet thundered past her and she rose, stumbling out of the crush of orcs eager for bloodshed, feeling soggy earth... water, grass...

Draka shrieked at pain so sharp it felt as if her child was slicing her belly from the inside. Her knees gave way and she collapsed onto the marshy earth, her heaving lungs inhaling damp air.

"Draka!" It was Durotan. On her hands and knees, Draka turned her head to see him racing toward her. Then, an enormous orc shot out a hand decorated with inky black markings and seized her mate.

"With child?" the orc bellowed. "You bring that wachook into my warband?"

"Let me go, Blackhand!" her husband pleaded. "*Draka!*"

She could hold her head up no longer. Durotan would not be at her side, roaring encouragement, as their baby slid into the world. Spirits... would it even survive, born so early, wrapped in his mother's torment? Draka sobbed, not with pain, but in anger and rage. This child deserved better! It deserved to *live*!

Suddenly someone was there, murmuring quietly, "Shhh… shhh… you are not alone, Draka, daughter of Kelkar, son of Rhakish."

She looked up, through the tangle of sweat-soaked hair clinging to her face, into the glowing green eyes of Gul'dan.

No!

Everything in Durotan's entire being cried out at the thought of Gul'dan, he of the green skin and death magic, standing in Durotan's stead while Draka gave birth. Durotan struggled against Blackhand's restraint, but the orc commander held him firmly.

"Push, little one," Gul'dan was saying, his voice uncharacteristically kind. "Push…" Durotan watched helplessly as Draka, on her hands and knees, threw back her head and screamed as their son entered the world.

The baby was still, so still, and silent. Durotan sagged against Blackhand's iron grip, his heart cracking inside his chest. *My son…*

But Gul'dan held the tiny thing, so small, barely as large as his green hand, and bent over him.

The little chest hitched. A heartbeat later, a lusty wail filled the air, and Durotan gasped as relief washed over him. His son was alive!

"Welcome, little one!" Gul'dan laughed, and raised Durotan and Draka's baby to the skies. "A new warrior for the Horde!" he shouted, and a deafening cheer rose up around Durotan. He paid it no heed. He stared, stunned, at the small being that was his son.

The child was green.

4

The city was dim, and loud, and hot. Fire burned in its center, as it had for years. The sounds of hammer on iron and the hiss of quenching water, too, were ceaseless. The air smelled faintly of smoke, though the cavernous construction made sure it was always breathable. Its name reflected its people—to the point, descriptive, and active: Ironforge.

The king of the dwarven underground capital, fiercely red of beard and bulbous of nose, escorted his guest through the main forge area. He was shaking his head, as if still disbelieving something, even as his feet moved purposefully. He pointed a sausage-thick finger up at his companion.

"You're the only man I'd make plough blades for, Anduin Lothar," he grumbled in his deep, melodious voice. "You and your army of farmers can attack the turf with dwarven steel, eh? It sends a shiver down my spine just to say it. What will my wives think?"

Anduin Lothar, the only man King Magni Bronzebeard would make plough blades for, smiled down at his old friend. Tall, well built but not massive, the "Lion of Stormwind" was easy in royal company. He had spent most of his life fighting—and drinking—beside the man who currently sat on the throne of Stormwind, and knew Magni well.

"The military man's curse, my lord," he said. Affection made the wry words warm. "The better I do my job, the less I'm asked to do it."

Magni harrumphed. "Well," he said, resigning himself to the situation, "it's still good to see you, old friend. We'll have your wagons packed and on their way as soon as they're ready."

Lothar paused beside one of the crates and ran his hand longingly—and carefully—along the glinting surface of what surely had to be the finest plough blades in existence.

"Come," Magni continued. "I've got something for you."

He had placed the hammer he had been carrying on a narrow table next to a small wooden box. Lothar stepped beside him, curious. Magni opened the box, and Lothar peered at it with interest. Inside, nestled against creamy white fabric, was an item the likes of which he had never seen. Made of metal, it had a wide mouth on one end, almost like a horn instrument. The other end was curved, and connecting them was a narrow rod. In a separate section was a collection of thumbnail-sized metal spheres. Lothar was at a loss.

"What is it?" he inquired.

"A mechanical marvel," Magni exclaimed, reaching for the thing with the same sort of doting expression some men reserved for their newborn children. "It's a boomstick." He lifted it out of the box, holding the curved end.

"Hold it like this," Magni said. "Put a bit of powder in here, quick tap down with the rod, ball in after, another tap, the flint goes here—"

He lifted the weapon and pointed it, staring down its length like an archer taking aim. Puzzlement drew his unruly scarlet brows together, and he lowered the weapon. "Odd," he murmured, absently returning Lothar's gift to him.

Lothar, tucking the weapon in his belt, looked where Magni was staring and saw one of the king's couriers running flat out toward them. He felt his spine straighten, his senses heighten, his whole body tensing—ready to spring into action as needed. Dwarves strode, stomped, ambled, and sometimes darted. They seldom ran—and certainly not like this. Something was very wrong.

The dwarf's face was nearly as florid as his king's beard as he charged up the steps, his pace never slowing until he dropped to his knees in front of Magni. He was too breathless for words, and gulped metal-tinged air as he extended a rolled-up parchment.

"Take water," Magni instructed the courier. The king's thick fingers were swift and nimble as he unrolled the missive. While Magni read, Lothar pointed the boomstick as the king had done, then peered curiously into the end of the metal cylinder, reaching for the small sphere inside and digging it out to examine it. Glancing back at Magni, Lothar saw his friend's genial face harden. Slowly he looked up and met Lothar's questioning gaze, and there was resolve and a hint of sorrow in his eyes.

"You might want to head home, big man. It seems someone has attacked one of your garrisons."

Lothar crouched low over the king's gryphon as she flew toward Stormwind. The creature, half-lion and half-eagle, was one of a handful that His Majesty King Llane possessed, and they were seldom ridden save for official business. His position on the gryphon's back told her that her rider wanted her top speed, and she was giving it to him.

Lothar's mind raced as fast as the gryphon's rapidly beating wings. Attacked? By whom, or what? The missive had been lacking in detail. No mention of casualties or numbers—just the simple facts that there had been an attack. Surely it was not the trolls. He, Medivh, and Llane had sent the blue-skinned, tusked creatures packing the last time they had come sniffing around Stormwind. Light, there was even a statue to Medivh for his part in the victory.

The gryphon tucked in her wings for a sharp dive and Lothar clung tightly to the saddle. Below, outside the Stormwind barracks, two of his lieutenants—

Karos, tall, sharp-featured, and rigidly at attention, and dark-skinned Varis, ever the more patient of the two—awaited him. They looked proper and professional, their faces composed, but Lothar had served with them and knew that he'd been right: something was terribly wrong here.

He vaulted off the gryphon as soon as she landed outside the royal barracks. She gave him a head-butt and he patted her neck, handing off her reins to an attendant. Lothar wasted no time, shoving the scroll in Karos's chest.

"This missive tells me there was an attack. Start talking now."

Varis nodded as they strode inside and hastened down the stairs into the infirmary. Chandeliers provided dim lighting, casting an eerie glow on the rows of white-shrouded, silent forms. "Yes, sir. We know about as much as you do, sir. The garrison sent a message asking for reinforcements. By the time we arrived, we—well... they were all dead, sir."

"No survivors?" Lothar was aghast. "Not one?" He looked from Varis's distinguished, dark face to Karos's pale one.

"No, sir. We found only the dead at the site," Karos replied. "We brought the bodies back here."

"Two search parties are unaccounted for," Varis said. "We've... the bodies are..." The two soldiers exchanged glances. Lothar had a reputation for inspiring men to follow him but right now, he wanted to knock their heads together. "You'd best come see, sir."

Lothar strode down the corridors of the barracks trying desperately to wrap his mind around what he was being told. "An entire *garrison*?" he demanded. "And no one who can tell us anything?"

Silence, broken only by the ring of booted feet on stone. Again, the two soldiers looked at one another.

"We did find someone," Varis said.

"He was searching the bodies," Karos said. Lothar glanced at him and saw that sweat was trickling down his temple.

"You found him at the site?"

"N—no, sir," Karos said. "It was after we brought them back. We found him here. In the barracks."

"*In* the barracks?" Lothar's voice carried in the hall, and he didn't care. "By the Light, what idiot failed to notice someone looting soldiers' bodies right here in the damned *barracks*?"

"We think he's a mage, sir!" Varis said quickly.

A mage. Someone who could make sure that he wouldn't be seen. Lothar's stride faltered, but he kept going. That would certainly answer the question he had just posed to his obviously rattled men, but it raised about a thousand others.

He kept his voice calm. "Were you able to restrain him, or did he turn you into sheep?" He didn't even try to keep the irritation out of his voice.

"Yes, sir," Karos said. "I mean—yes, we've got him. We're taking you to him right now."

They'd put the intrusive perhaps-mage in the barracks office and set a guard to watch him. The guard saluted smartly, stepped aside, and opened the door with a skeleton key.

Lothar had expected to confront an old man with a long white beard, who would fix him with an arrogant expression. He was not prepared to find what looked to be a rather dirty, scruffy teenage boy. He was perusing a book that had been left on the desk and looked up with huge brown eyes as Lothar stalked in.

The boy leaped to his feet. "Finally!" he exclaimed. "Are you in command—"

Lothar had already seized his arm, yanked him around, and shoved him down on the desk. He reached for the measuring compass and slammed it down, trapping the boy's left arm between the sharp edges and pinning it to the desk's wooden surface. He tugged the young intruder's sleeve down.

Varis had been right. Branded on the youth's arm was the image of an eye.

"Sha'la ros!" yelped the boy, his eyes glowing with blue light. Lothar's free hand covered the mage's mouth, muffling the incantation. Bright cerulean magic swirled in the boy's right fingers, fading without the power of words to feed it. Lothar pushed his face in close to the mage's.

"That's the mark of the Kirin Tor. What are you doing in my city, spell chucker?"

The young mage sagged, and lowered his hand. The magic he had summoned disappeared. Cautiously, Lothar removed his hand and let him speak. "Let me complete my examination of the body across the hall," he said calmly, as if his words were actually reasonable.

Lothar grinned ferally. "Now... why would I do that?"

The boy's dark brows drew together—frustration? Concern? "Within that body is the secret to your attacks." He licked his lips, suddenly looking like a teenage boy again. "I can help you."

Lothar's eyes narrowed as he searched the boy's face. He hadn't got to where he was without being a good judge of people, and there was something about the boy that was genuine. Lothar escorted the young mage to the room he'd requested—keeping a firm grip on the eye-marked arm as he did so.

Karos pushed back the curtain, revealing the corpse the mage had been caught examining. Lothar stopped so quickly that Varis, bringing up the rear, almost bumped into him.

Hardened soldier that he was, Lothar had witnessed myriad deaths, from the civilized to the brutal. But *this*...

Both eyes and mouth were open. The skin was gray and striated with darker threads, like gangrene but nothing so familiar. The cheeks were sunken and the eyes, encrusted with what looked like a rim of salt, were hard and glassy. Nothing about this... thing, if it could even be called a body, was natural.

The young mage didn't answer. He, too, looked repelled by what he saw, but resolute to continue with his investigation. He analyzed the body, observing everything, then his gaze wandered inexorably to the barely human face. Steeling himself, the boy leaned over and gingerly inserted two fingers into the open mouth, pulling the jaw down. Lothar leaned in to watch, disgusted and fascinated, as the mage's fingers probed.

A faint tendril of green mist spouted upward, then vanished. The soldiers—Lothar among them—gasped. The mage leaped back, covering his mouth and nose with his sleeve, clearly not wanting the strange green steam to touch him. His face was pale, and he swallowed hard before turning to face Lothar.

"What was that?" Lothar demanded.

The youth took a deep breath, trying to calm himself. "You must summon the Guardian. It should be he who explains it."

It was a statement, not a request. Lothar blinked. "Medivh?" asked Karos, eyeing his commander.

"We're wasting time!" the boy insisted.

Lothar regarded him with narrowed eyes. "Only the *King* summons the Guardian. Not I, and certainly not some scruffy puppy who barely has his first whiskers." To Karos, he said, "Get him to Goldshire."

The night was old, and dawn was not far away as Lothar's gryphon landed gracefully near the cozy Lion's Pride Inn. The air was damp and chill, the forest sounds that of the night creatures going about their business rather than the song of birds. A few yards distant, some of the locals had gathered despite the hour, making an outing of their own to ogle the king, his guard, and the flurry of activity.

"Beasts, you say?" The voice was calm, quiet, but commanding, and cut cleanly through the cacophony of several other voices all talking at once. Of course, Lothar thought as the Royal Guards saluted smartly and allowed him entrance into the Lion's Pride Inn, that might simply be how it seemed to him, considering how well he knew it.

King Llane Wrynn was tall, with dark hair, wise, kind eyes, and a neatly trimmed beard. He looked every inch the king even now, clad as he was in less formal clothing. The royal family had been enjoying a day's outing in Elwynn Forest when Llane had received a similar missive to the one the dwarven courier had given King Magni. They had retreated to the inn to begin analyzing the situation.

Lothar felt a stab of misplaced nostalgia. Until this very moment, the inn, located in the little village of Goldshire, had been a place where he, Llane, and Medivh had gathered to laugh, game, and drink. Now, it was a makeshift war room. Several of the inn's tables had been pushed together and maps, letters, and inkwells covered them. Lothar had to smile as he noticed beer mugs anchoring the curling edges of the parchment.

"What manner of beasts could do what you have reported?" Llane continued. He was visibly struggling to stay calm as he examined the shield of a Stormwind solider that bore a gash so enormous it had almost split the metal facing.

One of the officers, with dark hair and darker eyes, shook his head. "Rumors, Your Majesty."

"From *three* different valleys." Aloman, one of Lothar's finest soldiers, pointed out. Her blue-gray eyes were hard.

"I've heard a dozen conflicting descriptions," a third officer said.

"It's a rebellion, sire," a fourth chimed in.

"Rebels, beasts," the first offer said, exasperated, "we need more information."

Llane spotted Lothar, the furrow in his brow easing. "Lothar," he called, "have *you* learned anything that can help?"

"A little, perhaps," Lothar said. Queen Taria, standing next to her husband, also looked up at the sound of her brother's voice. Their eyes met, and she gave him a strained smile. Taria looked as regal as Llane, but Lothar well knew her doe eyes and demure demeanor hid a fierce intelligence and a stubborn streak as wide as—well, as his own.

Lothar spoke quickly, avoiding supposition and sticking to facts, telling them about the young mage, and the peculiar wisp of green that had escaped the dead man's lips. He finished with, "Also, my liege, I've been told to summon the Guardian. So, hop to it, man."

"I'll get right on it," Llane said wryly, then sobered.

"Is there still no word from Grand Hamlet?" Taria asked softly. Grand Hamlet, a town as quaint and quiet as Goldshire, had been where both she and Lothar had grown up. It lay to the south of Elwynn Forest and had fallen mysteriously silent, and unfortunately Lothar had no reassurance for his sister. He shook his head.

Llane gazed at him, utterly at a loss. "How does a garrison of thirty men disappear without a whisper?"

"The fel," came a young, strong voice, "or at least its influence."

The chatter faltered. Llane, along with everyone else in the room except for Lothar, looked to the door and the newcomer who stood there. The king raised an eyebrow. "Is this him?" he asked Lothar uncertainly.

"Mm-hmm," Lothar replied, distracted. His attention was drawn beyond the mage to the young soldier who had been chosen to escort him, now standing rigidly at attention.

Dammit.

Lothar pressed his lips together, nodding in answer to Llane's query. "Sergeant Callan!" Taria said, pleasure warming her voice.

Callan inclined his head. "Your Majesty." His voice, tenor, just a little too formal. *Was I ever that young?* Lothar thought.

"Thank you, Sergeant," he said, sharply, reaching to take the young mage and steer him toward Llane. Callan saluted, and took up a position beside the door, awaiting further orders.

"So," Llane said, his voice hard, "who are you, mage?"

"My name is Khadgar," the boy answered. "I am the Guardian Novitiate."

If the room had quieted when Khadgar first spoke, now it was so silent that the crackle of the fire seemed loud. He looked around, uncomfortable with the attention, and continued.

"I... well, I *was*. I renounced my vows." More silence. "There's, ah... not really a protocol in place *officially*, you understand. It was more of a—a personal decision. The ultimate result being my leaving Dalaran, and the Kirin Tor, and... I'm not Guardian material," he finished, rather lamely.

"You mean you're a *fugitive*," Lothar interpreted.

The boy—Khadgar—turned to him, bridling at the accusation. "I'm not hiding." Lothar redirected Khadgar's attention to the king.

"Your Majesty," Khadgar said, stepping forward, "I may have left my training, but I didn't leave my abilities behind. Any more than you could leave knowing how to swing a sword if you decided not to be a soldier. Look—" He ran a hand through his brown hair. "I've *sensed* something. Dark forces. When it's strong, it almost has a *smell*."

A chill crept along Lothar's skin and he knew the boy wasn't lying.

"Knowing that something so evil was so close... I couldn't just ignore it. I think—"

A sudden shriek from outside, followed by a babble of frightened voices, cut him off. Callan rushed to the door and opened it, calling for order.

"What's going on out there?" Lothar demanded of the youth.

The boy turned his impossibly young face to his

commanding officer. "Smoke, sir! To the southeast!"

"Your Majesty," Khadgar said, his whole body tense, "I urge you to engage the Guardian with all haste!"

"They've reached Elwynn Forest!" one of the guards declared. "Grand Hamlet is burning!" Lothar and Llane locked gazes, then Lothar strode to the window. The guard had been right. In the pre-dawn darkness it was ease itself to spot a sullen but sinister orange-red glow surging just above tree line. The wind shifted, bringing the acrid scent to his nostrils.

Taria was beside him, one hand on his arm. "An attack?" She was of noble birth, and royalty by marriage. She kept her voice steady. Only he, who knew her so well, could hear the slight tremor in it; feel her fear in the grip on his arm.

He didn't answer. He didn't need to. She knew. Her experssion changed as she analyzed his. "What?" she asked.

Lothar pitched low for her ears only, "Stop requesting Callan."

She looked at him, unable in this moment to feign confusion. He lowered his voice to a harsh whisper. "Stay out of my business."

Taria didn't deny it, only saying, as if the words explained everything, "He wants to follow in his father's footsteps."

There were ten thousand things wrong with that, and Lothar wanted to address at least three thousand of them, but there was no time. Instead, he said, "Stop helping him."

"Tread carefully," Taria said. "You talk to your queen."

That coaxed a sly smile from Lothar, and he leaned in to her. "You are my sister first," he reminded her. She couldn't argue that. Llane came up behind them, regarding Lothar with grave brown eyes.

"When was your last visit to Karazhan?" the king asked.

"With you. I don't know… six years?" Six years. A long time. How had they slipped by like this? The three of them had been so close, once…

Llane looked surprised. "You've had no contact with Medivh since then?"

"Not for lack of trying," Lothar muttered. "I know my letters were received, but I might have saved myself the trouble of hiring a courier and simply lit them on fire after writing them. I gather you've not heard from him, either."

Llane shook his head. "Well," he said grimly, looking at his hand, "he can't hide from us now." He pulled off a ring with a large, winking blue gem, and pressed it into Lothar's outstretched palm.

Their eyes met.

"The Guardian," said Llane, "is summoned."

5

Durotan, Orgrim, and two dozen other Frostwolves stood on a rise, watching what was unfolding below them. Durotan slowly stroked the thick fur of Sharptooth, scarcely believing what he saw. Orcs—the mighty, enormous, proud warriors—were setting fire to huts with thatched roofs, slaughtering livestock, and chasing after smaller, unarmed, soft-looking creatures that fled, screaming, from them. Gul'dan had promised the orcs food and clean water. He had delivered. The fields below them were golden with grain, littered with gourd vegetables that were bright orange.

The bellies of his people were full, but their spirits were still starved. Durotan's lip curled in disgust as the rout—it could not be graced with the name "battle"—continued.

Out of the chaos below, a wolf and rider separated from the others and surged up the hill toward them. Blackhand, the warchief, wore a thunderous expression. Tied down over his wolf's powerful shoulders was a prisoner. One of the "humans", as Gul'dan had called them.

She looked young, and terrified. Her hair was the color of the thatch that crackled and burned below them, and her skin was a strange shade of pink-orange. Her eyes were as blue as those of Durotan's son. Although she wept in terror, the infant she clutched close was too frightened even to cry. The female looked up at Durotan and pleaded silently, but he knew what she was saying without words. It was what any parent would say. *Spare my child.*

Detish…

"Frostwolves do not join the hunt?" Blackhand demanded.

Durotan regarded the weeping female as he answered. "We prefer our enemies armed with an axe, not a child."

An emotion flickered over Blackhand's face as he looked down at his prisoner. The expression was gone in an instant, but Durotan had glimpsed it. "We have been commanded, Durotan." And the voice held the faintest tinge of shame. "Respect the old ways." He resettled himself on his mount, gathering the reins of his wolf. So softly Durotan almost didn't catch it, the warchief muttered, "There must be a worthy foe somewhere in this dung-heap."

Durotan did not reply. Blackhand growled, then

jerked on the reins and wheeled his wolf around. "Find them!" he shouted to the rest of the war party. "Try not to kill too many. We need them alive!"

Quietly, Orgrim said, almost apologetically, "This is war, my chieftain."

Durotan continued to watch the terrorizing below him unfold. He thought of the cages, and the draenei, and he shook his head. "No," he said. "It isn't."

It was petty, Lothar knew, but dammit, at the moment, he was feeling angry and helpless, and yes, petty, so he did not tell the young mage where they were going. Khadgar had inquired, and Llane, obviously feeling similarly, said, "Wherever Lothar tells you to go."

He clung behind Lothar now as they flew atop the gryphon, this almost-Guardian mage boy not even as old as Callan. Lothar could feel him moving from side to side, peering down with the curiosity that marked his kind, asking questions which were, fortunately, snatched away by the wind. Lothar was in no mood to play tour guide.

The gryphon had leaped almost vertically into the sky, as if she had sensed Lothar's mood and she, too, felt like shaking Khadgar up. She had leveled out as they soared over the green treetops just now being touched by dawn. It was cold, this high in the air, and Lothar's breath came in white puffs. He yearned to direct the gryphon to serve as an aerial spy, to head straight for the fire, but he had his orders and was forced to watch the evil glow recede as they continued almost due east.

The rising sun spread a more benevolent glow over the awakening forests, until it it was fully daylight. A mountain crested ahead, a solitary giant among the lesser foothills and a gray smudge against the rosy hues of dawn. Something jutted upward even from this high peak. At that moment, the sun caught it, and light flashed off its windows. No, more than sunlight; there was light, blue-white and beautiful, emanating from inside the topmost chamber.

"Karazhan!" Khadgar's exclamation was not snatched by the wind, and all his enthusiasm, wonder, and trepidation was folded into the single word. Sour-feeling as he was, even Lothar could not begrudge him the moment. This, after all, would have been Khadgar's home, had he accepted his charge.

Lothar's eyes narrowed as the sun continued to illuminate the scene before them. Daylight was cruel to the place. The gray stone of the famous Tower of Karazhan had cracks that were visible even from this distance, and the closer they flew, the more Lothar realized that it was in a state of considerable disrepair. Ivy grew along the walls. The gardens and pasture, necessary to feed the Guardian and those who served him in so isolated a place, were tangled and overgrown. Some of the stables were even missing part of their roofs. His lips thinned. If the tower itself was so disheveled, what would this mean for its master? Six years was a long time to be silent.

As the gryphon wheeled gently, preparing to

descend, Lothar saw a single, straight-backed figure, his face a pale smudge over the flowing tabard depicting the Eye of the Kirin Tor, awaiting them at the base of the tower. Despite his trepidation, he felt the tension in his chest ease a little.

The gryphon landed gently, and a grin stretched across the soldier's face as he slipped from its back and strode toward the awaiting figure. Tall, thin but ropy with muscle, the man's skin and hair were both pale. Lines seamed his face, but his eyes were young, and they twinkled with pleasure as the castellan reached to embrace his old friend.

Lothar pounded the ageless figure on the back. "Moroes, you ancient beast! Look at you! Unchanged!" It was no idle compliment. Moroes had looked old to him when he was but a youth. Now, he looked much younger. Lothar realized with a wry mental shrug it was because he had aged, and Moroes had not.

"Would I could say the same for you, Anduin Lothar," Moroes replied. "You're an old man! What, is that gray in your hair?"

"Perhaps there is," Lothar allowed. There certainly would be, if his fears were confirmed. The thought sobered him. He turned to look at Khadgar. The boy's eyes were as big as two eggs set in his young face.

"Follow me, gentlemen," Moroes said. His old-young eyes lingered on Khadgar, but he asked no questions.

"Come on," Lothar said to Khadgar, adding, almost reluctantly, "I think you'll like this." To Moroes, he said, "Where is everyone?" as they stepped inside.

Sorrow flitted over those ageless features. Moroes didn't answer the question as he replied, "Many things have changed."

One thing that had remained the same, though, was the room they entered—the library. As high as the walls rose, so it seemed did the rows of books that encircled a winding staircase in the middle of the large chamber. They lined what felt like every inch of the curving stone wall: shelf after shelf, tome upon tome, boxes innumerable filled with scrolls, every last one of them, Lothar knew, rare and precious and most likely unique. There were so many of them that ladders had been erected connecting to a reading terrace above them—which was also filled with books. And, as if books in shelves or on a terrace were not sufficiently excessive, there were stacks of books as tall as Lothar himself scattered about the floor. The knowledge that lay within them could never be absorbed by a single person in his or her lifetime.

At least, no *ordinary* single person.

More striking than the almost obscene glut of priceless knowledge, though, were the veins of magic that provided light to read them by.

They flowed upward and along the shelves, bright, glowing white rivulets that seemed to burst into bloom across the ceiling high above their heads. Khadgar looked like a boy in a pastry shop, ready to devour everything, and Lothar supposed he could hardly blame him.

"These lead to the Guardian's font?" Khadgar asked, his gaze glued to the feathery tendrils of illumination. His voice shook ever so slightly.

Moroes's eyes widened a fraction and he threw Lothar an inquisitive look, as if to say *what sort of interesting tidbit have you brought me?* "Indeed," he answered. "Karazhan was built at a point of confluence—"

"—Where ley lines meet, I know," Khadgar breathed. He shook his head, obviously almost overwhelmed. "The power that must be locked away here... the knowledge!" He laughed, a surprisingly innocent sound. "I didn't know so many books even existed!"

Moroes looked even more intrigued. Lothar wasn't ready to answer questions from the castellan until he'd asked a few of his own. "Where is he?" he inquired bluntly.

Moroes gave his old friend a knowing smile. He extended an index finger, and pointed it directly up.

Of course. "Wait here," Lothar said to Khadgar, eyeing the winding staircase that went up... and *up*... and braced himself for the climb. He was certain the boy would obey this particular command. Mages. Ordinary youths Khadgar's age would have been more excited about entering an armory. Lothar understood the value of books, but this boy was just as Medivh had been—hungering for knowledge as if it were meat and drink. For them, perhaps it was. He added, "Try not to touch anything," but he harbored no illusions that this second instruction would be followed.

Moroes led the way. Lothar waited until they had made a few turns on the staircase and were safely out of Khadgar's earshot. "He sees no one?"

Moroes shrugged. "The world's been at peace."

Again, an answer that wasn't really one. "There were other obligations. The floods in Lordaeron. King Magni's weddings." He smiled a little. There had been a time when he, Medivh, and Llane would never have missed the opportunity for so much fine dwarven beer. The smile faded. "He was absent for all of them."

"Yes," Moroes confirmed. He was silent for a few steps, then, "I am glad you are here, Lothar. It will do the Guardian a world of good to see a friendly face beyond this old mug."

"He could have seen it at any time over the last six years," Lothar said.

"Yes," Moroes said again, with that irritating avoidance of any information that could be of actual enlightenment.

Damn, Lothar had forgotten how high the tower was. "Tell me what you can, Moroes," he said. "Let's start with who left, and why."

It was a good topic, and allowed Lothar to conserve his breath for the seemingly endless climb of the tight curve of the staircase. Moroes moved like a gnomish automaton, his pace regular, steady, and vexingly untiring.

The staff responsible for the care of guests were the first to be let go, Moroes informed Lothar; the maids, the footmen, much of the kitchen staff. Since he planned to have no more visitors, there was no need to have servants, Medivh had said. There was therefore also no need for extra steeds or hunting hounds. The master of Karazhan had let the grooms and kennel tenders have their pick of the beasts when they left, and the groundskeeping staff was cut to the bone. Even the animals were sent away; the inhabitants who remained relied on a few chickens for eggs and vegetables from the gardens.

And on it went. Lothar listened—he had to; he was becoming too winded to talk—with a growing sense of unease as Moroes continued the litany of those no longer present at the Tower of Karazhan. "The illustrators were the last to leave," Moroes finished up. The illustrators. Not those who grew the food, or prepared it, or kept the tower in a state of repair. Lothar did not like the image of his old friend Moroes had created.

"The Guardian keeps mostly to himself now," Moroes finished. "But he can't refuse you. Nor King Llane. Not if he's summoned." Lothar had subtly, or so he thought, leaned casually against the center column of the tightly winding stair in an effort to catch his breath. Moroes eyed him. He breathed in deeply, moving his hands to indicate that Lothar do likewise, said "Chop chop," and continued climbing briskly.

Lothar looked up at the seemingly countless stories yet to go, and in that moment would have liked nothing better than to hurl Moroes off the steps. Grunting softly, Lothar, looking daggers at the much older man's back as he ascended, followed with legs made of rubber.

They finally reached the topmost chamber of the Tower of Karazhan. It was open and airy. Alcoves bearing the Eye of the Kirin Tor alternated with stained-glass windows. The colored light that filtered in mixed with the illumiation provided by the room's central focus—the Guardian's Font. Like a gently roiling cauldron, the font bubbled and occasionally shot up a spray of pale blue mist; it was a pool of magical energy so powerful that Lothar didn't even like to think about it. A platform ringed the room, reachable by two sets of stairs, and housed Medivh's private sleeping area. This much, Lothar had seen on previous visits to Karazhan.

But the statue was new.

It was not a statue, not yet. At the moment, it was nothing more than a vaguely man-shaped hunk of clay towering fifteen to twenty feet over the glowing pool. The light cast shifting streams of white on its brown, lumpy shape. The thing was chunky, its limbs thick as tree trunks, with a featureless blob stuck on its enormous body. It was held up by scaffolding, against which was propped a staff with a carved raven.

Perched atop a ladder was its sculptor.

The Guardian of Azeroth was smaller than Lothar in height and bulk, and his power did not come from his ability to swing a sword, but he was still tall and well-formed. Sweat and clay decorated his bare torso as he worked, using tools as well as his hands to mold the earthen figure before him. His back was toward the newcomers, and muscles clenched and unclenched as he continued to work.

Without turning around, Medivh asked, "Did you send for him, Moroes?" His voice was clear and strong, the question seemingly idle, but there was a slight warning timbre to it.

"He did not," Lothar answered, trying and failing not to pant from the insane climb. A lump of clay sat on the table, and, still catching his breath, Lothar poked at it. "So," he said, to fill the silence, "you've become a sculptor?"

Now Medivh turned around. Lothar wasn't sure what he'd been expecting. The disrepair of the once-magnificent Karazhan, Moroes's story of solitude, six years of no contact whatsoever—but Medivh looked like... Medivh. His hair, long and loose and untidy, was the same shade of sandy brown, his beard the same hue. No sudden streaks of white, or deep lines on his brow, though the Guardian's face, like Lothar's, had a few more wrinkles than in years past. His eyes looked tired, but his body strong and fit as ever.

"Making a golem, actually," Medivh said casually. He eyed his creation for a moment, then, using a strand of wire between two wooden handles, shaved off a curl of clay on the thing's shoulder.

"A golem," Lothar said, nodding as if he knew exactly what Medivh meant.

"A clay servant," Medivh said. "Usually takes years for the magic to seep into the clay, but up here..." He gestured at the font of liquid white magic. "Much faster! Maybe Moroes can use it. Help around the house."

"There's no one else to help him," Lothar said bluntly, even as he gratefully accepted a cup of watered wine from the servant.

Medivh shrugged, leaping lightly down from the ladder and reaching for a towel. He wiped at his clay-spattered torso ineffectively.

"I like the quiet." The two old friends stood and regarded each other for a moment. Medivh's face softened into a genuine smile, and his voice was warm. "It's good to see you, Lothar."

"You've been missed, old friend," Lothar said, "but I've not come to reminisce and catch up. We need guidance now, Medivh."

He removed the ring with the royal seal that Llane had given him. It was a heavy thing. He held it between thumb and forefinger, showing it to Medivh. "Our king summons you."

A subtle mask of impassivity hardened the Guardian's features as he took the ring for a moment, regarding it as it lay in his palm. He handed it back. Lothar noticed that there was a smudge of clay on it, and he wiped it off before putting it back on his finger.

"Who's the boy downstairs?" Medivh asked.

The boy downstairs was presently happier than a pig in slop.

Bathed in the light of magic, he had spent the time waiting gleefully ensconced in books. He was raptly perusing one, hands covered with dust, when he caught a flicker of motion out of the corner of his eye. Suddenly acutely aware that he was reading books that did not belong to him—books that did, in fact, belong to the *Guardian of Azeroth*, he snapped the tome shut and replaced it guiltily.

A shape loomed, silent, at the far end of the room, dark enough that it was almost a shadow itself.

Khadgar swallowed. "Hello?" he called. The figure didn't move. He took a hesitant step forward. "Guardian?"

Now the shape did move, turning slightly to face a row of books and lifting a black hand. It extended a forefinger—pointing. It walked forward, one step, two—And *vanished* into the shelf.

Khadgar inhaled swiftly, striding forward, then breaking into a jog. What was the figure pointing at, and where had it gone? He skidded to a halt, his gaze flickering over the books. It had to be a doorway, unless the figure had been an illusion. What was the trick with books and doorways and secret rooms— ah, yes. A certain title was often a lever. Or so the old stories always said. Which one seemed likely?

Dreaming with Dragons: The True History of the Aspects of Azeroth? Unlikely… but interesting. He pulled it down. *What the Titans Knew*? Probably not… but still… Khadgar grabbed that one too. *Walking Through Worlds*—now that one had possibility.

He had just reached for it when he felt a tingling on the underside of his lower arm. Frowning, Khadgar returned the two books to their proper places and tugged down his sleeve. The brand that had once marked him as a future Guardian, the Eye of the Kirin Tor, was glowing!

Startled, Khadgar stepped back, and the glow and the warm, tingling sensation faded. He moved forward again—sure enough, it began to radiate once more. It... it was *guiding* him, somehow. The young mage moved his arm along the row of books, back and forth—cooler, warmer; by the Light, it was growing *hot*—

There.

The next-to-last volume on the shelf, squatter and thicker than most he had seen. Metal adorned its spine, and when he pulled it out, Khadgar saw the design on its cover had been inlaid with gems. But where was the title? He'd just started to flip through it when he heard footsteps.

Quickly, Khadgar shoved the book into one of the compartments sewn into his cloak. He took a deep breath, turned the corner and—

"Have a good look around?" demanded the Guardian of Azeroth. And his eyes blazed blue.

6

Khadgar was knocked off his feet, seized by an invisible grasp and tossed into the air. He cried out, squirming, and then was slammed against one of the bookcases with such force that the massive thing slid back several feet. "Taking measurements, perhaps?" Medivh accused. He strode toward Khadgar, eyes flashing with fury, his hands curled into fists. "Get some ideas what you might do with the place once it's yours?"

Lothar must have told him. And of course he'd think that, Khadgar thought. He was terribly intelligent, he knew. But sometimes, Khadgar also knew, he could be terribly stupid.

"Guardian!" he yelped. "I renounced my vow!"

"So I've been told." And, apparently, Medivh simply didn't care. Casually, the Guardian moved his arm, and Khadgar now found himself with his back against the great central staircase. Pinned like an insect to a board, the young mage dangled several feet off the ground, his arms and legs flailing. Khadgar struggled against the unseen force, but it was merciless and held him fast.

Medivh snorted in contempt, watching him. "Feeble," he said, his voice dripping scorn. He lifted a hand, almost casually, and the pressure against Khadgar's chest increased. His fear escalated as he realized he could barely breathe.

And yet, he had to speak. "I didn't want to come here! I swear, Guardian, I urged them to find you!"

He looked desperately to Lothar. The big man simply stood there, arms folded, watching. Why didn't he say anything? "I told them you should be the one to explain—"

"Explain what?"

Khadgar felt his heart slamming against his chest. His sight was beginning to dim. He struggled for another mere sip of air and managed a single word:

"*Fel!*"

The pressure vanished. Khadgar dropped, hard, to the stone floor and gasped as air flooded his lungs.

"In Azeroth?" Medivh demanded, striding over to him. Khadgar moved carefully, wincing. Nothing was broken, though he'd have some glorious bruises. He looked up at the Guardian glowering down at him.

"In the barracks," Khadgar panted, still catching his breath. "One of the bodies."

"Guardian," Lothar interjected, "what is the fel?"

Medivh did not take his eyes from Khadgar. "A magic unlike any other," he said, softly. "It feeds on life itself. It pollutes the user, twisting everything it touches. It promises great power—but it exacts a terrible price. There is no place for the fel in Azeroth."

He fell silent, and Khadgar had a very long moment in which to wonder if mentioning the fel had been the right tactic, and another in which to wonder if he'd be flung from the tower or simply turned into a small creature and fed to a cat.

Then Medivh nodded, once. "You've done the right thing." To Lothar, he said, "I will go." With a flurry of the folds of his crimson robe he moved past Khadgar, not sparing the younger man a second glance. Lothar stepped forward and extended a hand to Khadgar, but as the mage reached up to take it, Lothar withdrew it and followed the Guardian. Khadgar thought about all the spells he would like to summon at this moment and the things they would do to Lothar, and, wincing, got to his feet by himself.

Lothar carefully knotted the gryphon's reins so they wouldn't come loose, and adjusted them so they fit closely but comfortably around her feathered neck. He stroked her head and she cawed softly with pleasure. She'd been a reliable companion, and had helped him give Khadgar a good and proper scare, and he'd miss her.

He removed his hand and she opened her golden eyes in query. "Back home, you." Lothar gently knocked her beak twice. The gryphon shook herself, fluffing her fur and feathers, gathered her body like a cat, and leaped skyward, her wings catching the wind and propelling her back toward her Stormwind aerie and a well-earned meal and nap.

He watched her for a moment, envying the simplicity of her life when his was being upended, then turned and went toward the three mages. Medivh, clad now in a hooded cloak trimmed with raven feathers, had etched symbols at each of the four compass points and was drawing a circle in the earth with the end of his staff. The pale blue light of arcane magic trailed after it, sparking the runes to glowing light as well. Khadgar eyed the Guardian uncertainly as he worked, while Moroes stood back a slight distance with his hands clasped behind his back. Medivh looked up from his task and grinned at the boy's expression.

"They don't teach this in Dalaran."

"Teleportation?" Khadgar shook his head. "No." His gaze drifted back to the symbols.

"They're right to fear it," Medivh continued. He stole another glance at Khadgar and his eyes twinkled. *He's enjoying this,* Lothar thought. "It's very dangerous." He drew up the magic with delicate fingers, held his hand over his head, then brought his arm down with a swift, precise movement. The luminous strands he had gathered leaped up and joined, forming a dome of crackling illumination. From beneath it, his features thrown into sharp relief by the blue glow, Medivh gestured to the boy. "Go on. Step in."

Khadgar hesitated. "Come now," Medivh scoffed cheerfully. "Where's all that rebel spirit?" The boy's cheeks turned pink through the wisps of facial hair and he obeyed, though not without obvious trepidation.

Lothar smothered a smile himself as he stepped into the circle behind Khadgar. Mage though he was—nay, future Guardian, trained to be at least—it was almost too easy to rattle him.

As soon as both Lothar's feet landed inside the circle, everything—stables, the tower, even the earth beneath them—disappeared. Khadgar barely had time to gasp before other images took their place: polished white stone instead of brown earth, the blue and gold of banners, the gleam of metallic armor—

"By the Light, what—Halt!"

The voice floated to them, faint at first, but growing louder. The extremely sharp points of pikestaffs came into view, along with gauntlets, and then, finally, the angry and then confused faces of the king's guard.

"Commander?" The guard gaped first at Lothar in confused recognition, then his gaze went to Medivh. "Guardian!"

"Stand down," Lothar ordered, but not unkindly. Immediately the guards stepped back, snapping to attention, the butts of their staffs firmly on the floor.

Llane had risen from his throne and now descended, his eyes warm and a broad smile parting his neatly trimmed brown beard. Medivh bowed deeply.

"Your Grace," the Guardian said.

But Llane would have none of that. He reached out his arms to envelop Medivh in a bear hug. The

Guardian handed his staff to a startled Khadgar, who stared at it almost reverently, in order to return the embrace, clapping his old friend on the back. When they parted, both were smiling.

"Medivh… it's been too long!" Llane exclaimed. "Come. Help us get to the root of these troubles of ours." The king and the Guardian strode out of the throne room, heads already bent toward one another and talking quickly and urgently.

Khadgar stepped forward to follow. Lothar clamped a hand on the boy's narrow shoulder.

"Seen and not heard," Lothar warned. "Understand?" Khadgar nodded. He and Lothar followed the king into another room. Lothar knew it well. The throne room was for formal occasions and petitions—for when Llane needed to be king. The war room was when the king needed to be a commander.

Compared to the size and the formality of the throne room, this chamber was almost intimate. Lothar had always thought that fitting. A soldier could distance himself from the strategies, the master plans, the vast numbers of legions and the complexities of distributing both men and materiel. He—or she, for women fought in Stormwind's armies—could not, however, put distance from the fact that death would be dealt. Just as the act of creating life was intimate, so was the act that took it.

The ceiling was low, and the light came from a few windows and candalabras. The front part of the room was dominated by an enormous table upon which were spread maps drawn on parchment, and a second one peopled with small, carved figures representing weapons or friends or foes. Further in, the tools of war were on display: shields, swords, long and short, morning stars, pikes, axes. Khadgar, eyes wide, went straight for them, walking around the displays gingerly.

"These," Llane said, pointing at several clusters of red figurines, "are the beasts who have been attacking us so severely."

"What kind of *beasts*?" Medivh demanded, glaring at the maps.

Llane looked exasperated. "Giants—armed giants. Wolves carry them. Huge, unstoppable beasts—"

"It's the rumors that are unstoppable," Lothar interrupted.

"There's not much we can do about that," Llane said.

Medivh continued to examine the board, frowning. One hand reached out to touch the carved symbol of the mysterious foe. "What of the other kingdoms? Are they suffering the same?"

"All seek our protection, yet none trusts us enough to tell us anything." Llane had folded his arms and was glaring at the board as if his will alone could change something.

"In other words, little has changed in the last six years," Medivh said drily.

Lothar had had enough. "We know nothing about these so-called monsters." He grabbed one of the enemy markers, shaking it for emphasis. "We need prisoners. Even a corpse will tell us something."

Llane took the small figurine from Lothar, turning it over in his hands. He lifted his eyes to the Guardian. "I don't know what danger we're in, Medivh."

"I exist to protect this realm, my lord. It is my very purpose. I am the Guardian." Medivh's blue-green eyes went to Khadgar, who was holding the raven-topped staff and peering at the weaponry. "At least," he amended, "for the time being, anyhow."

Llane's gaze followed Medivh's and his eyebrows lifted. *He'd forgotten*, Lothar realized. "Yes," Llane said, straightening slightly. He placed the figurine back on the map in its former position. "What *are* we going to do about... what was his name?"

"*Khadgar*, sire." The young mage replied calmly, almost elegantly, but the effect was ruined when the staff struck a sword with a loud *clang* as he turned. Khadgar blushed.

"He will be coming with us," Medivh spoke before Lothar could.

Lothar rolled his eyes. "Well, then. We'd better get going."

Lothar requested three horses, a company of armed, armored soldiers and a sturdy, barred cart for the transportation of the hoped-for prisoners. As soon as word came that the company was ready, he, Medivh, and Khadgar strode through the main hallway of Stormwind Keep. Lothar grimaced as Sergeant Callan saluted him smartly.

"We are ready to depart when you give the order, sir."

"Let's give our guests the chance to get on their horses first, shall we, Sergeant?"

Callan's cheeks turned pink, but he nodded. "As you say, sir," he replied.

Lothar felt bad almost immediately. The boy had done everything right. By the book, even, right down to bringing Lothar's own stallion, Reliant, and two horses with good temperaments for Khadgar and Medivh. He hadn't earned Lothar's snide comment. The commander swung himself up into Reliant's saddle and patted the horse's sleek brown neck. Gryphons were fine, but horses were better.

Gruffly, he said, "Good choices for the others."

"Thank you, sir!" Callan's expression didn't change, but Lothar saw his son's shoulders relax, ever so slightly.

They rode at a slow trot through the streets of the city. When they reached the market square, they passed a towering statue with a very familiar face. Khadgar did a priceless double take, peering at the statue, then at Medivh, then at the statue again, and finally judiciously keeping his eyes straight forward.

Medivh's saddle creaked as he shifted. "I didn't ask them to put that up." It was true, Lothar knew. It had been erected by demand of a populace that was grateful to not have become a troll's supper.

"You saved the city," Khadgar replied politely.

The Guardian frowned slightly. "You think it's vain?"

"The people love you," Khadgar stated. Lothar fought back a smile.

"But that's not what I asked you."

Khadgar squinted up at the blue sky. "When the sun is hot, it makes excellent shade."

Medivh shot his old friend an impressed glance and, seemingly despite himself, couldn't hide a smile.

Once they had clattered over the bridge and through Stormwind's gates, Lothar gave the signal that the group should break into an easy canter as they headed down the road. A crowd had gathered to cheer the soldiers as they passed the Lion's Pride Inn. Lothar took care to make eye contact and return some of the children's salutes. Part of this battle, he knew already, would be won by keeping rumors to a minimum and the populace feeling safe, and a full company of fifty mounted knights in full plate armor thundering past certainly helped achieve that goal.

The company was too well trained to make idle conversation, so the way was silent save for the rhythmic sound of the horses' hooves and the fluttering and scolding of birds and squirrels. Lothar thought about what he'd seen; the vile mist surging forth from a dead man's mouth. He'd been quick to calm Llane, but in truth, he had no better idea of what these "beasts" were than a farmer gulping ale in the Lion's Pride Inn.

And Callan. He really didn't like the idea of the young man being involved, not until they knew what they were facing. Damn Taria anyway. She meant well, but she didn't...

He frowned. The forest was silent. Medivh, who rode a little ways ahead of him, had brought his horse down to a trot, then a halt. Lothar lifted his fist and the rest of the company clattered to a stop behind him. He kneed Reliant forward to the edge of the clearing beside Medivh.

What had once been an ordinary broad path through a pleasant part of Elwynn had become a battlefield. Not a proper one, consisting of soldiers and armies, but the worst kind—the kind where the weapons were scythes, pitchforks, and small axes, and the "soldiers" were farmers and townspeople. Carts lay everywhere, smashed and overturned. Some cargo, like linen and wool, had been rummaged through and discarded. Other carts, presumably carrying food, had been picked clean. Several of the trees had their limbs hacked off or smashed by weapons so large Lothar was having a hard time grasping the size of them.

And there was blood—both the red of human blood and also splashes here and there of a thick, brown fluid. Lothar dismounted, removing his glove and touching the liquid, rubbing it between his fingers. Something very important was missing—bodies. Medivh and Khadgar, too, had dismounted. Medivh strode ahead, absently planting his staff in the ground. Khadgar caught it before it tumbled to the earth. The Guardian was staring at a burned tree trunk that gave off a sickly green smoke. Glowing embers in the blackened wood winked like emeralds.

"It can't be," Lothar thought he heard Medivh murmur.

He saw Khadgar's attention shift to something behind one of the carts. "Here's a body," the boy said, then called out, "Guardian!"

There was a blur of motion. Lothar's head whipped around just in time to see one of his knights go flying, his mail and chest crushed in by a thrown hammer a third as large as he was.

The hitherto silent forest was now filled with a terrible roaring sound, and the beasts they had been hunting poured into the clearing, exploding out of nowhere, dropping from the trees.

Giants—armed giants.

Wolves to carry them.

Huge, unstoppable beasts—

Lothar's first, absurd thought was that the rumors hadn't gone far enough.

7

"Mother of—" Sir Evran whispered. He, like the others, like Lothar himself, was frozen, rooted to the earth as the monsters charged forward.

Like the trolls, they were tall, had tusks, and adorned themselves with tattoos and bones and feathers. But they were not just tall, they were massive. Their chests were enormous, their hands large enough to envelop and crush a man's skull without effort, and the weapons designed to fit such hands—

The biggest one of all silenced Sir Evran before he could even finish his sentence. Towering above the others, tattoos crawling over his hands, he sprang with the speed and power of one of Stranglethorn's great cats, bringing an enormous hammer crunching down on the hapless knight. The gargantuan thing turned, and, almost casually, hefted a shrieking horse into the air and tossed it as if it were little more than a sack of grain. Two soldiers fell, crushed beneath its weight. A female, her skin more green than brown, laughed maniacally at the spectacle.

It all happened in the span of one heartbeat to the next.

Sir Kyvan roared in response, his voice sounding thin and high next to the bellow of the beasts. He brought his blade swinging up, knocking that of a greenish-tinted monster to the side. The creature grunted in surprise, then—it looked like he grinned as he engaged the brave Kyvan in earnest. Though the enemy was twice his size, Kyvan managed to hold his own until the creature almost casually tore a wheel off one of the carts and slammed it into Kyvan's skull.

It looked up, grinning around those hideous tusks, only to stumble as Lothar's shield bashed him in the face. The thing's head jerked back, and Lothar swung his sword, slicing across the beast's jugular. Blood as green as its skin spurted forth, and the creature fell—dead.

The rumors had been wrong about one thing, at least. The beasts were *not* unstoppable.

Khadgar gaped at the enormous thing that had hurled a fully-grown horse fifteen feet. Obviously the leader of the monsters, it rampaged through the clearing, reached for a battleaxe that was almost as big as Khadgar, and swung it in a wide, low arc, severing the bodies of two armored knights. Blood spattered everywhere, and the thing threw back its head and bellowed joyfully. All around him, wolves nearly the size of bears, white and gray and terrifying, were killing with the same speed, power, and ferocity as their riders.

Khadgar dragged his horrified gaze from the carnage to see what Medivh was doing, thinking he could help. His bowels clenched even tighter when he realized that what the Guardian of Azeroth was doing was absolutely nothing. Medivh simply stood, staring.

One of the beasts charged toward Khadgar. The youth shouted a spell, and a blast of arcane lightning shot from his hand. It struck the creature full in the chest and sent him flying. Khadgar shook himself and, speaking quickly and clearly, cast a protective circle about himself and Medivh. The air shimmered, encasing them in a small, shimmering blue bubble. If the Guardian wasn't ready to attack, at least the former Novitiate would see to it that those things didn't slice them both in half.

A shrill whinny behind them caused the young mage to whirl around—

—and come face to face with one of the beasts.

Lothar's sword dripped greenish-brown blood as his gaze flickered over the scene. His knights outnumbered the beasts almost four to one—yet the monsters were overcoming them. Several good soldiers lay on the ground, either dead or dying, and—

Callan.

Callan didn't see the axe that was about to—

Lothar was moving even before his brain realized

it, lunging forward, using body, shield, and sword all as weapons. The beast was caught completely off guard and Lothar's sword found its mark, plunging deep into the thing's unprotected chest.

Callan stared gratefully up at his father. "Don't try to take them on with brute force," Lothar panted. He kicked at the creature's corpse, rolling it off his son. "They're stronger. Be smarter."

He extended his free hand to his son. Callan reached up to take it. But even as Callan's eyes flew wide in warning, Lothar felt something go around his waist that was as thick and strong as a tree trunk and he was hurled backward. He landed hard and painfully, his sword knocked from his hand, his own armor a liability as the monster, the leader of the whole horrifying group, advanced on him, leering.

The giant axe that had cut two men in half mere moments before was nowhere to be seen. The beast had thrown it, or abandoned it, or simply decided he didn't want it any more. Lothar neither knew nor cared. Hot saliva dripped onto his face as the beast leader raised a hammer with an oversized right hand, reaching for Lothar with the other.

Refusing to accept the inevitable, Lothar put his hands down beside his waist in a doubtless futile attempt to rise. His right hand brushed something unfamiliar, and for a moment he didn't realize what it was. And then, he remembered.

It's a boomstick.

He'd stuck it in his belt and completely forgotten about it—until now. Lothar was able to get Magni's gift out far enough to aim it at the descending hand. The beast's enormous fingers clamped down on the weapon. Lothar squeezed the small movable part. The resulting blast almost deafened him, but the scream that followed was still audible. The beast staggered back, staring at the smoking ruin of flesh at the end of his arm.

The beast was huge, with brown skin and two yellowed tusks jutting upward from his oversized lower jaw. Two thick braids hung down on either side of his ears, the rest of the black length braided or flowing freely. Ears the size of Khadgar's hands were pointed and pierced. Like the other beasts, this one wore primitive jewelry of bones and beads. He held an enormous axe in one hand. With the other, he touched, with surprising delicacy, the magical field that was all that stood between him and the mages.

His eyes were clear, brown, and calm. Behind those eyes, Khadgar realized, was an intelligent brain.

And *that* was the most frightening thing of all.

"Guardian!" Khadgar shouted, his voice climbing.

The cry seemed to knock Medivh out of whatever trance he was in. He began to chant, light following the motions of his weaving fingers like ink from a pen until a sigil hung in the air.

The beast lowered his hand, his too-intelligent eyes going at once to Medivh, watching closely—curiously.

There were several sudden blazes of sickly green light. Khadgar gasped and the beast leaped back, both sets of eyes focused on the clearing.

Khadgar had noticed that some of the beasts had undertones of green in their skin—the color of fel magic. He had not had time to discuss—well, *anything* with Medivh upon their arrival, but he was certain the Guardian had noticed it as well. Now, as he stared, all the beasts who had that peculiar coloring dropped their weapons and started to convulse, screaming. Jagged, spindly fingers of green lightning leaped from the stricken creatures, arcing directly back to Medivh, who stood with his hands outstretched, palms up. Before Khadgar's eyes, the beasts' skins paled, their muscles atrophied, and one by one, they fell, crumbling, like pieces of hard earth in the hands of a child.

A spontaneous cheer of relief went up from the knights as they saw their chance. "They're all dying!" someone shouted.

"Only the green ones!" another cried. They fell on the spasming beasts, impaling them with swords and then turning on their shocked brethren. "Kill that beast bastard!" an officer shouted, pointing toward the leader. The beast with the ruined hand looked around in obvious confusion. Khadgar flinched as another boom from Lothar's weapon resounded. A hole appeared in the massive chest of one of the monsters. He stared down at it for an instant, then tumbled, stone dead.

The beast who had been standing outside the protective circle whirled, catching his companion. He cradled the monstrous form, grief plain on his ugly face. Khadgar blinked. Somehow, this surprised him. But the creature's expression shifted from concerned and caring to coldly furious as he looked at the man who had slain his friend.

"Let's put some steel through these bastards!" Lothar's voice rang out.

The beast rose, simultaneously releasing the corpse with gentleness and preparing himself to attack Lothar. Before Khadgar could even form the words of a warning, though, the beast's comrades seized him and hauled him off. With a final, furious glare, the beast leaped onto Medivh's horse, yanked on the reins, and galloped into the woods. The others followed, most on their wolves, but many with stolen horses, and in a heartbeat the clearing was as empty as it had been when the knights had arrived… save for the grim scattering of corpses.

Behind Khadgar, Medivh gave a low, soft moan. Khadgar turned to see the Guardian of Azeroth down on one knee, pale and exhausted, the heels of his hands pressing into his temples.

"Guardian!" Khadgar stammered. He started to move toward Medivh, but the other waved him off as he got unsteadily to his feet. "What—did you do?"

Medivh ignored him utterly, focusing his attention on swiftly drawing another circle in the dirt. Frustrated, Khadgar persisted.

"The fel. I was right, wasn't I? It's here." Again, he thought of the green tint to the skin of some of the beasts, and the lightning that leapt from them to Medivh as they flailed and grew weak.

Then, abruptly, he recognized the sigils the Guardian was sketching into the soil. Another teleportation! "What are you doing? Where are you going?"

Now, Medivh did look at him, his green-blue eyes piercing, it seemed, straight into Khadgar's soul. "Get these soldiers safely back to Stormwind." He stepped into the circle. "I must return to Karazhan." He paused. "You did well today."

There was a pulse of white light. Khadgar was left, blinking from the brightness, staring at exactly nothing.

"Where's he gone?" Lothar's shout was both worried and angry as he cantered up to Khadgar.

Khadgar realized his mouth was dry. He clenched his fists to stop his hands from trembling. He knew it wasn't the fight that had stunned and spooked him so badly.

"Karazhan," he told Lothar, quietly.

Lothar swore, pressed his lips together, then shook his head. "We need a prisoner. Where's your horse?"

"They *took* my horse!"

"Really?" Lothar's look of contempt could have withered an entire forest. "Just... stay there." Lothar galloped off with a pair of knights. Khadgar fought back the urge to knock him off with a spell, looked at the empty space where the Guardian of Azeroth ought to have been, and, sighing, turned his attention to examining the body of one of the beasts.

* * *

Nothing was as Durotan had expected. He had backed down in his earlier clash with Blackhand, but the longer this... this *harvesting* of the creatures he was told to call "humans" continued, the less he liked it. Today, at least, he did not feel sullied by his actions. Today, the humans had fought back— even taking Kurvorsh and others with them. It was unexpected, but at least Kurvorsh had died in battle, and Durotan would sing a lok'vadnod for him.

At least he would, if he lived long enough. The humans had rallied after the strange attack from the older human in the unpassable circle. Until he had agreed to join Gul'dan on this trek to this world of Azeroth, Durotan had never seen anything like it, and now, he had seen two similar spells. What had their shaman done? Or was he a warlock? Perhaps Drek'Thar could help him understand.

The Frostwolves had lost only a few warriors, but the humans were still in pursuit. Durotan had no desire to add any more of his clan to the ranks of the fallen until they understood what they were up against. He crouched low over the stolen riding beast, his huge hands on its head, directing its panicked flight.

He caught movement out of the corner of his eye—something green. It was Garona, Gul'dan's slave. She was still a prisoner, except now she was bound to the dead. The length of chain that started at her scrawny neck led to a pale corpse—one of the green-tinged orcs that had been so mysteriously killed. She was struggling, trying to break the chain, glancing back the way Durotan had come.

With no weapons, bound to a dead minder, and so much weaker than a true, full-blooded orc, she was pitifully easy prey for the humans. They would cut through her tiny body with a single stroke of one of their small swords. Durotan should just leave her; such a thing as she was not worth risking his people for.

But it had been Garona, the slave, who had tried to warn Durotan against Gul'dan the second time the warlock had visited the Frostwolves, and certainly since the clan had joined the Horde, Durotan had started to regret not heeding her words. And Draka had felt sympathy and kindness toward her, seeing in the half-orc a reflection of her own temporary Exile from the Frostwolves.

Durotan made his decision. He turned the animal's head toward the female, lifted Sever, and brought the great war axe crashing down on the iron chain. It parted easily, and he reached out his hand to her, ready to swing her behind him and bear her to safety.

Garona stared at his extended hand. Her gaze flickered to his face, and for a moment she hesitated.

Then she ran, darting into the forest—back the way they both had come. She would rather die as an orc than live as a slave.

It was a choice that almost guaranteed her death, but Durotan understood it. And he found he could not blame her.

* * *

Fel. It was, Khadgar was almost certain, what he had seen flowing between the beasts and Medivh, but there was no sign of it in this corpse any more. No telltale green mist seeping out from its mouth when, mindful of the seemingly razor-sharp teeth, Khadgar had opened its lips to test for the taint.

He paused. Something wasn't right here. He got to his feet, looking around. The remaining knights were tending to the wounded, preparing the human corpses for respectful transportation home and the beast corpses for a somewhat less respectful journey.

The young mage closed his eyes for a moment, tuning in to the natural world around him. The rustle of leaves in the wind, the hum of insects. Birdsong.

No birdsong. Just as there had been no birdsong when—

He whirled around, hand outstretched, fingers splayed. Magic crackled in his palm and he shoved, hard.

The intruder who had just leaped from above him was struck by the spell. The beast was pinned in the air, its back against the rough bark of a huge tree, snarling down at him and writhing impotently.

Khadgar's eyes widened as he got a good look at the beast he had just captured.

"Over here!" he shouted, not taking his eyes from his prisoner. He heard the sound of hoof beats behind him and then Lothar was there. So was a huge beast, unconscious and strapped across a second horse.

"You got a prisoner," Khadgar said.

"So did you," Lothar replied. "You took it alone?"

"Yes."

For a moment, Lothar looked impressed, but then the expression was gone. He eyed the captive. "Looks like the runt of the litter."

Khadgar sighed.

8

The human youth had looked like a reasonable target. Garona had not realized he knew magic—and was so proficient in it. The mistake had cost her. Now she jolted along in a barred wagon, a bleeding, battered orc warrior in chains across from her, staring at her. In the enclosed space, she wondered if she should have gone with Durotan. Maybe he would have agreed to hide her from Gul'dan. But no—he was too honorable. He would have felt the need to tell Gul'dan about her. And more than anything, Garona desired to be away from the warlock. Whatever the humans might do to her, it would be better.

Over the rumble of the wheels and the clopping sound the riding beasts made, one of the humans, the man who had used the loud weapon which hurled small missiles, called out to them.

"You. What are you?"

The orc across from Garona looked at him, then turned back to Garona.

She stayed silent, too. The human, riding atop his mount beside them and gazing at them through the bars of the cart, continued.

"Why do you attack our lands?"

Garona sat for a moment, thinking. Weighing her options. Then, she said in the human's own tongue, "He does not know what you speak."

The human turned toward her, alert as a predator. His eyes were... blue, his hair and beard pale, more like sand than earth. "You speak our language!"

There came a sharp clang as the bloodied orc lunged for Garona and was brought up short by his chains. "Say one more word in their language, slave, and I will wear your tongue," the orc rumbled.

"What is he saying?" the human demanded.

"He does not like that I am speaking to you," Garona said.

The Frostwolf was well and truly angry now, and he again pulled hard on his chains, the veins in his neck standing out like ropes. "I will not warn you again," he snarled.

"He keeps threatening me, but I care not for—"

The Frostwolf lunged forward a third time, bellowing in fury, straining to reach Garona. The metal groaned in protest. Garona inhaled swiftly, her eyes widening. The human saw it, too.

"Tell him to stop—" he began.

"*You* tell him," Garona retorted.

A final rush forward, and this time the chains pulled from the wood to which they were secured. The Frostwolf reached out for her throat, his mouth open in furious cry. Garona retreated as far as she could, but it would not be far enough—

He froze, gurgling. Brown blood seeped from his throat and his mouth, oozing down over the bright blade that was impaled halfway up its length. The light in his eyes faded, and when the human tugged his sword free, the Frostwolf slumped over, quite dead.

Garona stared at her savior, impressed. Somehow, he had been both swift and strong enough to leap from his mount and strike the Frostwolf through the bars in time. Now, he looked at her again with those uncanny blue eyes.

"You're welcome," he said.

"Have you a name?" Llane asked of the strange prisoner.

Lady Taria stood in the throne room, off to the side with Lothar, Khadgar, Callan, and some of her husband's guards. She couldn't keep from staring at the female prisoner Lothar and Khadgar had brought in. She looked so *human*... except that she didn't. She was of human size and shape, and would have been pretty save for the small tusks jutting out of her lower jaw.

She was bleeding here and there, and there were nasty, festering sores on her green skin where her manacles had rubbed. What passed for clothing, and it was very little, was stained and torn. Her thick black hair was tangled, and dirt smeared her emaciated body. And yet—she stood as if she were queen here, not Taria. Her spine was erect, her demeanor calm. This female might be in chains, but she was neither tamed nor broken.

"You understand our language," Llane said, reminding her that they knew this. "Again… have you a name?" He walked down the steps from his throne. The prisoner stepped forward boldly toward him. One of the guards stepped forward, his hand on his sword hilt, but Llane lifted a hand to stay any interference. The green female stroked the king's tunic, lingering over the lion head brooches, then continued upward to the great throne of Stormwind itself.

"Garona," said Lothar. He sat on the top step, his eyes following the female as she stepped past him. "She calls herself Garona."

"Garona," Llane said, addressing her directly as she stooped to touch the life-sized, golden lion at the throne's base. "What kind of being are you?"

Garona did not reply, sniffing at the gold beast. Her dark brown eyes scanned the room and those inside it. Curious? Anxious? Evaluating? Taria couldn't tell.

"She seems more like us than those… beasts we fought," one of the soldiers said.

His words made Garona pause in her exploration of the room. "Orc," she said.

Llane seized on this. "Orc? That's what you are? Or what the beast in the cage was?" When she didn't reply, he regarded her intently, looking her up and down. Some might have thought it an intimidation tactic, or perhaps a gesture of contempt. Taria recognized it for what it was. When her husband's father was killed and Llane took the throne, he had vowed to learn all he could about not only the kingdom he was to rule, but the world in which it was located. Standing before him was something utterly new. He was excited and fascinated by that, and Taria knew it pained him to permit the use of violence against beings so, in his view, marvelous and remarkable. She noticed that the young mage, too, seemed enthusiastically curious, as if he were stifling questions with difficulty. Perhaps, though, that was due to the fact that he was a young man, and the being before them was exotically beautiful.

"I know every race in the Seven Kingdoms, but I have never heard of an orc." Llane pointed toward the ceiling. Painted above their heads was a detailed map of Azeroth—all its islands and continents, its kingdoms and oceans. All that was known. There were patches that were as of yet unknown, wide expanses of open, blank mystery. "Show me where you come from, Garona."

The orc tilted back her head and examined the map. She frowned, then shook her head.

"This is not orc world," she said bluntly. A hint of a smile curved her lips. "Orc world is dead. Orcs take *this* world now."

"Not from this world?" Llane looked completely bewildered.

So, frankly, was Taria, and likely everyone else in the room. Khadgar seemed to be almost physically silencing himself. But she realized that they were all focusing on the wrong thing. Llane was an idealist. While it was part of what made him a fine king, he was wise enough to ensure he was surrounded by others who were more pragmatic. It was, if true, a revelation—but they needed to save lives, not draw new maps.

"How did you get here?"

The voice cut through the air of the room like a knife. Medivh stood in the doorway, his body taut as a bowstring. *How long has he been here, listening?* Taria wondered.

Garona snapped to attention at once, her eyes trained on Medivh. She strode toward him, seemingly as unafraid of him as she had been of any of them.

"The Great Gate. Deep in ground. Ancient magic brings us here."

Medivh strode forward. "You went through a gate," he confirmed.

"But how did you learn our language?" Khadgar burst out, unable to contain himself any longer.

The orc turned her dark gaze to the youth. "Orcs take prisoners for the gate. I learn from them—"

Llane interrupted, his voice and body taut with tension at her words. "Prisoners like us? Our people? Are they alive?"

"Yes. Many," Garona replied.

"Why?" Khadgar asked.

The orc looked at those who had been questioning

her in turn and lifted her chin. Her eyes blazed as she replied, pride in her posture and voice, "To feed the Gate. To bring the Horde. To take your world."

No one spoke. Taria could hardly believe what she had been hearing. A Great Gate, hungry for human prisoners. A horde of beings like Garona, flooding into Azeroth. To take it for their own. Her husband ruled, not she, but he shared almost everything with his queen, and she had learned many frightening things in their years together. But nothing as terrifying as this.

To take your world.

"You'll take us to them." Her brother, slicing through the sick silence in his usual manner.

Garona smirked. "No."

Lothar smiled. Taria knew that smile. It did not bode well for those at whom it was directed. "You'll take us to them," he repeated, almost pleasantly, "or you'll end up like your friend in the cage."

Garona strode toward him slowly, kneeling beside him on the step and bringing her face close to his. "You think you are fearsome?" she murmured. "Orc children have pets more fearsome than you."

Taria believed her.

"We are not trying to be fearsome, Garona," Llane said, speaking calmly in an effort to diffuse the tension. "We are trying to protect our people. Our families."

It was, it seemed, the wrong tactic. A mask seemed to settle over Garona's attractive features. "What do I care about families?" she replied in an icy tone, her gaze still locked with Lothar's. And Taria realized that Garona cared very much indeed.

"If you help us," Llane said, "I give you my oath that I will protect you, too."

Her brows, dark and elegant as raven's wings, drew together. At last, Garona looked from Lothar to the king.

"Oath? What is… oath?"

Durotan and Orgrim stood with the rest of the chieftains and their seconds in Gul'dan's hut. He, the Frostwolves he had commanded, and Blackhand had returned several hours ago, but they had been made to wait until after the sun had descended. The Frostwolves had used the time to mourn their dead, doing what they could to honor their passing without a ritual funeral pyre. The only light in the great tent was from a huge, burning brazier to the left of and slightly behind Gul'dan ornate chair.

The fire's light, a sickly shade of pale green, threw the features of both Gul'dan and Blackhand into sharp relief. The warchief knelt before the warlock, one of them muscular and strong, the other hunched and seemingly withered. But everyone present knew which of the two was the most powerful.

Including Blackhand.

Gul'dan leaned on his staff and looked Blackhand up and down. "Fearsome Blackhand, warchief of the Horde," he said, and his voice dripped scorn like ichor. "You have allowed the smallteeth to kill your warriors! Worse, you have shamed your people, by running from an enemy."

Blackhand did not reply. Durotan saw him clenching and unclenching his remaining hand, the dark ink on it almost absorbing the green illumination of the fel flames. He tried to keep his face impassive, but Durotan could see the pain in his eyes.

Gul'dan prodded the larger orc with his staff. "Are you too weak to talk, Destroyer?"

Blackhand shook his head, but even now, did not speak. Orgrim leaned over to Durotan and said quietly, "I have no love for Blackhand, but even I feel for him, watching this."

Durotan shared that feeling. The Frostwolves had been one of the last clans to join the Horde, and he was well aware that in the years since its formation, there had been many power struggles. Order and ranking had been established, reward and punishment doled out. Blackhand had already lost his hand in the battle. Durotan did not think he wanted to see what else the failure was going to cost him.

Gul'dan used his staff to straighten up slightly. In a heavy, angry voice, he said, "The Horde has no use for weakness. Respect our traditions. You know the penalty."

Blackhand looked out over the sea of silent, watchful faces, although he had to know there would be no help forthcoming. He lowered his head, resigned, then got to his feet, shuffling toward the green brazier.

"Death," said Gul'dan.

The warchief extended his mangled hand over the flickering, hungry green flame. Then, taking a breath, he pushed forward, shoving the limb deep into the glowing embers.

Durotan watched, horrified. The fel fire did not simply burn Blackhand's flesh. It ate it, like a living thing, curling upward along his arm like an invading army.

Blackhand did not cry out. He lifted his mutilated, green-shrouded limb, awaiting his death as the fel crawled upward.

Durotan could not bear it. Before he even realized what he was doing, Sever was in his hand, and it lived up to its name as he lifted the axe and brought it down, cutting cleanly through Blackhand's arm. It fell to the floor, writhing and twitching, and Blackhand collapsed. The green limb abruptly crumbled into scorched chunks.

Gul'dan fixed his glowing green eyes on the Frostwolf chieftain. "You *dare* interrupt this judgment?"

Durotan stood his ground. He knew he was right. "We fought hard. Their warlock used your fel against us!"

It was completely true. All those who had been present had seen it. And yet, they stayed silent as Gul'dan's body trembled with fury.

"Only I can control the fel!" he shrieked. He leapt to his feet, his eyes glowing even brighter as the green flames flared to new life, flickering and licking hungrily. Many orcs gasped and drew back. Even

Durotan retreated a step. "I have heard that most of the Frostwolves survived." He sneered. "Perhaps Blackhand kept you safely away from the battlefield. Maybe he knows you are weak, too."

The ludicrousness of the accusation rendered Durotan momentarily mute. Twice Gul'dan had made a difficult journey to ask the Frostwolves to join the Horde. In the end, it had not been Gul'dan's pleas, but the brutal and inescapable fact that Draenor could no longer support the clan which had made the Frostwolves trek south. Gul'dan knew this.

Orgrim surged forward, looming beside his friend and chieftain's shoulder, his fists clenched. Others saw the gesture and turned to Orgrim. Durotan had no desire for a fight to break out. Violence was not the answer, not now, and he lay a calming, but firm, hand on his second's arm. *Stand down.*

Orgrim all but choked on his rage, but he obeyed the unspoken command. Blackhand was struggling on the floor, and now he managed to make it to one knee, clutching the stump of his arm.

"I was not strong enough to defeat their champion," Blackhand grunted. "If I had, the battle would have turned—"

Durotan would have none of this. Gul'dan was being stubborn and arrogant, and Blackhand should not believe the warlock. "Warchief—"

"Your pride blinded you," Gul'dan barreled on. "Only my magic can defeat our enemies!"

The words burst forth from Durotan before he could halt them. "Your magic is what got them *killed*!"

Gul'dan turned, slowly, toward Durotan, his eyebrows lifting in surprise. "Do you wish to challenge me, little chieftain?"

Durotan glanced around. Everyone present was silent, their attention focused on him. He thought of the thousands of innocent draenei—children included—whose lives the fel had claimed simply to open the portal to this world. He looked at the green flame in the brazier, and in Gul'dan's eyes, and spoke carefully.

"I do not question Gul'dan," he said. "But the fel is born of death. It must have a price."

Gul'dan relaxed, ever so slightly, his brow unfurrowing. He even smiled.

"Yes," he agreed. "A price paid in lives taken."

Later, much later, he entered his tent. Draka was there in the firelight, the good, true firelight, bathed in its orange glow. She was cradling their child, and looked up as he entered. Her welcoming smile faded at the look on his face.

He told her what had happened in Gul'dan's tent. She listened without comment, as she had done the first night she had returned home from Exile, under the stars of Draenor.

When he had told it all, he sat at the brazier, gazing into the flames. Draka understood his need for silence, murmuring gently to their baby as she moved the little head to the side and extended a clawed forefinger. She pricked her breast, and a trickle of blood, black in the firelight, appeared. She guided the baby back to her nipple, now feeding him his mother's blood as well as mother's milk. It was fitting nourishment for a proud orc, a Frostwolf child, a future warrior. Draka glanced up at Durotan, and their eyes met over the head of their contentedly nursing infant. For the first time in what felt like forever, Durotan's heart knew a small brush of peace, here, alone with his mate and child.

He wondered if they should talk about what to do, how to react, what this meant. But what could he say? What could he do?

Draka rose and went to him. "Will you hold your son?" was all she said.

She extended the small, precious bundle, wrapped in a woven blanket with the Frostwolf symbol embroidered on it. Slowly, Durotan held out his hands.

He was small, so small, so vulnerable. He barely covered one of Durotan's great palms. He was whole, and perfect... and his skin was the color of the fire that had raged across Blackhand's body.

"He will be a great chieftain, like his father," Draka continued, sitting nearby and watching. Her voice was warm, soft, confident. "A born leader."

The words stung. "I was no leader today," Durotan said.

The baby's eyes, blue and bright, went right for his father's face when he spoke. No orc had ever had blue eyes...

The baby gurgled happily, his tiny legs kicking

energetically. One small hand reached up and unsteadily closed on Durotan's tusks. Durotan leaned forward, wrinkling his nose playfully. The baby grunted, a tiny sound. His face scowled, before he giggled.

"Ha!" said Draka, smiling. "He challenges you already!"

From somewhere deep inside Durotan's aching soul, a chuckle emerged. The baby laughed in response, his entire torso moving with his breath as he patted the tusk gently, mesmerized, utterly focused on his father's face.

Durotan's smile grew for a moment, then, unbidden, the thought of what he had witnessed snuffed out the joy. His eyes burned with unshed tears.

"If Gul'dan can infect one as innocent as him, what chance do the rest of us have?" Draka looked at him mutely, having no answer for him. "Whatever happens…" he began, but couldn't finish.

"Whatever happens," she replied.

9

Lothar's mind was a whirlwind as he marched into the throne room. His men, who had known he was interrogating the prisoner about the enemy's position, snapped to attention as he entered. Without preamble, he began firing questions at them.

"The Black Morass. What do you think?"

Karos raised his eyebrows. "You *could* hide an army in there."

"Or lose one," Varis countered. "You believe her, sir?"

"No." It was blunt, and it was true. Lothar had noticed Khadgar's reaction to the female, and he had to admit that she was attractive, for all her strangeness. And she wasn't quite like the monsters that had descended with such terrifying violence in Elwynn Forest. But he would be a fool to blindly trust this Garona, and King Llane Wrynn did not tolerate fools.

"But… it's what we have to go on," he continued. "Best horses, small escort. Let's see if this orc can be trusted. We leave at dawn." They nodded and hurried off. He watched them go for a moment, then turned back to the throne room.

Medivh was there, waiting for him. "I won't be going with you," the Guardian said.

Lothar ground his teeth. What had happened to Medivh in the last six years? He, the Guardian, and the King had been friends—more than friends, brothers in all but blood. They had fought together, suffered together. Been there for him when he had lost—

"Well *I* need to see what we're up against. You don't think seeing the enemy force firsthand is useful?" He couldn't quite shove back the anger, and the concern that fueled it.

Medivh didn't meet his gaze. "I have things to attend to."

Lothar gave up on subtlety. He marched up to his old friend and looked at him searchingly. "What happened to you today?" It was both true query and an accusation.

"I was studying our foe—firsthand," the Guardian replied slowly and deliberately.

Lothar snorted angrily. "If the kid hadn't been with you, you'd have been studying the edge of an axe."

Medivh shrugged laconically. "He had it in hand." An idea seemed to occur to him. "You should take him with you. He's more powerful than you think."

"Medivh—" Lothar began, but there was a flurry of motion and he found himself talking to a raven. The bird flicked its tail and took wing, soaring out of the window.

"I hate it when he does that," Lothar muttered.

It was a room in one of Stormwind's inns, not a cell this time, but as he nodded to the guard stationed outside his door, Khadgar accepted the reality that he was, after a fashion, still a prisoner. He did not mind. He was where he wanted to be. Lothar had asked— well, all right, told him to come to the Black Morass to investigate the lead that Garona had given them.

He quickly lit a lamp, his mind racing. Garona. Orcs. Fel. So much information. As he closed the door and bolted it, Khadgar had to admit, he had missed learning things. His life here in Stormwind as an ordinary person was better than being, essentially, the ultimate errand boy for the Kirin Tor, but it had been rather unstimulating until now.

The Black Morass—big enough to hide an army. A good guess for someone who wasn't from this world. That is, if Garona was telling the truth. His thoughts lingered on her for a moment—so strange-looking, and yet he was drawn to her. She was so strong, so confident even though she was a prisoner.

But now, something else demanded his attention. He reached beneath his shirt and brought out the book he had stashed there what seemed like ages ago. Khadgar had been terrified that it would fall out at some point, but it had stayed secure. Remarkable.

He placed it on the rough table, took a breath, and opened it. It was a slim tome with an unprepossessing cover, but the first few pages took his breath away. Runes filled the pages, and as he turned them, carefully, his eyes widened as he beheld a lavish illustration.

It depicted a wave of creatures that greatly resembled the beasts he had fought today. They were clustered together, a tight, unified mass, holding weapons of all varieties. And this mass of warriors was pouring forth from an enormous stone structure like water from an upended jug.

"A 'great gate,'" Khadgar whispered, his skin prickling with gooseflesh.

His eyes wandered from the sight of the roaring, maddened orcs to the runic text above the art. Two glyphs had been circled, and someone had scribbled in the margins, *From light comes darkness, and from darkness, light. Ask Alodi.*

Khadgar repeated the words to himself, unpacking his writing supplies and inking his quill. Taking a deep breath, he laid the thin parchment over the book, and began to trace the disturbing image.

It was the king's private prison, they had told Garona. It was not a place of torture. There were even windows to the outside and above. The moon shone down, silvering the room, and Garona's heart cracked to see it. It was still a cage, and she was still not free.

It was small, and it was barred on three sides.

There was something called a "cot" that was intended for sleeping. It was covered with cloths that were strange to her, and she saw no sleeping furs at all. In the corner was a small pot, for what she did not know. There was a table and a pitcher of water along with a uselessly small receptacle. They had left food for her, also alien, but she had eaten every bite to keep her strength up. Now, she lifted the pitcher and drank the cool water.

As she placed it down and wiped her mouth, she said to the shadow in the room, "I see you."

The one they had addressed as the Guardian stood there, his arms folded, his eyes, bright and curious as a bird's, fastened on her. Now, he stepped forward into the light provided by a few torches, walking around her prison.

"This gate," he said. "Who showed it to Gul'dan? Who led him to Azeroth?"

He cut straight to the heart of the matter. She liked that. Garona debated answering, then said, "Gul'dan called him a demon."

The Guardian—"Medivh" someone had said at one point—did not react. "Did you see it?"

It was a memory Garona did not want to revisit. She was quick with languages, but the orc tongue was richer when it came to some things, and she struggled to put the experience into human words. "Not the face. Just the voice. Like…" Her eyes fell on the flickering torchlight. "Like fire and ash." It did not describe the sound. It described what one felt upon hearing the sound. Very orcish.

He ceased his pacing and turned to her, regarding her with eyes that seemed to stare straight into her heart. "How old are you—"

The creak of the metal, barred door to the room interrupted him. Garona turned briefly to look at it. A rustling sound, like a bird's wings, brought her attention back to Medivh—but he was gone. A prickling sensation, as of eyes upon her, caused her to look up. A raven perched on the barred widow, silhouetted against the full moon, then flew off.

Shaman, she thought.

Garona took a deep breath and turned to see who else had come to visit her. It was the one called "Lothar," who had had killed the Frostwolf to protect her, but who later had threatened her. With him was the lone female who had been present during her interrogation earlier. She was so thin and fragile, like a woman made of twigs. Her eyes were large and brown and soft, like a talbuk's. She bore a piece of thin wood that held one of the small vessels and another vessel Garona could not identify. Steam escaped from them. Behind her trailed a servant girl, who was even smaller than she, bearing a thick pile of furs.

Lothar put a hand on the female's narrow shoulder. "I'm nearby if you need me," he told her, then shot Garona a warning look. The female nodded, stepping back as the guard entered the main area and stepped briskly to Garona's cell.

"Stand back," he ordered the orc. She didn't move for just long enough, then did as he had said, lifting her chin as the female entered. The guard closed the iron-bar door, then retreated back into the shadows, watching.

"Your mate," Garona said. "I could kill you before he even reaches me."

The woman looked confused. She followed Garona's gaze then laughed. "Lothar? He's my brother! The king is my… mate."

The king. The leader. Llane. "You are a chieftain's wife, then?"

The dark, delicate brows rose at the wording. "I suppose so."

Garona stepped closer, towering over her. "Then killing you would bring me even greater honor." Garona watched the female's reaction. She was so frail-seeming, Garona wondered if the words would frighten her. They were certainly true.

But the female simply shook her head. "Not among my kind." She nodded to the girl, who walked past Garona and placed the furs on the bed. "It's a cold night. I thought you could use these."

The girl smelled of fear, but not the cheiftain's wife. She moved forward in her long robes, the fabric rustling, and set the items she bore on the table, filling the cup with a hot liquid. She held it out to Garona, who eyed it.

"It will warm you," the female said. The beverage smelled clean and herbal, and Garona found herself welcoming the warmth as her hand closed around the ceramic. "It's my favorite. Peacebloom." Garona took a cautious sip, then, finding it delicious, drank it down despite its heat.

"More of our villages burn tonight," the female said as Garona drank. "One is the village of my birth." She gnawed her lower lip, then continued. "I see your wounds—old ones. Scars. I cannot imagine what horrors you have been through, Garona, but this doesn't need to happen. We have had peace in these lands for many years. Peace between races from all over the world."

Peacebloom, Garona thought. She wondered if the female had selected the drink intentionally, or if it was a simple coincidence. She turned away and picked up a cloak that had been placed atop the furs. The motion made her chains rattle and the manacle about her neck rub.

The female extended an uncallused hand, reaching to touch Garona's throat, saying, "I can have it removed—"

The orc jerked back, spilling the tea, instantly alert. The cheiftain's mate drew her hand back, and her face was unspeakably kind. "I'm sorry, I didn't mean to startle you." She took a deep breath. "There's a life with us here, Garona. If you want it."

Only once before had anyone even attempted to touch her with kindness. Another female—Draka, the mate of Durotan. Draka had worn a similar look to Taria's—compassion, and anger at what Garona had been forced to endure.

She had fled even from Durotan, in order to escape her life in the Horde. Garona well knew what she had been running from. Was this what she had been running *to*?

* * *

The pebble bounced harmlessly off Durotan's skull. He turned to the orc beside him, raising an eyebrow, to see his second in command looking unconvingly innocent. Durotan tried to scowl, but he couldn't keep up the pretense, and started laughing. Orgrim joined him. They chuckled like children for a while.

"It is good to see trees again," Orgrim said. He and his chieftain were sitting on a rise. Below them was the grunt work going on near the portal and the ugliness of cages filled with human slaves. But above that, in the distance, lay a scene that almost... almost... reminded Durotan of home. The trees were different, but they still grew straight and tall. They still bore fruit, or smelled fresh and clean.

"And the snow," Durotan said, wistfulness creeping into his voice. "Even from a distance."

Orgrim scratched idly at his healing wounds. "When the humans are beaten, we can journey to the mountains. Feel the cold on our skin." He spoke eagerly, and Durotan understood the yearning. Ever since they had left the north of Draenor, he had felt the pang of missing snow.

But Durotan had not asked his second-in-command to join him so they might gaze upon a snow-covered mountain together, beautiful though it was. He had brought Orgrim here to remind him what life looked like. Durotan could not find that reminder below, with the cries of the sick, starving humans and their children, and the grueling labor of hauling and carving stones. He rubbed his neck, not relishing the task before him, but there were things that needed to be said.

"Remember when we would track clefthooves through the Frostwind dunes? Whole herds of them, everywhere. And when there were no clefthooves, there were talbuks. There was always meat. Always life. We would dance in the meadows at Midsummer, and even in winter, we never hungered."

"But our world was dying," Orgrim said. "We *had* to leave. You stayed as long as you could, Durotan, but you knew what we had to do to survive."

Thoughts crowded Durotan's mind. What he had to say was dangerous... but necessary. His mind went back to when he had made the excruciating decision to follow Gul'dan, and the words he had told his clan. *There is one law, one tradition, which must not be violated. And that is that a chieftain must do whatever is truly best for the clan.*

"Orgrim... Do you not think it strange that we lost our home when Gul'dan came to power?"

Orgrim scoffed, prepared to laugh. The smile faded as he realized Durotan was deadly serious. "One orc cannot kill a *world*, Durotan."

"Are you sure? Look around you. Does it not remind you of something?" He directed Orgrim's gaze not to the beckoning forest and distant snow, but to what lay behind them. To the Great Gate, and the land around it. Orgrim's brow furrowed for a moment in confusion, and then Durotan saw understanding spread across his friend's face.

When they had entered this world, the land near the gate had been a swamp. Draka had birthed the son of Durotan on her hands and knees in stagnant water. Now, there was only dirt, parched and thirsty. What plants there had been were long dead, brittle and ground to dust beneath orcish feet as Durotan's people moved giant stones to build a doorway.

It did remind him of something.

It looked exactly as the other side of the portal had looked, in the land they had fled. Emotions warred on Orgrim's face.

Durotan knew what he was asking. But he also knew he was right. "Wherever Gul'dan works his magic… the land dies. If our people are to make a home here, my friend," Durotan said, his voice rough with emotion, "Gul'dan must be stopped."

Orgrim took a long time before he replied, but when he did, he did not disagree. All he said was, "We are not powerful enough to defeat Gul'dan."

"No," Durotan agreed. He scratched thoughtfully at his chin with a sharp thumbnail. "But with the humans' help, we could be."

10

It had been a dangerous gamble, and Llane had been anxious every moment since Lothar and Taria had departed the throne room. But he had felt it was the right decision, and he kept telling himself that as the moments ticked past. He was on the balcony, overlooking the dark city and thinking equally dark thoughts, when Taria returned.

She slipped an arm through his. "You were right," she said. "A woman's hand was needed. She will take Lothar to their camp, the poor creature."

"Thank you," he said, taking her hand and kissing it.

"How did you know I could reach her?"

It was hard to put into words. Garona was an adult female, and, from all reports, a fierce fighter. It was hard to think of someone like that as "vulnerable," but he sensed that her wariness wasn't hate-fueled, or cruel. There was something about her that reminded him of the children he had seen in the orphanage—wild, feral, but desperate for someone to look past that and see who they truly were.

"She needed a mother's care," he said at last. He squeezed his wife's hand, then pulled her into his arms. "I know of none better."

"Flatterer," she teased, and kissed him.

There were five of them in the mounted scouting party: Lothar, Garona, Khadgar, Karos, and Varis. The three soldiers had spent a great deal of time away from Stormwind, but of course, to Garona, everything was new. She was alert and attentive, her dark eyes taking it all in and evaluating it. *For what?* Lothar wondered. *Hiding places? Weapons? Escape—or attack—routes?*

She was clad in Alliance armor, and he noticed her hand wandering to the breastplate now and then, as if surprised each time at the golden lion's head there. His attention lingered on her perhaps longer than it should have. This morning, he had helped her get into her armor. She had asked for a weapon, and he had replied as he laced her gambeson closed, "You'll have me to protect you."

"I need no one to protect me," Garona had asserted. He had paused then, with his face inches from hers, a witty retort dying unsaid on his lips as their eyes met. He had realized almost at once that, despite her tusks and green skin, Garona was beautiful. But now, standing so close, Lothar understood that she was more than just physically appealing. She was right. She *did* need no one to protect her. She was likely as strong—perhaps stronger—than he was. But as he looked at the scars that crisscrossed her skin, he, the soldier, wanted nothing more than to keep her safe. It was ludicrous, it was likely insulting…but it was true.

"What are you looking at?" she had demanded.

He himself wasn't sure.

Lothar's mind returned to the present. He smiled to himself as he noticed that Khadgar's gaze was fixed to whatever it was he was reading. He missed the sole pleasant part of the journey, through the safe areas of Elwynn Forest, only looking up when they paused as the foliage gave way to bare stone. Below them, Elwynn lay spread out like a lush tapestry. Behind, Stormwind's white towers jutted skyward, looking as small as a model on King Llane's battlemap, and even Khadgar admired the sight.

Before them lay Deadwind Pass, a fitting name for an unhospitable, desolate canyon of sheer walls and cutting, whistling winds. One branch of the trail culminated in a ledge, where Lothar declared they would camp for the night. It was useful to have a site with only one direction to guard. They could have pressed on, but Deadwind Pass was a tricky enough path in the daylight. He could not risk a horse making a misstep in the growing shadows.

"Bookworm," he said to Khadgar as the mage dismounted, wincing, "take the first watch."

Garona, slipping lithely to the ground, looked both perplexed and amused at the word. She watched Khadgar, to gauge his reaction.

The boy tucked the book in the waistband of his trousers while reaching for his bedroll, but the look he gave Lothar was *not* one of amusement. He had not missed Garona's look, either. "Respectfully, Commander, my name is Khadgar," he said.

Lothar brought a hand to his chest in mock horror. "My apologies, Khadgar. I thought we had bonded when I didn't put you in a prison cell for breaking into the royal barracks." The two glared at each other. "Now. *Take the first watch*."

Khadgar's lips thinned, but he nodded. "Yes, Commander."

The meal was simple—bread, chicken, apples, and hot tea. No wine was passed around tonight—the party was too small and the danger too great for even a little intoxication. Thankfully, the sobbing wind eventually stopped, although the silence that replaced it was perhaps more unnerving. They ate, cleaned up, and spread out their bedrolls while Khadgar glumly wrapped himself in his cloak and perched atop a boulder, looking back at the path they had traveled.

Lothar's mind was too busy working out scenarios for him to sleep at once, so he gnawed on a leftover piece of chicken and watched the watcher instead. To his credit, the boy seemed to take the duty seriously. Lothar half-expected Khadgar to have sneaked his book with him so he could read by moonlight, or firelight, or maybe a tiny point of blue flame dancing at the end of his fingers. Who knew what sort of things mages could do.

Instead, the youth's head turned, rather shyly, in Garona's direction. She lay facing away, her distinctive curves soft and rolling and green as the hills of Elwynn. Lothar was amused—but he also didn't like it.

"Well," he said, shattering the silence, "at least you're not reading."

Khadgar jerked his head back toward the path. Lothar smiled to himself.

"He wishes to lie with me." Garona's voice was matter-of-fact and Khadgar cringed, almost squirming with embarrassment. She propped herself up on one arm, watching them both.

"I beg your pardon?" Khadgar tried to sound perplexed by the accusation, but his voice climbed a little too high for it to be convincing.

"You would be injured," she stated.

"I *don't* want to lie with you!"

It was all Lothar could do to not laugh out loud. Garona simply shrugged. "Good. You would not be an effective mate."

This time, Lothar couldn't help it, and a snort of laughter escaped him. "Why do you laugh?" Garona asked, and it was Lothar's turn to feel uncomfortable. "I cannot see how you humans survive such a thing. How you survive anything. No muscles to protect you. Brittle bones that break."

"You don't look that different to us. How did you survive?"

She went still. Her voice when she replied no longer held mirth. It was careful; cool. "Broken bones heal stronger. Mine are very strong."

The humor bled out of Lothar. He thought of her green skin, soft as a human woman's, lacerated by the manacles at her wrists and her throat. Of the massive males of her species, with enormous hands and torsos and tusks. Of the weapons that probably weighed as much as he did. His mind went to dark places at her words, places that made him grow angry, as well as sombre.

But yet, "I'm sorry," was all he could find to say.

"Do not be." The silence resumed. The fire crackled.

"My name, 'Garona'," she said at last. "It means 'cursed' in Orc. My mother was burned alive for giving birth to me."

Lothar's hands hurt. He looked down at them, surprised to see he had clenched them. *Monsters.*

"They kept you alive, though," he said. *Why?* He wanted to know. *How badly did they hurt you? What can I do to help?*

"Gul'dan did." She rolled over on her back. In the flickering firelight, he saw what she held: a cord, from which dangled a delicate tusk, only about the size of her little finger. "He gave me this. To remember her."

Lothar watched the slowly moving object as if mesmerized by it. It both repelled and fascinated him, but clearly Garona cherished it. He wondered if, truly, it was so different from a lock of hair, treasured as a keepsake after a loved one had died. He had tried to argue Llane out of letting Taria talk to the orc. Now, listening to her speaking so openly, he realized that his friend had insight he did not possess. She was obviously beautiful, obviously strong. But she was also, as Llane had sensed, someone who responded to kindness. Someone who had been wounded more than physically.

"My parents gave me to the Kirin Tor when I was six years old." Khadgar's voice was soft, a confession that, like Garona's, was better suited to being uttered in concealing darkness. "That's the last time I saw them or any of my brothers and sisters. It brings a family honor to offer a child to the Kirin Tor. To have their son taken up to the floating city of Dalaran and be trained by the most powerful mages in the land. " He smiled self-deprecatingly as he looked at Garona. "Less so to have them run away."

The orc woman held his gaze, then she nodded.

"Well," Lothar said, "That was cheerful."

He lay back down on his bedroll, hearing the other two shift positions. Lothar closed his eyes, seeing behind his closed lids firelight shining on an orc tusk held by a strong, beautiful green hand.

The night was lit by fire, painted with blood, and its songs were all of slaughter.

Gul'dan watched it all with quiet glee. Beside him stood his mentor, his advisor, the one who had kept his promises. The one without whom this night would never have been possible.

"North, south, east, west," he intoned, sweeping a hand over the scene, "all will be ours."

Movement caught his eye, and he frowned slightly. Some of the humans were escaping. There was a trail, as of busy ants, fleeing the conflagration. They carried things on their shoulders, and followed a long, winding path. "Tell me, teacher," he inquired, "where do they run?"

"Stormwind," the figure standing beside him intoned. The word was raspy, but powerful. It burned, as its speaker's heart burned. "Their greatest city." So much contempt. So much certainty that the flight was futile. As, of course, it was. There was no standing against the Horde... or fel.

"Ah," said Gul'dan, "where Garona ran to." Now was the moment. He turned to his mentor. "I brought her here. For you."

Surely, his teacher would be pleased, would heap praise upon his faithful pupil, who had learned so well. But there was no reaction at all; not pleasure, not annoyance... only silence, from within the deep shadows of the cowl. Gul'dan felt disappointment— and a stirring of unease.

He tried to correct any possible misstep. "When the portal opens, we will take this city first." He looked directly at the figure. "And we will name it... after *you*."

11

Lothar had thought he would be prepared for anything he would behold. He was wrong. Now, standing beside Garona and the others as they stared at the horrifying panorama spread below them, Lothar felt both stunned and sickened. War was never tidy, or clean. It was never like gazing at one of Llane's maps, even when strategy was orderly and victory was certain. But this…

Tents, hundreds of them, dotted the landscape, punctuated by watchtowers and larger constructions. There were cages, too. Not as many as he had initially feared, but enough to make Lothar's hands clench in anger. Cages crammed with humans: men, women, even children. So this was where they had gone— seized and carried off while their homes burned about them, taken like animals.

And further on, enormous, chiseled hunks of stone hauled by the labor of the physically powerful orcs and arranged in a pattern. A flat, level base, like the foundation of a building. Or something much worse.

"The Great Gate," Garona said, pointing to the stones.

"Why do they need so many prisoners?" Lothar asked. The breeze caught Garona's black hair, playing with it. Her gaze did not leave the terrifying diorama as she spoke, and her words made Lothar's heart sink.

"Like wood for fire," she explained. "Green magic takes life to open the gate."

Lothar's gaze was dragged back inexorably to the scene below them. "How many more orcs are they planning on bringing?"

Her reply was simple and stark. "All of them." She waved her hand at the scene. "This—this is just the war band. When the portal is opened, Gul'dan will bring the Horde."

And all at once Lothar understood what, subconsciously, he had been denying. These hundreds of tents were, essentially, just the beginning...

A Horde.

"Get them back to Stormwind," he snapped at Karos, already heading for his horse. "Varis and I will ride ahead."

Garona gazed after Lothar and Varis as their horses galloped off. Thoughts crowded her mind. Was she truly doing the right thing? Why did she even have any loyalty to the orcs? They had murdered her mother, and she had only been spared from the fire herself by the will of Gul'dan. He had taught her how to read and write, and ordered her to study and learn other languages. But she was always a slave. Always bound, always sneered at or spat upon.

Except by a few. Every time she was filled with hatred for her treatment by her so-called "people" she recalled Durotan, twice a voice of reason for his people, and his wife Draka, who had treated her with gentleness and care. Other orcs might drown sickly children at birth, but the Frostwolves gave their weaker members at least a chance to earn their way back into the clan. Draka herself had been one such, and she became the mate of a chieftain.

Garona had hesitated when Durotan freed her and extended his hand. But she knew if she returned with him, Gul'dan would simply reclaim her. And in that moment, Garona had tasted freedom, and knew she would die before relinquishing it.

She thought of Queen Taria, treating her even more kindly than Draka had. Of course, Taria wanted something. Garona fully realized that. But what she wanted was to save her people. So did the orcs—but they were doing it by killing those who were not orcs. First the draenei, now the humans. She thought of Khadgar; such a pup, so eager, but with a power she respected and didn't understand.

And… she thought of Lothar. He had saved her from the furious Frostwolf. He had not been as overtly kind as Taria, but Garona understood his mistrust. She knew enough of darkness to know when it had touched someone, and Anduin Lothar surely walked with shadows. She had seen the pain in his eyes at the loss of his men in the recent battle, the horror at the thought of the innocent farmers being held captive, their lives fodder for more orc destruction. He was... good, she decided.

Though he had a sense of humor. She recalled the term Lothar had used to Khadgar, "bookworm." Garona smiled, turning to look at the young mage—

An orc stood in the shadow of tree branches. He held Khadgar under one arm, his massive hand clamped over the boy's mouth. The young mage stared at Garona with wide, alarmed eyes. A few feet away orc lay the body of Karos, unconscious, but still alive.

"Durotan!" Garona gasped.

He grunted in acknowledgement. "To the north is a black rock that touches the sky. I would meet with their leader there."

A sliver of fear sliced through her. "To challenge him?" She was surprised at how much she did not want Llane to die... nor, truth be told, Durotan.

He shook his head. "I saw you lead the smallteeth to our encampment," he said, stepping closer, still holding Khadgar, but with care. "They have seen what is being built, but only you know what Gul'dan has planned for my people." His eyes bored into hers, and he spoke as if the words tore at him. "You warned us, Garona. You told us he was dark and dangerous. I only came, in the end, because there was truly *no* other choice."

Garona knew Durotan might have chosen death for himself, but he did not have the luxury. He was a chieftain, and he took care of his clan as best he knew how.

"This magic is death," he said. "For *all* things. It must be stopped."

So he had seen. He knew. Their gazes locked for a moment, then Durotan nodded. "Tell him. The black rock. When the sun is highest."

"I will," Garona promised.

Durotan nodded. He seemed unaware that he had completely shattered everything Garona had believed she could ever expect out of her life. If Gul'dan fell—

She surged forward. "Chieftain! If I return, would you take me into your clan?"

Durotan's eyes traveled to her throat, her hands. A throat and hands free of chains. "You are safer here. With them."

And she knew he was right. The hope died, and she simply nodded. The chieftain looked thoughtfully at the boy he still restrained. The mage, still as death, stared up, barely blinking. Durotan released him. Khadgar made no move to run, or to utter a spell. Durotan punched him, very gently, in the chest—a comradely gesture. Then, pressing a hand to his own chest in a gesture of respect and gratitude to Garona, the half-breed slave, he stepped back into the shadow dappled light and vanished into the trees.

* * *

The raven soared, its superlative vision taking in the scene below in in detail that ripped at his heart. Even those with poorer sight would have been able to see the destruction, though; it was blatant, excessive, and seemingly everywhere. Amidst the healthy green of foliage, the bare spots, gray and black and burning, stood out starkly. One, and another, and another—

Medivh collapsed beside the font, barely able to plunge a hand into its restorative depths. Energy infused him, but more slowly and less thoroughly than it had in the past. He was drained dry, and recovered less completely each time he pushed himself. But he had to. It was his charge.

Moroes knelt beside him, calm, steady, eternal. The castellan had dwelt at Karazhan for a very, very long time. Longer than Medivh had. Longer than the previous Guardian, or the one before that. In his own way, he was as much a part of Karazhan as its stables, or its kitchen, or even its font of magic.

Quietly, sorrowfully, the older man asked, "Is it as you feared?"

Medivh pressed his lips together and nodded. He kept his arm in the font as he replied, his voice weak and cracking, "The fel. It's everywhere."

"Then you mustn't leave again," Moroes stated.

"They need a Guardian's help now more than ever," Medivh answered. His voice was so hollow, so terribly weary, even in his own ears.

"Maybe the boy could help," his old friend suggested.

Could he? Khadgar had shown initiative and

courage. Maybe he could. Wearily, Medivh turned his head to look at Moroes—and froze. He stared over the castellan's shoulder, his eyes fixed on something or someone that might—or might not—have been there; a ghostly black form, pointing directly at him.

"Begone!" hissed Medivh. Moroes turned, but saw nothing.

Llane sat upon the great throne of Stormwind, and despaired.

It had taken this—an incursion of bestial creatures determined to wrest the entire world for themselves—for the diplomats currently scowling in front of him to even agree to meet. And now that they had gathered, no one seemed to want to listen.

Taria had often commented on her husband's cool head—one that had not been nearly so cool in years past. Now, it seemed that he alone was keeping even a semblance of calm as those assembled ranted, protested, and took below-the-belt verbal strikes at one another.

The representative from Kul Tiras was holding forth. His people had recently tasted the fury of the orcs, and he was not about to let Llane forget it—though he himself seemed to forget that Elwynn Forest had been among the first targets.

"Stormwind, the high and mighty—always thinking itself better than the rest of us. You knew what would happen to us, yet we fought and fell alone. Where was your army as our ships burned?"

"My army is losing a regiment a day," Llane replied. His voice was tight, even though he fought to stay calm.

"Stormwind, Kul Tiras, Lordaeron, Quel'thalas. Dwarf, human, and elf. All of us in peril—and all of us squandering precious time arguing among ourselves. We need to work together!"

The representative of Lordaeron scowled. "What we *need*," he snapped, "are more weapons! Dwarven forges must work overtime." He turned and regarded King Magni with an expectant expression, as if the dwarf ought to immediately start spitting out swords and battleaxes.

Magni was apoplectic. When he was able to manage words, they came out in strangled, staccato bursts. "You treat us no better than *dogs*! You refuse to protect us with the very weapons we *make* for you! We shall supply you *no more*!"

Llane leaped to his feet. "Enough!" he shouted. The raised voice of the normally mild king silenced the bickering—for the moment. Everyone turned to look at him. "All of you have called on Stormwind in the past. Either for troops or arbitration. If we do not unite to fight this enemy, we will perish. Stormwind needs soldiers, arms, horses—"

"Ha! We have our own kingdoms to look after!" shouted Magni.

"Fight your own wars!" added the Lordaeron representative.

The doors swung open. Lothar marched in, Varis following a step behind. Everyone turned at the interruption. Both men were dirty and sweaty, and Lothar had a wild but determined look in his blue eyes that Llane recognized. Whatever this was, it was bad.

"The orcs are building a portal," Lothar stated bluntly, "through which they plan to bring an army. If we do not stop them now, we may never get another opportunity."

The two old friends locked eyes. Unspoken was the question that the elven representative had no trouble articulating.

"Where is he?" he demanded, his musical voice rising with his anger—and, likely, his fear. His robes whirled about him as he turned back to Llane. "Where's the protector of Azeroth?"

"Aye!" the Kul Tiras representative chimed in. "Where is the Guardian?"

Taria leaned over and whispered to her husband, "Where *is* Medivh?" Llane's jaw clenched and he took a deep breath, forcing calm upon himself as he turned to address the gathering.

"I suggest we take a recess—"

"Take as long as you like," the Lordaeron representative interrupted as he and his companions rose. "We're done." A courier shoved his way through the departing Lordaeron group, handing a missive to Varis. Varis read it quickly, then approached Lothar.

"Commander," Varis said quietly, "what's left of the Fourth has retreated from Stonewatch."

"What's *left*?" Lothar echoed. His face had paled beneath its layer of sweat and grime.

Varis hesitated, then said, "Callan is among the injured."

Llane had overheard, and despite the disaster unfolding in front of him, he did not hesitate. "Take the gryphon. Go."

Lothar flung open the canvas door of the makeshift field hospital tent, heading straight to the figure on a bed. His boy's eyes were closed, but as if sensing his father's presence, Callan turned and managed to partially sit up.

His boy. His, and Cally's.

Light, but the boy looked so much like his mother, it cut Lothar every time he laid eyes on him. The sandy brown hair, the gentle hazel eyes. Seeing him lying here reminded Lothar of the last time he'd seen his wife. The beloved face had been pale as milk, circles of pain underneath her eyes like bruises. She'd always been so fragile, his little Cally. Too fragile.

There were no bandages wrapped around his son's slender body, no white saturated with red, and he remembered a day when there had been red, too much red. Callan had only a gash on his forehead. It did not look too bad, but Lothar took his son's head in his hand and turned it this way and that, checking. Callan regarded him almost sheepishly, with his mother's hazel eyes.

"Dad," he said. "I'm fine. It's fine."

Lothar forced a smile. Those eyes had nothing of him in them, they were all *hers*.

"You had me worried," Lothar admitted. There was an awkward silence, then he added, trying for a little levity, "You should have been a baker, like I wanted."

"Too dangerous," Callan deadpanned. "All those oven burns."

Lothar found himself chuckling. When he was very young, Callan had stated that he wanted to be a soldier. Lothar had replied, "Wouldn't you like to be a baker instead? Think of all the cakes you could eat!" Callan had thought about it for a moment, head cocked to the side in a gesture so much like Cally that Lothar's heart had felt like lead. And the child answered, "Well, I bet lots of people would be happy to bake cakes for soldiers, 'cause they're so brave." When Lothar had mock-complained that no one made cakes for him, Callan had suggested that Lothar himself become a baker.

He was surprised, and moved, that Callan remembered the moment. He ruffled his son's hair, his hand not quite knowing how to do so, and looked around. He'd been so focused on his son that he hadn't realized that Callan was the infirmary's sole occupant. A chill settled over him.

"Where's the rest of your troop?" Callan shook his head. "They can't all be dead!"

"They took most of us alive," Callan answered. "They—people are saying that they *eat* us—"

"Fear-mongering," Lothar said, though the reality facing the prisoners was possibly even worse. Callan winced slightly at the harshness of his father's voice, and Lothar gentled his tone. "You hear the same stories about every enemy, every war. Don't worry, son. We'll get them back." Callan immediately sat up, as if he was about to head out right now. Lothar placed a hand on his chest. "Don't be in such a hurry." He played with Callan's rumpled uniform, smoothing it, as he had done when the boy was small. "You're all I have," he said, softly.

Callan endured it for a moment, then squeezed his father's arm—a gesture of appreciation, but also of rejection. Lothar removed his hand.

Callan's face looked strangely old on such a young man; the expression of one who had seen too much. "Dad. I can do this. I'm a soldier."

Lothar thought about the violence the orcs had displayed in their attack. He imagined his gentle-natured, somewhat shy son battling for his life against the oversized monsters, which were shockingly strong and eerily fast for their size.

Tell him, he thought. *Tell him that he's brave— maybe braver than you were, at that age. Tell him you love him, and you're proud of him.*

Tell him... it wasn't his fault.

Lothar only nodded, and turned to leave.

12

"Garona, pull your hood down and ride between us," Karos said in a low voice. His head was bandaged and his face was bruised, but considering he had been knocked unconscious by an orc chieftain, he was in good shape.

Garona heard the sound of horses and carts behind them. They were no longer alone on the road, now that they were on the outskirts of Elwynn. She was not afraid of a handful of farmers, but a scuffle would serve nothing. She obeyed, and observed. More and more humans joined them on the road, funneling in like small rivulets that swelled a stream to become a river, until at last, at the castle gates, it was not even a river any longer, it was an ocean.

Thousands of refugees thronged here, with the wide, frightened eyes that Garona recalled from countless cages. She caught sight of one of the short, barrel-chested beings that were known as "dwarves." He was attempting to lead a spooked pony pulling a small wagon. A female dwarf and two small children clung to one another inside, glancing about worriedly at the angry human tide swirling about them.

One of the harried-looking guards held up a mailed hand, forbidding the dwarf passage. "Them first!" he shouted.

The dwarf's brows drew together. "I work in the Royal Armory, man!" he bellowed.

"Find a cave to hide in, dwarf!" a human, safe in the anonymity of the crowd, shouted angrily. Others began to jostle the cart, and one of the children cried out for her father. Any patience the dwarf might have had had clearly evaporated long ago, and he reached back into the wagon and grasped a hammer so large Garona marveled that he was able to wield it.

"I'll 'cave' your *skull*, you stinkin'—"

"This is unacceptable," Karos muttered. Louder, he called, "Sergeant! Muster a line up here! We'll have order or we'll be closing the gates until we do!" He turned on the people who had been shoving the cart. "Kaz is making weapons for all our safety. Not one more word out of you."

The dwarf nodded his thanks, his face flushed, and was permitted through. Karos and Garona started to follow, but Khadgar caught Garona's arm. "I need to gather my research. Tell the king what happened. I'll be there as soon as I can."

* * *

Khadgar's mind was awhirl. The same orc who had looked at him with calm intelligence when he had erected a protective dome around himself and Medivh during the initial fight with the orcs had captured him, covered his mouth with a hand the size of a trencher, and then released him unharmed. Not just unharmed—with a request to work with the humans to bring down Gul'dan and the fel.

He inserted the key in the lock of his room's door. He had never been more afraid in his life, and then never more... well... honored, than when this powerful orc chieftain, Durotan, had given him what was obviously a friendly—

"*What is this?*"

Khadgar jumped about a foot in the air and lifted his hands reflexively for an attack spell, but recognized the intruder in time to bite back the incantation.

"Guardian!" He felt the panicked energy bleed out of him, leaving him weak with relief. He struggled to get his mind working again and answer the obviously furious Medivh's question. The Guardian was gesturing at the clutter of notes, open books, and drawings that papered the room. When Khadgar had run out of flat space, he had taken to hanging them from string, as if he were a washerwoman hanging laundry. Notes were, almost literally, everywhere. "The gate... We saw it! In the Morass! I've been putting together all the clues I can about it."

"This," Medivh demanded, gazing at a sketch he held. "This drawing. Where did you copy it from?"

Khadgar felt like a bird mesmerized by a snake. He stared, knowing he looked foolish, feeling even more so as he tried to collect his thoughts. He didn't understand Medivh's anger. "G—Guardian?"

Medivh snatched a piece of parchment dangling from one of the loops of string "And this? And *this*?"

Another, and another. He marched up to Khadgar and shoved one of the pieces in the boy's face.

Khadgar's hands and his voice both shook as he replied, the sweat of genuine fear popping out on his brow. What had he possibly done wrong? He swallowed, his mouth as dry as the parchments that were crushed in Medivh's hands. "I've been researching ever since I felt the presence of the fel."

"*I'm* the Guardian! Me." Medivh moved closer, forcing Khadgar back one step, then another, bearing down on him. "Not you. Not yet."

Khadgar tried one last time. "I just thought that you might appreciate some help…"

Khadgar stared into the bloodshot, blue-green eyes of the one who was supposed to be the protector of the world. And who, he was fairly certain, was about to kill him.

A heartbeat later, every single note, scribbling, illustration, and map that he had worked so hard on went up in magical fire. They burned swift, hot, and utterly, not even leaving behind ashes. It was as though they had never been.

"Don't presume you can aid me. You have no idea of the forces I contend with." He took a deep breath and steadied himself. "If you want to help, protect the king. You leave the fel to me."

He turned to depart. Khadgar sagged against the wall, relieved. For exactly one heartbeat. Then he saw what was on a chair beside the door.

The runic book he had "borrowed" from Karazhan.

Don't let him see it, Khadgar willed. Medivh was halfway through storming out the door. *Don't let him see it, don't let him—*

The Guardian paused midstride. He froze, then as Khadgar shrank inwardly, Medivh's head turned slowly and he stared directly at the book.

Silence.

The Guardian, moving deliberately, picked up the book and looked at it. He did not turn around. The young mage was slightly surprised he wasn't incinerated on the spot.

"Interesting choice." The Guardian's words were icy.

"Guardian…" *I can explain,* Khadgar thought wildly. There was a sudden flare in his hand as the sketch he'd forgotten he was holding turned into a sheet of flame and disappeared. By the time he looked up, Medivh had already gone.

"He would not ask for this meeting if he thought he could defeat Gul'dan alone," Llane stated. He was seated on his throne, flanked by Lothar and several other advisors whom Garona did not know. His queen sat in her own throne beside her husband, smiling kindly down at the orc woman. "The fel must truly terrify him."

Garona bridled on the Frostwolf's behalf. "Durotan is scared of nothing."

Llane glanced over at Lothar and lifted a brow, wordlessly inviting his friend to speak.

"The location, the suddenness of the meeting… it sounds like a trap, Your Majesty."

Garona shot him an angry look. "It's not."

"It *could* be."

She glared at him, her nostrils flaring at the implied insult to both her and Durotan. Lothar returned her gaze without flinching, his blue eyes boring into hers. "It is *not*!"

"What do *you* think?" Lothar asked, appealing to his friend.

Llane. "It's too good an opportunity to ignore. I think we have no choice. We must stop the orcs from opening the portal. That's a given. But we will need help."

"And if he's lying?" Llane wanted to know.

Garona shot him a look. "Orcs do not lie."

"What if he is?"

"There is no honor in it!" Garona said, as if that explained everything.

"And where's the 'honor' in him betraying his own people?" Lothar challenged.

She turned back to him, to the assessment of those strange eyes. She had learned the human language enough to converse, but she was far from a master of its subtleties. How to convey who Durotan was? She was silent for a moment, choosing her words with care. Finally, she spoke.

"Durotan is protecting his clan. His enemy is the fel. Gul'dan is the betrayer."

Still Lothar regarded her, gazing into her eyes as if searching her soul. She was not accustomed to such scrutiny. Most orcs treated her as if she were not even present. If they did acknowledge her, it was only to jeer at or spit on her—or worse. She had not lied to Khadgar and Lothar when she had told them her bones were very strong. She lifted her chin and did not look away.

Taria's voice came to her. The queen seemed to have something on her mind. "This orc, Durotan... how do you know him?"

"He freed me... and he is loved by his clan. He puts their needs first. Always. He is a strong chieftain."

"Strong chiefs must earn their clans' trust." Taria regarded her steadily, as Lothar had done, but with a compassion that made Garona shift her weight uncomfortably. Then the queen seemed to reach a decision. Her hand went to her narrow waist and deftly unfastened a small dagger. "If we are to expect you to join us, we must earn yours." She handed the dagger to Garona. "To defend yourself."

"With this?"

"Yes."

Garona stared at it. It suited Taria, not her; it was pretty, and delicate. Not at all like a solid orcish dagger. The hilt was decorated with jewels, and at

Taria's nod, Garona drew the dagger from its finely wrought leather sheath and examined the blade. She revised her initial impression of it. It was well made, for such a slender thing.

She could kill Taria, Lothar, and maybe even the king before they'd be able to stop her. Taria's gentle smile widened. *She knows what I'm thinking,* Garona realized. *And she knows she is safe.*

Kindness. And more important—trust. Garona's eyes burned suddenly. She could not speak, merely fastened the exquisite weapon around her own waist.

Llane nodded firmly. "Find the Guardian. We'll need him."

Khadgar had used the ride to calm himself. He was beginning to think the Guardian had gone stark raving mad, but Medivh's attempt to terrorize him into forsaking his research had instead merely made him more determined than ever to pursue it. A reaction that strong meant something, surely.

He was waiting outside Stormwind Keep for a meeting to finish up. A meeting he should have been at, but as usual, he was not involved. It was, at first glance, just as chaotic here as it was at the city's gate, but after a few moments Khadgar saw an order to it all. People moved with purpose and direction, and he heard snatches of military jargon here and there. He paced and fumed, watching as as Garona emerged, a stern-faced guard behind her. Her hood was up again, concealing her beautiful face in its shadows. He looked around for Lothar, but the commander was still inside. Still, Garona might be of very great help.

"There you are!" He rushed over to her. "Tell me—what do you know of the warlock's magic?"

She peered around, tense, even now ready to fight should she have to. "What are they doing?"

"Getting ready for war," Khadgar answered absently as he tried to get an answer from her. "Garona, I need your help. I found—"

She had started to smile, and now she burst out laughing. He went red right to the tips of his ears. "What? What's so funny?"

Garona tried to compose herself, but her eyes still danced with mirth. "How can you not be ready for *war*?"

"Some of us are ready," Khadgar replied defensively.

"Oh yes," the orc agreed, still smiling. "You... and Lothar. A man and a boy. The Horde *trembles*."

He bristled at being referred to as a "boy" and could not help but snap, "Two *men*—and many others." He reached into the folds of his robe and pulled out the solitary item that had survived Medivh's inexplicable rage—a single sketch. "Here. Look at this," he said, handing it to her. "Have you heard of someone called Alodi?"

"You drew this?" She peered at it critically, and he stifled a smile.

"Yes, but... you've got it the wrong way." His voice was warm with humor at her innocence. "Let me..."

The words died in his throat. He had sketched it horizontally, but she was holding it vertically. The orcs he had drawn coming out of the Great Gate now no longer appeared to be running on flat ground. They seemed to be climbing, as if out of an enormous hole.

And waiting for them, beckoning, was a hooded figure.

"You drew our arrival in the Black Morass. How would you know what that looked like?"

He didn't reply. The heat of his prior embarrassment had faded. He felt cold, terribly cold. All he knew was that he had to take this to Lothar. Now.

Without another word, he ran up the stairs, taking them two at a time, shouting the name of Anduin Lothar.

When Lothar spied the crate stamped with the symbol of Ironbeard and the Bronzebeard crest, he headed straight for it. Aloman, trying to impose some sort of order on the chaos, inquired, "Commander? What of these?"

"From King Magni," Kaz said, peering around a corner of the crate. "He says they might come in handier than plow blades."

Despite the direness of the situation, and that he had been running on too much adrenaline and too little food and sleep, Lothar found himself smiling as he opened the crate to see several of the "mechanical marvels" that had done such damage to the tattooed orc's hand. "Boomsticks," he said, pleased.

"Lothar!" Khadgar's voice echoed from outside, and the youth came pelting into the room, skidding to a halt. Panting, he said, "I need your help!"

"What's happened?"

Catching his breath, Khadgar said, "I found… a book."

Lothar tried and failed not to roll his eyes. "Of course you did." He nodded at Aloman, and she helped him lift and maneuver the crate to one side.

"No, wait, you don't understand," the boy persisted. He pulled out a rolled-up parchment. The words were coming out of him at a thousand leagues a moment, as if afraid he'd be silenced before he could get them all out. "Let me explain. There was an illustration that showed a gate, like the one we saw being built. I tried to show the Guardian, but he became furious. Burned all my research. He would have burned this, too, if it hadn't been hidden in my robe."

Annoyed, but now at least slightly interested, Lothar perched on a nearby crate and took the parchment Khadgar was waving at him. The mage sat next to him. As Khadgar had said, it was was a sketch of the Great Gate. This one was intact, and through it rushed a mass of armed orcs. The gate itself was only the length of Lothar's hand, and the orcs were tiny figures as they flowed out. On each side of the gate was carved a hooded figure, head bent. Surrounding the scene were the hills and stagnant water of the Black Morass. He glanced at Khagar, raising an eyebrow in confusion.

Khadgar reached over. "No—turn it this way." Now the page was vertical, not horizontal. "Look," he said, trailing a finger over a curve that previously depicted the roll of a hill. Illumination flared beneath his touch, enhancing the the sketch. "See?"

The hair at the back of Lothar's neck lifted. Turned this way, what had once been a landscape was now clearly a figure: Hooded, face hidden, like the stone ones that flanked the opening of the portal. It bent over a gate that was now beneath its feet, towering over the cluster of orcs who raced up out of the gaping earth. Its arm was raised, as if beckoning.

Lothar fought to keep his voice calm. "What do you think the image means?"

"The orcs were summoned… from *this* side of the gate." His eyes burned with certainty—and fear. "They were *invited in*!"

Lothar glanced around, to see if anyone had overheard the unsettling conversation. "And the Guardian burned your research," he said, slowly, sickly. Why? Why would the Guardian of Azeroth become so angry he'd destroy the boy's notes? Was he that jealous of the Novitiate? Khadgar was doing good research, though Lothar was pained to admit it. None of this was making any sense. The more they learned, the muddier things got. *Medivh, old friend… what's going on?*

Lothar groped for something to say. "The Guardian was probably trying to protect you."

Khadgar looked at him searchingly, his brows, dark and elegant as raven's wings, furrowed in worry that was not entirely erased by Lothar's words. "Now," Lothar said amiably, "go away."

Khadgar nodded and obeyed, accustomed now to Lothar's teasing. The smile faded from Lothar's face as he watched the mage depart.

13

They had spent the morning in preparation. Durotan was gladder than he could say that Orgrim had given his full support to the plan. His second had insisted on taking a few scouts out to the appointed meeting place. They would set up, Orgrim told his chieftain, and then Durotan and the rest could join him. The Frostwolf chieftain, meanwhile, had quietly alerted his clan to his intentions, speaking with them and allaying their concerns. Now several warriors stood ready beneath the black rock. They burned evergreen boughs, sending up a fragrant, smoky signal that would, Durotan hoped, guide the humans to the specific spot.

The area was stony and bare. The black mountain and its foothills towered over the single, narrow switchback path that was the only road to the meeting place. Orgrim stood beside him. Durotan's eyes were on the path, watching for any sign of movement. He had told Garona to be there when the sun was highest, and that had passed. The humans were late. Would they even come at all? he wondered morosely. Had Garona—

Something glinted along the trail. Durotan slitted his eyes, straining to see. There came another flash, and he realized he was looking at a long line of armored humans, riding atop their hooved mounts.

"Weapons," Durotan shouted. At once, his warriors stopped feeding the fire, and went to arm themselves just in case. They were on edge, as was Orgrim. Durotan had never seen his friend this ill at ease. He understood. He, too, had never been so unsettled before either a parley or a battle. These were strange times, but he was firm in the correctness of his choice.

"A good spot for an ambush," Orgrim commented, looking up at the peaks that closed in around them.

"Our sentries are well placed."

Orgrim grunted. "I will check again," he said, and moved off. Durotan nodded absently, his attention fully on the line of soldiers winding their way toward him. Forty, perhaps fifty of them, all told. Beside him, the warrior Zarka snorted. "So many, they bring," she said. "They must be very fearful."

"They could have brought many more, Zarka," Durotan said.

"Perhaps they did."

"If so, Orgrim will find out."

"Chieftain..." Zarka looked at Durotan. "I follow you, but I mislike this."

"We did not like being forced to leave our home, but we had no choice. I do not believe we have one now, either."

Zarka looked at her chieftain searchingly, then thumped her fist over her heart in a salute. Durotan glanced up, seeking Orgrim. His second-in-command stood on a ridge above him. He turned to Durotan and made a broad signal with his arms: *All is well.*

They were closer now, the stream of humans and beasts spreading out onto the valley floor. Finally, about fifty feet away, the human in the lead lifted his hand, and the soldiers halted. He wore armor that seemed to Durotan to be delicate and decorative. His head was bare, as was that of the man who rode beside him with a blue-eyed gaze as sharp as a sword. The two men slipped off their mounts, and Garona followed.

Kill them, something inside him shouted. *They are not orcs. Kill them!*

No. The lives of my people are more important than bloodlust.

He clenched his hands tightly, not to make a fist, but to stop them from trembling in their desire to fasten about the slender human throats. The humans walked several steps toward him, then halted, waiting for him to close the distance.

Durotan did, striding to within a few feet of them. *How small they are*, he thought. *How fragile.*

More like Garona than us. But how brave.

"You asked to speak with the human king," Garona said to him. She gestured to the dark-haired, dark-eyed human. "Here he stands."

Durotan couldn't bring himself to utter a word. He was too busy trying to control his instincts. The humans exchanged glances, and the king broke the tense silence with his strange, clipped language.

"This is King Llane," Garona said. "He says, he was told you wish to talk."

Durotan inhaled a deep breath, willing himself to be calm, and nodded. The other man next to Llane said something quickly, looking at Durotan with more than a hint of wariness.

"Anduin Lothar wishes to know if you plan to return to your home through the portal you are building," Garona translated.

"Our world is dying," Durotan said. "There is nothing to go back to."

"We are not responsible for destroying your world," Llane said, through Garona. "War with us will solve nothing."

Durotan sighed deeply, and thought of Orgrim's words earlier. "For orcs," he said, "war solves everything."

"Then why are you meeting with us now?" The question was from Llane, who regarded Durotan fixedly. For the first time since the parley had begun, Durotan met those eyes. He saw no fear in them, only watchfulness, steadiness and... curiosity. This Llane did not know how honorable orcs were, or how much

Durotan had wrestled with this decision. He knew nothing other than what Garona had told him. And yet, he had come.

He had come for the same reason Durotan had.

"To save our people," Durotan told him.

When Garona translated, the king looked surprised. He exchanged glances with the one called Lothar, and Garona looked at Durotan expectantly.

"The fel takes life from more than its victims," Durotan explained. "It kills the earth and corrupts those who use it. We saw this happen before, in my world of Draenor. The land died, the creatures were twisted... even the Spirits were harmed. Gul'dan would poison everything with his death magic here, as he did there. If my people are to survive, Gul'dan must be destroyed. In two suns, the humans we have captured will be used to fuel the portal. If you attack our camp and draw his warriors away, the Frostwolf clan will kill him."

Llane listened intently as Garona translated, nodding now and then. He and Lothar conversed. Then, he turned again to Durotan. "Two days... if we do this, you will protect my people until then."

Durotan thought of the cages, of the torment those inside them endured. Most of the orcs ignored the humans, but some did not. But this king wanted them safe—just as Durotan would want the same if their roles were reversed.

"I will try—" he began, unwilling to give his word on something he could not necessarily offer.

His words were drowned out by a roar behind

him. All around them, green-skinned orcs leaped up from where they had been concealed by rocks, scrub trees, and cracks in the stone cliffs, charging at the Frostwolves with axes, hammers, and maces. Durotan saw the comprehension in Llane's brown eyes just as he himself realized what had happened.

They had been betrayed.

And Durotan's heart cracked as he understood by whom.

"Get back!"

Lothar, the lifelong soldier, had recovered from the shock first, drawing his sword and leaping atop Reliant. Llane was right behind him, already mounted on his own steed. Garona, her head swimming with shock at what she had just witnessed, was jolted out of her horror by a thunderous crashing sound. She whirled, seizing the reins of her horse, to behold a massive boulder hurtling down the cliffside toward them. Her mount neighed with terror, bolting and tearing the reins from her hands. The other riderless horses joined him. Lothar had told Garona the beasts had been trained for combat, but clearly not for this.

Garona howled with rage at being weaponless, save for the queen's gift of the small, bejeweled dagger. It would be less than useless against maces, axes, and morning stars. Frustrated, she looked about wildly. She saw small, green-skinned figures atop the canyon's walls; those orcs had doubtless been the ones to roll down the boulders. More orcs were flowing down behind the king's soldiers, blocking the sole escape route. Others exploded out of seemingly harmless piles of stones along the path.

The battle was on in earnest. Llane and Lothar rode their steeds through the chaos, attempting to defend those who had been a moment too late and were now fighting unmounted. A massive bellow of gleeful bloodlust came from her right, and Garona turned.

This orc's skin was not just tinged with green, but saturated with it. He was enormous, almost as big as Blackhand, and held a huge shield adorned with the skull of a twin-horned horned beast in front of him. The orc was, very effectively, using that shield as a second weapon. He barreled through the cluster of armored soldiers like a charging animal without the faintest slackening of speed. He scattered them as if they were nothing more than the tiny toy soldiers Garona recalled from the strategy maps, knocked aside by a casual hand. The twin great, sharp horns on the shield found a target—Lothar's horse.

Fear descended upon Garona unlike anything she had ever known. Anduin Lothar would surely die, right in front of her, and she could do nothing to help. She had witnessed battle and death before, but always she had felt nothing but resentment and anger toward those who had fallen.

She did not feel that toward Lothar.

Even as the unfamiliar clutch of terror seized Garona's throat and turned her gut to ice, Lothar leaped clear of the dying animal as lightly as if he wore no armor at all. As he sprang, he raised his sword and brought it down, angling behind the great shield and into the orc's throat. The orc toppled down, following the dead horse by seconds.

Lothar whirled, then stooped to pick up a pike dropped by one of Llane's soldiers. He raised his head and met Garona's eyes. For a heartbeat, their gazes locked. And then, reaching a decision, Lothar tossed the half-orc the pike. She caught it easily, her fingers curving around the weapon. Tempered joy rose inside her. She could now defend herself with honor, and Anduin Lothar had just demonstrated that he trusted her.

As another orc surged forward, Lothar whirled, sword glinting in the sunlight. It clanged against the metal of an axe blade, but did not break. Steel on steel shrieked, and sparks flew as Lothar's blade slid off, down the shaft, and bit deep into the orc's arm. Suddenly the great axe dangled masterless as its wielder's hand, still clutching it, swung by only a few sinews from the orc's arm. Lothar took advantage of the orc's momentary pause to drive the blade through his enemy's chest.

A third charged toward him. Lothar ran toward it, not slowing as he approached a mounted knight, instead dropping and sliding beneath the horse's body to emerge, sword ready, to stab upward and gut the startled orc.

"Llane!" he shouted above the din of battle, "You're no good to us dead! Get out! I'll get the others!"

The king, too, was holding his own as he shouted back, "We're *all* getting out! Medivh will cover our retreat!"

Lothar hadn't paused in his attacks. The men were gravitating toward him now, as if he were a living banner and they were drawing strength from his seemingly limitless supply.

Medivh.

The Guardian's name roused Garona from her rapt fascination with Lothar's astounding ferocity. As they had approached the meeting site, Medivh had told them he could protect them better if he could see them all. He had taken his horse up, to watch them from above. Now, Garona tore her gaze from Lothar to gaze upward, trying to spot Medivh. Where was he? Why was he not acting?

She did not see him. But she did see someone else.

Blackhand, mounted atop a wolf, peering down at the ambush.

And beside Gul'dan's warchief stood Orgrim Doomhammer.

14

Anger, white-hot and pure, fueled Garona. Against all reason, she started to move toward the cliffside. Gaze locked on Orgrim, she didn't see the orc who was charging at her from the side until he started screaming. She whirled, snarling, to behold the orc writhing in agony. Small pieces of liquid orange fire were bombarding him. Garona hissed as she smelled his cooking flesh. He died quickly, but in obvious torment.

Over his fallen body stood Khadgar. "Are you all right?" he asked.

She had been saved by a boy. A boy who could wield magic like a shaman or a warlock, and who could summon and direct lava—but a boy nonetheless. She nodded her thanks, then turned, ready to fight her own battle with the Stormwind pike. A green-skinned orc charged her, woefully underestimating her as she shrieked and jabbed him square in the throat. As Garona tugged the blade free, she realized she was looking directly at the king. He was fighting desperately, utterly unaware of the orc rushing up from behind him, the huge, curved blade of his war axe lifted to deal a death blow.

Garona was not about to let this human, who had trusted her, whose mate had even armed her with her own blade, fall to a treacherous orc. With the full force of her body and her speed, Garona opened her mouth in a battle cry and raced toward the would-be killer. Llane's eyes flew open wide as she charged, seemingly directly at him, and he dived to the side. Garona impaled the huge green orc as if he were a haunch of meat.

It should have killed him, but seemed only to anger him. His body a green almost as bright as that of her former master, the orc snarled an insult at her. She did not want to wait for him to die. Howling, she drew Taria's knife and slashed his throat. Green blood flew, arcing from the severed artery and spattering both her and a startled Llane. She yanked the pike free and the orc fell heavily to the dirt, spun round, his attention diverted from the king.

Garona's eyes met the king's over the body. Panting, Llane nodded; he knew she had saved his life today.

* * *

"Where's the bloody Guardian?" Lothar muttered. He was hip-deep in enemies, dodging and swinging and ducking. His sword found an open spot as an orc raised its axe and he lunged. Distantly, he realized that orc anatomy was similar enough to human for his purpose as the creature toppled almost at once.

He risked a quick glance to see if he could find Medivh and instead saw his son. Callan was holding his own, ripping a spear out of one orc's huge paws while ducking in time to avoid the swipe of another wearing an enormous warclaw.

Beyond the boy was a cluster of soldiers. They looked pathetically small as they battled the giant monsters. Lothar glanced back at Llane, anguished. Protect the king—or his soldiers, who were outnumbered and ruthlessly being beaten down?

"I'll get them!"

The voice was youthful, but determined. It was Callan's. Lothar was first surprised, then terribly proud. His son had seen, and had known immediately his father's dilemma. The boy had killed the orc he was fighting, and now moved determinedly to aid his companions.

Dad... I'm a soldier.

Lothar spared a moment as his son raced toward his brothers in arms, shouting out, "Shield formation!" The soldiers drew together and raised their shields in front of, and over, themselves. Why was—

And then Lothar understood. A monster of an orc on one of those overgrown wolves charged them, leaping at, then, incredibly, *climbing up* the layers of

Stormwind shields. Swords, spears, and pikes jutted between the shields, and the wolf howled piteously, scrambling as its red blood stained the shields. It was dead a moment later, but the soldiers collapsed under the weight of wolf and rider.

It happened in the span of a few seconds, but the brief glimpse was sufficient for Lothar to recognize the orc. The last time Lothar had seen him, the beast had been ordering a retreat, his right hand burned, bloodied, and minus several fingers courtesy of Magni's boomstick. But now, he had a new and more horrifying limb—a claw, enormous, monstrous and shiny, with five blades to replace his five fingers.

Lothar looked up anxiously at the plateau. "*Medivh!*" he bellowed. He turned back to the soldiers who had escaped the collapse of the shield barrier, fighting desperately.

And into the merciless eyes of the claw-handed orc.

He now understood what was so terrifying about these creatures. They were huge, and some of them had green skin. Some wore skulls around their necks, and their weapons were almost the size of the humans they slew with them. They had ugly, jutting jaws and tusks in their mouths. But what made them so very horrifying was not any of these things. It was the fact that they were not, indeed, mere "creatures". For in those tiny, dark eyes, Anduin Lothar saw not just bloodlust and hatred—but a fierce intelligence.

And at this moment, in those eyes, Lothar saw recognition.

The orc began to stride purposefully toward him, hacking at any who would dare impede his descent upon the human who had deprived him of a hand.

All right then, you bastard, Lothar thought. *Come on, and I'll lop off the other—*

Light exploded in front of him, accompanied almost simultaneously with a deafening peal of thunder. He heard Llane shout, "That's the Guardian's work! Quick! Retreat to the plateau!"

Another blinding flash and ear-splitting roll of thunder, and another, and another. They came hard on one another's heels now, hundreds of sizzling, bright shafts of lightning that struck the earth and lingered side by side to form a wall that spread out to separate humans from their attackers; a fence of deadly energy that stretched across the valley.

And the monstrous orc with the artificial hand was on the wrong side of it. Lothar couldn't help laughing, mostly in relief, as the orc threw back his head and raged impotently.

"Let's go!" cried Llane, spurring his horse into action and riding among his men, herding them toward the plateau and an open area. Lothar used the moment to catch his breath, and smiled with relief as he gazed upward. "Medivh," he whispered. Until this moment, he hadn't realized how worried he had been that his old friend might not be—

Where was Callan?

No...

He turned. A small handful of soldiers were still fighting, still trying to retreat. And they, like the tattooed orc, were on the other side of Medivh's wall.

"Down!" The word was half demand, half sob. Lothar looked up at the plateau, trying to find his old friend. "Take it down! Medivh! *Medivh, please!*"

His world narrowed, and he sprinted toward his boy only to be brought up short by the spitting, captured bolts of lightning. Furious, he tried to reach through the spaces between them, to see if there was any place he could cross. His armor sizzled as he touched it, shocking him and knocking him back, but he again rushed forward, trying to find a space, a crack in the lightning-spear wall, a place where a slender sapling of a young man, a boy with his mother's eyes, could slip through—

It was futile. There was only the erratic, flashing wall, the straight backs of Callan and the handful of other soldiers who had been trapped, alone with the maddened green-skinned monsters who now advanced upon them.

"Medivh!"

Desperately, Lothar gritted his teeth and pushed his arm through. The lightning did not like such a violation of its power and punished him for his arrogance, turning the armor red where it touched. Lothar persevered, straining until his hand closed on his child's shoulder. Callan turned. Their faces were only a few inches apart, but it might as well have been a thousand leagues. "Callan!" he cried, "Hold on, son!"

"Dad...!" The lightning cracked and Lothar was forced to stumble back. Callan looked at his father with that strange, old, knowing expression he had worn in the infirmary. He smiled sadly, almost sweetly. He knew. Cally had known, too, when the shadow of death had stretched across her. Even as her lungs had filled for the last time, she had used the precious breath to form words of comfort for her devastated mate. Enraged, Lothar scrabbled furiously at the soil, reaching his arm through again. *He's right here—he's so close, I can reach him, I—*

Lothar met his gaze, held it, as his wife's eyes smiled back at him from a boy's—a man's—face.

"For Azeroth!" And Callan turned and charged into the approaching sea of brown and green skin.

Lothar went mad.

He flung himself at the lightning barrier, trying to break through, perhaps through sheer force of will. This time, he gritted his teeth against the jolts of energy and kept pushing. His armor sizzled, glowing orange where the white lightning shafts touched it, and he heard it snap.

He endured it as long as he could, but at last he stumbled away, nerves afire with pain, watching the huge monsters with their scraps of armor and obscenely sized weapons close in around the handful of soldiers, blotting out their bright armor.

Lothar sobbed, a harsh, racking cry that tore at his throat and his heart. His head whipped around wildly, searching for Medivh, anyone, anything, for aid, unable to help his boy, unable to abandon him.

His eyes fell on Reliant's body—and the shield with the horned skull that had taken the horse's life. Lothar raced toward it and heaved it up, arms quivering beneath the weight. He kept his feet by sheer effort of will and charged the sizzling wall once again, trying to push through using the shield as a battering ram. Through one of the skull's empty eye sockets as large as his whole head, he could see Callan fighting with skill and strength Lothar had not realized his son possessed. He was holding his own.

Then the throng of brown and green bodies stepped back. Some of them stared down at the center of their circle, others had their gazes turned elsewhere. The lightning wall hissed and spat. Another blast sent Lothar hurling backward. He landed hard, his body spasming. Two of his soldiers lifted him to his feet.

Callan was engaged in combat with one of the green orcs, a massive beast with a topknot and a jaw tattooed entirely black. The boy lunged forward with his sword, but the orc trapped the blade with his own—a primitive, jagged thing that looked like an animal's jawbone. He yanked the weapon from Callan's hands.

Callan grunted, but stayed on his feet. The orc's lip curled. He lifted Callan's blade, intending to shame his enemy by felling him with the hilt of his own weapon, but the leader shouted a protest. The orc lowered the sword and stepped back, ceding his prey. A black hand shot out, spun Callan around, and then wrapped about the boy's throat.

"Callan!" cried Lothar. "Look at me, boy."

The orc turned, staring at Lothar, his grip on

Callan never slacking. Slowly, carefully, Callan moved his head to look at his father. There was fear in those eyes, as there would be in in any sane creature's. Lothar could not bear to see it, not in Cally's eyes. He, too, was afraid, horribly afraid, more frightened of what was unfolding with a dreadful inevitability than of his own death.

And so, for Callan and not for himself, Anduin Lothar did not hurl himself against the lightning again. He did not scream in fury. He stood, quietly, even peacefully, Callan's hazel eyes locked with his own. Lothar kept that gaze, even when the orc, finally understanding the significance of the prize he clutched, grinned with deep satisfaction, the expression stretching his hideous, misshapen face around the jutting tusks.

He turned back to Callan, lifted his arm and the bloodstained claw that was grafted onto it, and brought it down.

It felt as though the weapon had plunged into his own body, carving out his heart as it sliced though Callan's armor and flesh. The orc lifted the body of Callan Lothar as if it were a piece of speared meat. He hurled Lothar's boy toward him, to crash and sizzle into the blue-white spears of lightning, then fall, limp, to the uncaring stone.

Slowly, Lothar raised his eyes. Hatred, cold and cleansing, replaced his anguish, for this moment at least. And as he gazed at the smug, grinning orc who had eviscerated the last thing Lothar loved, Lothar made them both a promise.

I will kill you. However long it may take, whatever it will cost me... I will kill you, for what you have done here today.

"He's here!"

At Garona's shout, Khadgar closed his eyes briefly in relief. He hastened over to where she knelt beside what at first looked like a discarded pile of clothing. As he drew closer, he sucked in a breath at the sight of the Guardian.

The only motion was the faint rise and fall of Medivh's chest. Otherwise, he was terribly still. Cheekbones jutted out in a hollow, pale face dotted with sweat.

"What's wrong with him?" Garona asked. Khadgar had no decisive answer, only suspicions he was not willing to share. Not yet. "We need to get him to Karazhan," he said.

Garona nodded. "I'll get horses."

"You won't make it in time by road." Llane's voice was clear and strong. "You'll take one of my birds."

The king lifted his hand in a signal to one of his men, who nodded and unfurled a long, leather tube. He raised the tube and began to spin it around his head. The device caught the air and produced a sharp whistling sound. The response was swift: A dot appeared in the sky, dropping down toward them. It was one of the royal gryphons, its white feathers and brown lion's body a welcome sight. Its powerful wings created a wind that blew back Khadgar's hair as it landed, shook itself, and looked at the gryphon master expectantly.

A few days ago, Khadgar had never even beheld the creatures. Now, he had ridden them more than once, and this time he was the more experienced of the two who now climbed into the gryphon's saddle. Other events that had occurred had more importance and urgency, but he cherished this little pleasure in the midst of all the horror.

Settled astride the beast, Khadgar and Garona reached to accept Medivh's frighteningly limp body. Without even thinking, Khadgar let Garona hold the Guardian, knowing her arms were stronger than his. As her green arms wrapped around the Guardian, the young mage suddenly realized what a great gesture of trust this was. She knew it, too, and nodded, the barest trace of a smile curving around her tusks.

Llane caressed the head of the great beast, looked it in the eyes, and commanded it: "Karazhan! Go!"

Moroes was waiting for them as they rushed down the stairs from the landing to the main chamber, Medivh slack in Garona's muscular arms. Khadgar saw that the servant didn't seem in the least bit surprised, although his already lined face was further furrowed in worry.

"Place him in the font," Moroes instructed.

"Moroes," Khadgar demanded. "What's wrong with the Guardian?"

As Khadgar himself had done when Garona

had posed that question, Moroes did not answer, just shook his white head. "I told him not to leave Karazhan," he said, more to himself than to them.

Together, Moroes and Garona placed Medivh in the magical font, arranging him carefully, leaving only his head and chest floating above the white wisps of living magic. Khadghar had wrapped his cloak around Medivh to help protect the Guardian from the cold air during the flight. The cloth had bunched up beneath the Guardian's head when they had placed him in the font. Gently, Khadgar lifted Medivh's head to remove the cloak.

Now, at last, Medivh showed some signs of life, if vague and confused. His eyelids flickered, then opened. The young mage's heart spasmed as he saw the faintest flicker of green light in Medivh's eyes.

His gut clenched, and he swallowed, his mouth suddenly dry. "I have to go," he blurted. "We need the help of the Kirin Tor... Now!"

"Go," Garona urged him.

As he pelted up the stairs, Khadgar heard Moroes tell Garona, "There are medicines I must prepare. Sit with him."

Khadgar did not want to leave the Guardian, but there was no choice. His mouth was set in a grim line as he raced for the loft, the gryphon, and, Light willing, some help for this world, before it was too late.

15

Draka was a warrior. Until now, her place had always been fighting at the side of the orc who was her husband, chieftain, and best friend. The birth of their yet-unnamed baby here, in this new fertile but hostile world, had changed all that. The infant was not just her child, or the son of the chieftain—he was the *clan's* child, the only one born to the Frostwolves in far too long, and despite his unsettling coloring, he was loved by all of them. In addition, there were few orcs here in Azeroth who were not needed, almost daily, to fight.

She had shared her husband's sentiments regarding Gul'dan, his evil magic, and the wrongness of this battle against the humans. But every moment that they were separated was a trial. It was one thing to go into battle together, knowing death was a possibility. It was another to be left behind to wait, not knowing anything at all.

As if sensing her distress, the baby started to fuss in his basket, opening those beautiful, peculiar blue eyes and reaching out his tiny fists to her. Gently, Draka took one of the little hands in hers and kissed it. "This hand will hurl your father's spear, Thunderstrike," she told him. "Or maybe you would prefer the great axe Sever, hmm?"

The baby gurgled, seemingly happy with whichever weapon he would wield some day in the future, and the trepidation in her heart eased somewhat. "My precious little warrior," she murmured, "you are a true orc, no matter your skin color. We will teach you that."

He had drifted off to sleep when the hanging skin that served as a door was flung aside. It was Durotan, sweating, panting, every line of his body telling her before he even spoke that everything had fallen apart.

He clasped her close for a moment, then told her quickly what had happened. She said nothing, but kept shaking her head. No. No. this could not be. Orgrim could not... would never betray them. But he had.

"You and the baby must leave," Durotan said when he had finished. He reached for the infant, lifting him tenderly, even in this moment of crisis. "Now!"

A shape moved to fill the doorway. Blackhand. He was spattered with gore, but had no weapon. He did not need one, not any more. The claw where his hand had once been would serve. He seized Durotan by his scalp and hauled him backward. The baby, cupped in his father's palm, squalled.

"You are a traitor, Durotan!" Blackhand bellowed.

Everything in Draka urged her to attack, but instead she kept her eyes on Durotan. He was not fighting—not with weapons, and she would follow his lead.

"No." Durotan spoke calmly, and from a deep place of certainty. "One who values what we once were. Like you used to."

"That time is past," he said angrily. Then, more softly, "We are but fuel for the fel now." The warchief's face held not fury or hatred, but only detached melancholy.

Draka was moved to speak, surprising even herself. "We are more than that. *You* are more than that. There is still hope, Blackhand. We do not have to take another step down this path."

Blackhand looked at her, his eyes narrowing, then down at Durotan. For a long, tense moment, the three stood, while the child cried. Then, growling, Blackhand released her mate, shoving him away. Durotan went at once to Draka, giving their child to her. She clasped the infant close. There was still no anger in Blackhand's voice when he spoke, but even so, Draka's heart ached with despair. "Do not make me take more innocent lives, young chieftain."

She held the baby tighter still, her eyes darting from Blackhand to Durotan. Durotan straightened, steadying himself. "If I submit..."

Draka's hand shot out and gripped her mate's arm, her nails digging into his flesh. He kept his gaze on the warchief. He continued, "… will you leave my people be?"

Blackhand did not answer. Draka knew that he could not. He was the warchief, but he answered to Gul'dan. Blackhand knew it, too. He merely opened the tent flap, and waited.

A chieftain must always do what is best for his people, Draka recalled. She refused to utter the sob, to give voice to the sound of her breaking heart. She would show her husband courage. *And besides,* she thought with determination, *I will not let this be the end.*

When her heart turned to her, she made sure he would only see determination and love in her eyes as he gazed intently into them. They were Frostwolves. They knew they loved. They would make no scene in front of Blackhand.

Whatever happens.

I've thought of a name, she had said to him.

I'll choose the name when I've met him… or her.

And how will the great Durotan name his son, if I do not travel with him?

"What will I call our son?" she asked him, chagrined but unashamed that her voice broke, Durotan lowered his gaze to his son, and for a moment, his composure slipped as he caressed the tiny head with unspeakable tenderness. "Go'el," he said, and it was at that moment that she knew he did not believe he would return. He caressed her chin with one finger. Then he turned to Blackhand, striding out of the tent, and out of her life. But never out of her heart.

Blackhand looked at her for a moment, his expression unreadable, then he followed. The great spear Thunderstrike, which had belonged to Durotan, and Garad, and to Durkosh before them, fell from where the Frostwolf chieftain had placed it to land on the hard-packed earth.

Slowly, Medivh opened his eyes, blinking. He remembered the battles. One he had shared with Lothar and Llane, fighting alongside them as he had before, in earlier times. He recalled the orcs, and the wall of lightning.

But there had been another, a battle in which his friends could have no part. Before he could help them, Medivh had been forced to struggle against the hooded figure that seemed to him to be formed out of the thunderheads themselves; a figure whose eyes glowed green.

He forced the image away. He had not succumbed. He had stood with his friends. He realized he was back in Karazhan, but could not remember traveling here. He turned his head, and saw *her*.

"You."

Warmth filled him and he smiled at Garona. She sighed a little, relieved at seeing him awake. His eyes took her in. So strong. So beautiful, and so proud, despite everything she had seen, everything that had been done to her. "Where's the old man?"

"He asked me to watch you," she replied.

"He did?" *Thank you, Moroes.* The pleasure

ebbed somewhat. He asked, almost afraid to know the answer, "And the king?"

"He is alive," she reassured him.

Thank the Light. But her next words dimmed his pleasure.

"Lothar's son is dead."

Not Callan. Medivh closed his eyes and sighed, pained. He had not known the boy well. Lothar had always kept his son at a distance, not only from himself, but from others. It had been Taria's kindness that had found Callan a place in the king's guard, not Lothar.

"I do not think Durotan knew about the ambush." Garona spoke intensely.

Medivh wondered where this was going. "I agree."

"I argued for the meeting," Garona continued. Her dark eyes were pools of regret. "Lothar will hate me."

As Medivh himself well knew, six years could change a man. He did not know if, in truth, Lothar would hate the orc woman sitting beside him, and so did not tell her no.

"That upsets you," he said instead.

"He is a great warrior," she continued. Her cheeks darkened slightly. "He defends his people well."

Ah, thought Medivh. Anduin. It made sense. He examined his feelings for a moment, then made a decision. "A good mate for an orc," he said, carefully.

Garona frowned and shook her head. "I am no orc. I am no human either. I am cursed. I am Garona."

The self-loathing and hopelessness in her voice made him ache. He regarded her for a long moment, then reached a decision.

"When I was younger," Medivh began, letting the words come as they would, "I used to feel apart from my kin." Part of the Kirin Tor, but not really— their project, their pet. Separated from his blood family, creating a "family" in the company of two devil-may-care companions. And the aftermath of their adventures...

"I traveled far and wide, looking for wisdom. How to feel a connection with all the souls I was charged with protecting." Garona listened with her whole body, eyes wide, nostrils flaring as she breathed. *Orcish concentration,* he thought, and a bittersweet ache such as he had not felt for years gripped his heart.

"On my travels I met a strong and noble people, among them a female, who accepted me for what I was. Who *loved* me."

Part of him did not want to continue. This was his burden, his great joy and secret; his and his alone. Except, it wasn't. It couldn't—shouldn't—be. He paused before continuing, meeting her gaze steadily.

"It was not a life I was fated to have, but it taught me something. If love is what you need," he said, softly, his voice trembling with intensity, "you must be willing to travel to the ends of the world to find it. *Beyond,* even."

Garona looked down for a moment, emotions warring on her face, usually so closed. "You left your mate?"

"Go find Lothar," he said, sharply. He looked away. Even now, even with her, this, he could not share. There was so much he wanted to tell her, but now was not the time. Maybe afterward. If there was an afterward.

"I must stay and watch you." Honor. Loyalty. Things he had loved so much about…

Medivh squeezed her shoulder. "That is Moroes's job," he said.

Medivh was still weak, but strong enough for what he needed to do now. He rose from the couch, moving his hands deftly, effortlessly, conjuring a circle for her. It was no great mystery to him where Lothar would be at this moment. Part of Medivh's energy came, of course, from the magical font's healing. But part of it was his own doing. His choices. His decision to, finally, after so many mistakes and disasters and broken lives as consequence, do something good. Something right. Something true and worthy of the one he had loved so long ago; loved, lost, but never forgotten, not for a day, an hour, a moment.

He would pay dearly for what he was doing. But that was all right. Some things were worth the cost.

This is for you, my heart.

She stared, as the circle shimmered into being; pulsing, radiating blue light. Medivh reached and gathered a small bit of magical energy into his hand, and crafted a small, perfect flower. It was exquisite and beautiful, light made into a palpable thing, its hues shifting like an ember in a blue fire. Garona had seen him work magic before—dangerous magic, designed to cause harm. But this was only for healing. For hope. She understood that, as he knew she would, and her eyes were wide and soft with wonder.

"Step inside the circle," he instructed. Garona looked at him, then the circle, then, slowly, mesmerized, moving more delicately than he had ever seen any orc save one move, she obeyed.

"This," Medivh said, his voice rough with emotion as he held out the luminous flower, "is my gift to you." He allowed himself to savor this moment, giving her no hint as to what this was costing him. She accepted it, her green fingers closing so very gently around the magical flower, looking first at it, then at him.

Peace filled him, and he stepped back. The circle's white illumination spread upward, becoming a sphere, encasing Garona safely within its cocoon. The white glow increased, its brightness becoming almost blinding, then it disappeared—Garona along with it.

Medivh collapsed.

The Lion of Azeroth had been drinking.

He lay outstretched on the bar in the Lion's Pride Inn, surrounded by empty bottles. An equally empty tankard dangled from his fingers. His eyes were closed, and Garona wondered if he was unconscious.

She took a step forward, trying to move quietly, but even so Lothar heard her and his eyes opened. He didn't look at her, but kept his gaze fixed on the ceiling. Garona wondered if she had should have come. Perhaps Medivh had been wrong. Perhaps this was foolishness, to think that a human could care for an orc, particularly one who could easily be held responsible for the brutal murder of his only child.

But she thought of the Guardian's words. She was here. She would speak. At least she would know that she had tried.

"I'm sorry."

He didn't answer, and Garona had almost turned to leave when, at last, he spoke.

"Callan's mother died in childbirth. I blamed him for it. For years. I'm not going to blame you."

His voice was less slurred than Garona had expected, and he was obviously aiming for a conversational, relaxed tone. But she, who had tasted so much pain, could recognize its sharp, bitter notes in the voice of another.

Her eyes widened at the words. Lothar had been carrying such a burden... She moved forward. He sat up and slipped off the bar, stepping back as she drew closer. She halted. He looked almost as awful as Medivh: pale, save where his cheeks were flushed with drink. His eyes were bloodshot and swollen, and he trembled. Suddenly he whirled, flinging the tankard against the wall. It shattered with a musical crash.

He was in a place Garona knew well. A place where anger and grief and guilt collided in an unholy trinity of torment. He was a soldier without his armor in front of her now, raw and aching and unable to hide any of it. She stepped forward, reaching to touch his face, wanting to do whatever she could to ease a pain that was obviously ripping him apart.

"He was so young," Lothar whispered. His eyes were red from weeping. She trailed her lips over his bearded cheek, mindful of the sharpness of her tusks, then pulled back, gazing at him. "My whole life," he rasped, "I've never felt as much pain as I do now…"

Lothar's voice, and Garona's heart, broke on the last word. Then he whispered, "I want more…"

Garona understood at once. Her whole life, she, the cursed, had been in pain. It was never the physical pain of broken bones or ripped skin that hurt the most. It was the pain that stitches and poultices and healing drafts could not mend: the pain of the soul, the heart. More than once, she had found healing, respite, from that torment in physical pain, which provided a distraction and allowed the spirit to, somehow, find its own way. Sometimes it did not work, but sometimes it did.

He lifted his eyes to her, and if there had been any question that she loved, and that she belonged here, at this moment, it vanished like mist beneath the sun.

She reached out to him, gently touching his face. He closed his eyes and tears, warm and wet, slipped beneath the tightly shut lids. Then, slowly, ready to stop if he did not wish this, Garona began to dig in her nails.

His eyes flew open wide, and in those blue depths Garona saw desire. Lothar reached out, pulled her to him, and pressed his mouth on hers.

And then, there was no pain at all.

16

Day or night, it made no difference. Work continued on building the Great Gate, whether that work was done by sunlight or torchlight, as it was now. Orgrim glanced briefly at the orcs laboring in the flickering firelight, and at the construct that disappeared up into darkness. It was coming along swiftly. It would be ready in time.

There was more on his mind than the portal, though. Before this day's decisions, his life had seemed simple. Choices had been clear to him. It was Durotan who had always seemed to agonize over the gray shades when, to Orgrim, things were either black or white. But now that he had made his decision, he suddenly understood what his friend had wrestled with. Orgrim now stood beside Gul'dan, who occupied an ornately carved chair on a platform above the gate, supervising the work as ordinary orcs might observe ants.

On Gul'dan's other side huddled a human slave. It seemed that with his pet Garona turned traitor, the warlock felt the absence of someone crouching at his feet. Garona, though, had never looked like this: pale, emaciated, staring at nothing. Orgrim could count the human's ribs.

It was not a pleasant sight, so Orgrim looked to the Great Gate. He pointed to the two statues that flanked what would be the portal's opening. They were representations of the same figure—a tall, too-slender being whose face was hidden by a cowl. "Who is it?"

"Our… benefactor," Gul'dan said, his voice a rough purr on the word.

Orgrim scoffed in surprise. "A new world in exchange for a statue? Gods are strange creatures."

Gul'dan chuckled. Ever since he had first arrived at Frostfire Ridge, asking the Frostwolves to join the Horde, Gul'dan had unsettled Orgrim, and never more than when he laughed.

"Frostwolves," the warlock said. "You are a practical people. Those of us from the south have always admired that about you." He turned to look down at his slave, smiling with apparent affection. He extended his hand, and both his eye and the tips of his fingers burned bright green. He waved his hand, languidly. A thin, misty trail snaked from the human to Gul'dan's green-tipped fingers. The human's eyes widened in terrorized agony, but he made no sound. He began to struggle, weakly, and choke, withering before Orgrim's gaze. It was as if Gul'dan was literally drinking the creature's life energy.

He is, thought Orgrim. *Spirits help us, he is.* He found he had to fight an instinct to flee.

Gul'dan dropped his hand, and the human sagged back, his thin chest heaving.

"When the portal opens," and Gul'dan's voice was relaxed, almost dreamy, "and the rest of the Horde joins us, we will gift them the fel. All of them."

Orgrim's fists clenched. "Durotan did not agree to this," he said snapped, angrily.

"And why would you care what that traitor thinks?" Gul'dan's eyes were radiant with the bright green hue of fel. *How much of this thing is still an orc?* Orgrim wondered with a surge of horror. When the warlock spoke, his voice was strident, harsh, and biting. "It is time for a new leader of the Frostwolf clan. One who has the best interests of his orcs in mind. One," and he placed a hand immodestly on his own chest, "who appreciates Gul'dan's vision. His power!" His green lips stretched in a wide smile, and again extended his hand to the slave, taking another sip of that pathetic creature's life energy.

"Come," Gul'dan said, as the human, little more than a skeleton now, drooped, panting. "I will grant you the fel."

My master is dark and dangerous. Garona had said this to Durotan, to the Frostwolves. Garona, who had arranged for the humans to meet with Durotan. Garona, as green as Gul'dan, but as unlike him as could be imagined.

She had said this, and she had been completely right. Was she—was Durotan—right about allying with the humans against him?

"Durotan, he…" Orgrim struggled to appear sincere, though his heart was pounding. "He has poisoned the Frostwolves against the fel. Let me gather them. Bring them here. Grant me the fel in front of them—let them see how much stronger I become."

Gul'dan's eyes narrowed. Orgrim forced himself to project calm, meeting those eyes evenly, even as at the corner of his vision he watched the human gasp for breath. The warlock considered.

"As I said," Gul'dan said finally, "a practical people. Summon them, then. This is not Draenor, Frostwolf. This is a new dawn! The time of the Horde."

He turned his attention again to the slave, lip curling in contempt as the man reached out to him imploringly. "Be feared," Gul'dan said, said, "or be fuel."

Gul'dan abruptly closed his fist and tugged. The cord between them snapped. The human's eyes rolled back in his head and he collapsed. Orgrim stared at the corpse, a papery, withered husk. He inclined his head, and left. As soon as he was far enough away from the torches, he broke into a run. He was certain that Gul'dan had not believed him. He only hoped that he had bought his clan enough time.

But he had not.

Howls and shouts pierced the night air and as he approached the Frostwolf encampment, Orgrim saw one hut go up in a sheet of flames. "Gul'dan does not want to waste his power on the Frostwolves!" he heard a large Warsong, green with the fel, declare. He would never say anything else. Orgrim closed the distance between them, hoisted the other orc, then slammed his head down at an angle on his own bald pate. The Warsong's neck snapped. Orgrim hurled away the body and continued on.

Durotan, my old friend, forgive me.

He rushed to the chieftain's hut. Draka whirled, one arm on her child in its cradle, the other holding a huge, wicked-looking dagger that could slice Orgrim's throat just as easily as it had once opened a talbuk's belly.

"I'll bathe in your blood!" she snarled, her eyes hard with loathing.

"Maybe," he agreed sadly, "but not now. I can't give you long, but I can give you a head start." He moved to close the tent flap. The instant he turned back to face her, she had the blade to his throat. He knew how badly she wanted to slash it across his jugular. He saw it in her eyes, could feel it in the slight trembling of the metal against his flesh. And she was right to want to do so.

She spat at him. "Why should I trust you? You have betrayed us all!"

Orgrim gestured to the baby. "Do you recall what I said to you, before we left to join the Horde? I swore I would *never* let harm come to you or the baby, not if I could prevent it. I cannot halt what I have put into motion, but let me at least keep that promise. For your son's sake, Draka. Leave! Now!"

Draka looked at him, listening to the sounds of murder and chaos outside the tent. At last, her expression as cold as winter in Frostfire Ridge, she lowered the blade—but not without leaving a small, bloody cut on his neck. Frustrated, she whirled and directed her fury at the back of the tent, slicing a hidden exit.

Holding her and Durotan's child in its cradle, she turned and gave him a final, contemptuous glance. "You should have trusted in your chieftain, Orgrim Doomhammer." Sick with shame, Orgrim found he could not bear to look at her as she slipped out into the darkness, instead checking to make sure no one was coming to the tent.

Once he heard her leave, he went to the rift she had made and looked out, watching her race for the trees and, Spirits willing, safety. Out of the corner of his eye he saw movement, one of the Bleeding Hollow orcs rushed the tent, his eyes on the fleeing Draka. Casually, Orgrim swung the Doomhammer, crushing the other's skull. He looked up from the corpse, and saw no sign of Draka or other pursuit.

Now, to see if there were other Frostwolves he could help before it was too late. And then, he would do what he could for Durotan.

Khadgar had leaped from the gryphon's back while it was still in flight, landing on the stairs that led to the Chamber of Air and racing up them. He knew this room well. Here, he had stood as a boy of eleven, while the same mages who stood on the ringed platform now had tested him and found him worthy. Here, silvery white magic had burned its Eye into his arm. It tingled now, as he returned to this place; something he had never imagined happening.

"Khadgar!" another mage shouted. "How dare you return here!"

"Get out!" another cried.

Khadgar turned his face up to the thin, elderly Archmage Antonidas, catching his breath as the Council of Six, clad in their violet robes embroidered with the Eye of the Kirin Tor scowled down at him. "I come seeking your wisdom," he said.

Antonidas's scowl deepened. "There's nothing for you here now."

"The Guardian Medivh is unwell."

Murmuring broke out as the six exchanged glances that ranged from shocked to furious to offended. Antonidas looked thunderstruck. "What?

The young mage took a deep breath. "He has been poisoned by the fel."

Silence. Antonidas strode to the edge of the platform. He looked as if he wanted to bring lightning down upon Khadgar, but didn't want to damage the precious inlay of the floor. "Ridiculous," the archmage all but snarled.

Archmage Shendra, who never had much cared for Khadgar, stepped forward. "It was *you*, Khadgar, who was weak!" She didn't even attempt to disguise her loathing as she stabbed a bony index finger in his direction. "*You* who felt the need to study that wretched magic the Kirin Tor had so specifically banned!"

There was no time for lectures, no time for posturing or arguing about who was right or wrong or anything other than what was going on with Medivh. Khadgar was not the boy who had left only a few short months ago. He had seen more horrors in the last few days than, he suspected, had any of these old mages in their entire lifetimes. He did not rise to challenge Shendra's accusations, keeping his gaze on Antonidas. "What do you know of the Dark Portal?" he demanded.

"You come back," Antonidas sneered, "and accuse the Guardian—"

Khadgar lifted the sketch he had showed Lothar—the one of the Great Gate, and the mysterious figure inviting the Horde into Azeroth.

"What," he asked, "is Alodi?"

The chamber fell silent. Antonidas looked stunned. Whispers came: "Who is he to speak of that?" "How does he know?"

They took him to the bowels of the Violet Citadel. Khadgar had known the Citadel had a prison level, but had never been here. It was not deemed necessary; he was to be the Guardian of Azeroth, and the archmages would take care of Dalaran. He looked about, frankly stunned at the myriad magical wards, until at last the door was opened to a single large cell, and his eyes widened as he was escorted inside.

The humming sound of voices was oddly soothing as Khadgar tried to take everything in. Four mages were stationed at the compass points. They stood stiffly, their bodies held taut in almost unnaturally perfect stillness, their eyes closed. All that moved was their mouths, a regular incantation flowing from their lips. In front of them floated placidly bobbing purple sigils, and from these flowed a steady stream of magenta magic.

In the center, surrounded by the mages and the sigils, was an enormous black cube that hovered about a foot off the floor. The inky surface rippled, as if the cube were composed of thick, sludgy fluid. As the spells reached the cube, they revealed swirls and markings on its surface in no language that Khadgar recognized.

"Alodi," was all Antonidas said.

This was decidedly unhelpful. "What is it?"

His eyes never leaving the form, Antonidas replied, "An entity from a time before the Kirin Tor existed. We think it once served a function similar to that of the Guardian."

Ask Alodi. "A protector…" Khadgar whispered, his eyes glued to the languidly rippling surface of the cube.

Antonidas turned to him. "No one beyond the arch-council knows of its existence… and it *will* stay that way!" Khadgar hesitated, then nodded his agreement.

The archmage scowled, but he looked more lost than angry. At last he said, "For you to mention it by name in the same breath as the dark portal is too much to be mere—"

Movement caught their attention. A fluid... crack? Line? Khadgar wasn't sure which to call it—began to make its way vertically up the side of the cube that faced them. A semicircular segment shimmered, and Khadgar caught a glimpse of his and Antonidas's reflections. Then, it simply vanished, leaving an open area. More slick blackness gushed forward from the newly-created entrance and rippled, forming stairs that led to the dark interior.

"—coincidence," Antonidas finished, weakly.

Khadgar's mouth was desert-dry. "Do... do I go in?" he managed, his voice cracking slightly.

"I don't know." Antonidas stared with open astonishment. "It's never done that before."

Ask Alodi.

Well, Khadgar thought grimly, *here's my chance.* And slowly, his heart in his mouth, he stepped forward, climbing up the slightly vibrating stairs, into the heart of the thing called Alodi.

17

The cube was as black inside as it was outside. Khadgar ascended, pausing on the final stair, then stepped forward to enter. Instantly the wall behind him sealed shut and the wall in front of him emitted a slitted light. He felt the surface upon which he stood undulating. It was silent—utterly so, a stillness such as Khadgar had never experienced.

"Alodi?" he asked, and his voice was loud and strangely flat; no resonance, no echo, swallowed up as if he had not spoken, had never spoken.

Then, the silence was broken again—but not by him. "We do not have long, Khadgar," said the voice—husky, warm, feminine. Khadgar gasped as he saw a lump materialize "I have used the last of our power to bring you to us." The lump shifted, elongated. Now it resembled a person standing up, still covered with the black, slick substance that comprised the rest of the cube. As Khadgar stared, enraptured, the form refined itself. The black material began to look more like cloth, the shape fleshed out, becoming more detailed.

Khadgar gasped.

"I know you! The library—"

That mysterious shape, which had pointed out the book to him and then vanished. The book that had "Ask Alodi" scribbled on its pages.

"All are in danger," Alodi continued. "We are counting on you.

"The Guardian has betrayed us," she said, sadly.

Khadgar thought back to the flicker of green in Medivh's eyes that had prompted his journey to the Kirin Tor. He had hoped he had been wrong. "I saw the fel in his eyes," he told Alodi.

"He has been consumed by it," Alodi went on. "If he is not stopped—this world will burn."

Khadgar shook his head. This wasn't possible. "But he's… How could this have happened?" How could the one person who was entrusted with the welfare of a whole world want it destroyed? What had tempted him so, to betray his charge so utterly?

Alodi regarded him with great compassion from beneath her hood. The reason she gave shocked him.

"Loneliness," was all she said.

Khadgar stared at her. Could something so simple truly have undone someone so strong?

"Like all Guardians before him, Medivh was charged by the Kirin Tor to protect this world, alone.

His heart," she said gravely, "was true. So devoted to his charge was he that he took it upon himself to find and master all forms of magic."

The young mage listened, his soul sick. He didn't want to hear. He didn't want to know, but he had to.

"It was during this search, in the depths of the void, that he came upon something insidious, a power of terrifying potency…"

Alodi waved her hand. The black confines of the cube disappeared. Khadgar found himself floating in space as colors, images, and shapes whirled about him. Some he could recognize and name: Oceans, stars, purple, blue. Other concepts were so unfamiliar he could not even wrap his mind them. And at the center of the exquisite, roiling, beautiful chaos stood the Guardian of Azeroth.

His face was young, alight with joy in what he beheld. Fierce intelligence shone in those eyes, and there was both kindness and a sense of friendly mischief in the little lines at the blue-green eyes and slightly parted mouth. This was the Medivh that Llane and Taria and Lothar had known. And all at once, Khadgar understood why they were so loyal to him. Medivh embodied all that a Guardian should be.

And then, all at once, the hue, like a flaw in a perfect weaving, began to stain the celestial images of a Guardian at work. Its evil, glowing green tendrils, like blood poured into a bowl of pure water, seeped through the scene. More and more colors fell to the green, and the beautiful images turned ghastly and malformed. Medivh closed his eyes, grimacing, and when he opened them, they glowed as green as the mist that Khadgar had first beheld issuing from a dead man's throat.

He had all but forgotten Alodi, and her voice was a welcome reminder that what he was seeing was in the past. "The fel," she said.

Khadgar took a deep, shuddering breath. "Despite his best intentions, it consumed him—twisting his very soul. It turned his love for Azeroth into an insatiable need to spread the fel." Alodi paused. "You must face him, Khadgar."

He felt blood draining from his face. "I—I don't have the power to defeat a Guardian!"

Alodi smiled. "'Guardian' is but a name. The true guardians of this world are the people themselves. I know you see what the Kirin Tor cannot—that's why you left them. No *one* can stand against the darkness alone."

She was right. He had always believed that the Guardian should not be isolated, that the entire burden should not rest on a single pair of shoulders. He thought the Kirin Tor should become more involved with the people they shared the world with, not stay aloof and apart from them. But even so…

"I don't understand what you want me to do."

Alodi stepped closer to him, her strange wispy form flowing around the outlines of her body as she turned her head to him, letting him fully see her face for the first time. He gasped, softly. Around her face were the unmistakable, spider-web traces of fel magic. But they were not green and sinister. They were scars left behind, remnants only of something that had once been there, but was no more. Of a wound that had healed.

"Yes," she said. "You do."

And he did. He did not suffer as Medivh had. He was not alone. Medivh once had friends in the form of Llane and Lothar, but he could not stay close to them. His charge—to hold himself aloof from others ostensibly to protect them—had made him vulnerable. It was a vulnerability that Khadgar did not share.

"Lothar," he breathed. "Lothar will help me."

Even as Alodi's fel-scarred face smiled approval of his understanding, her form was starting to melt away. Her voice came to him still, but faintly.

"Trust in your friends, Khadgar. Together, you can save this world. Always remember—from light comes darkness, and from darkness... *Light*!"

Moroes rushed to the crumpled, panting lump on the floor that was his master. Quickly, he scooped up Medivh and bore him to the font. Where was the girl? He had asked her to stay with the Guardian! Then his eyes fell on the runes the Guardian had scribbled on the floor, and he understood.

Moroes blanched as he supported his master as they stumbled toward the font.

Carefully, moving as if drunk, Medivh stepped forward to the center of the pool. The white energies gently seeped into the Guardian's body and spirit, soothing him, caressing him, washing away the demonic grip of the fel. His gaze became lucid, and he tried bravely to smile.

"Thank you, Moroes," he said, his voice so very weak it cut at the old servant's heart.

"You'll recover, Guardian," he said with a certainty he was far from feeling. "You always do."

Medivh waved a too-thin hand. "No," he said, "for Garona. Thank you for the time with my daughter."

Moroes's shrewd gaze softened. He started to speak, then froze. A thin wisp of green was starting to tinge the whiteness of the font. He blinked, hoping against hope that he had imagined it, but the hideous, glowing green hue bled into the pool.

"I'm sorry, old friend. It seems I have led the orcs into this world."

Moroes shook his head, disbelieving. Medivh had wrestled with this for so long. He couldn't fail, not now, not when—

"The fel… it's twisted me, I… I don't even know what else I may have done." His voice cracked. "I just don't *remember*." Moroes, his heart breaking, moved around the circular pool, watching as the white magic struggled, then ceded to the green. "Everything I've thought to protect, I have destroyed." Broken, he lurched to one side in the font, his head hanging in defeat.

"I can't control the fel. No one can."

Abruptly Medivh shot to his feet, his body strong once again. His body was bathed in green light from the polluted magic, but his eyes—whites and irises—

were inky black. Moroes backed away. He wanted to urge his beloved master to fight it, to turn it back, as he always had before. But there was no trace of the Guardian he had tended to for so long in that face any more; no hint of friendly good humor, or pain at the thought of another's suffering, or love for the young woman who—

It was gone. All of it. And the only thought Moroes—old beyond reckoning, who had taken care of so many Guardians of Azeroth—had, as the demonic figure before him began to draw out his life, was that he wished he had died ere this moment had ever come.

Llane had been worried about Lothar. His friend had watched his son die, right in front of his eyes, unable to do anything about it. Llane knew that if he had lost his own boy, Varian, something in him would have broken irreparably. And so, he had said nothing when Lothar had left afterward, saying only he was "going to Goldshire." How often had he, Llane, and Medivh done so in years past? Except then, the drinking and carousing had been to celebrate the joys of life, not to drown its pain. And yet, this morning, when Llane had sent Karos to fetch Lothar from the Lion's Pride Inn, deep as his agony ran, his old friend had honored his duty to the man who was both friend and king and come at that man's command. Karos intimated that Garona had been with the commander. Llane could only assume that Medivh, having noticed the attraction between the two, had seen to it that they were together. Llane trusted Garona. He was certain that the ambush had not been of Durotan's making, and if she and Anduin could comfort one another, Llane would not judge, so long as the commander was fit to carry out his duties. Lothar seemed able, but there was a hardness to him that had not been there before. A stubbornness and a determination, and they had been locking horns for an hour on strategies. Llane was exhausted. He had returned only to cleanse himself of the sweat and blood of battle, kiss his wife and son, seize a few hours of sleep, and had been in the map room for hours before Lothar's arrival.

For what felt like the thousandth time, and might well have been, Llane, Varis, and a handful of others perused the model of Stormwind with red-rimmed eyes. "Five legions to block Deadwind Pass," he said, plunking a marker into position. "Another ten here, here, and here, along Redridge Mountains. Supply lines here. While the Eastern Sea hems them in south and east." He looked up at Lothar. "If we hold these positions, we will be at our strongest."

"Containment," Lothar said.

Llane sighed and rubbed his eyes. "Until there a better option, yes."

"And when there are ten times as many?" Lothar challenged. "What then?"

Llane looked down at the board. "If there were easy answers—" he began, but Lothar cut him off.

"Our priority has to be to stop this gate from

opening. Fail there, and it's just a matter of time before they beat us with sheer numbers."

Llane replied tightly, "What do you suggest?"

Lothar leaned against the table, his face close to Llane's. "Send everything we've got. Destroy the gate, free our people, and end the immediate threat."

"And what of the orcs that remain?"

"We'll take care of them later."

It was not good enough. "After they've ravaged the entire kingdom?" Llane shot back.

There was a sharp sound, a flash of blue-white light, and the Guardian of Azeroth appeared at the end of the table. "My lords."

Llane's heart surged with relief. Medivh looked better than he had since he had rejoined them after a six-year absence. His color was good, his face looked much less angular, and his body was straight and tall.

A grin stretched across Llane's face that he couldn't have suppressed even had he wanted to. "Medivh!" he exclaimed. "You are up and well!"

"I am," his old friend assured him. "I feel restored."

"We need you." Llane indicated the map. "We've been agonizing over our options." He gave Lothar a look and added, "Some of us feel that there *are* no options. We need fresh eyes."

"I not only bring fresh eyes, I bring fresh hope," Medivh replied. "I've met with Durotan."

"You met with Durotan," Lothar repeated. Was that truly skepticism in his voice? Worried now, Llane turned to see his old friend playing with one of the map's figurines.

"He *survived*?" Lothar looked astonished.

Medivh turned to him. "Indeed. He's assured me the rebellion against Gul'dan is gaining strength. With the help of the Frostwolves and their allies, we can destroy the gate."

Medivh always did have a flair for the dramatic, coming in at the nick of time to save the day. As he was doing now. Llane felt hope rise within him again.

"That doesn't change my plan." Lothar's words were blunt.

"What plan?" Medivh asked.

"Anduin believes we should attack with our full force," Llane explained. "I'm concerned it leaves the rest of the kingdom defenseless. I cede his point, that we should prevent reinforcements and try to save the prisoners. But the orcs have already clearly demonstrated that they can do a staggering amount of damage and cause much more loss of life."

Medivh nodded, considering. "How many legions would you need to hold the orcs in place and defend the kingdom?"

Llane shot Lothar an annoyed glance, and answered Medivh's question. "Twenty-five total. Five to hold the Pass, ten to guard the Redridge, ten to hold the city."

"We've already lost eighteen legions. That leaves only one... two... three!!" Lothar brandished the figurine, plucking the metal standards inserted in its back and flinging them on the table as he counted.

Llane ignored him. "Can it be done, Medivh?"

Lothar flung the figurine onto the table. "No, it

can't be done!"

There was an awkward pause. "With three legions, the Frostwolves, and my power," Medivh began, "we—"

Lothar turned his intense gaze upon his old friend. "With all due respect, Guardian," he said tightly, "your power has recently proven to be unreliable at best." He turned back to Llane. "I can't lead a mere three legions into that Horde waiting for him to magically save our backsides!"

Medivh did not seem upset. He turned his attention to the king. "Llane. Have I ever let you down?"

"Let him down? Where have you even *been* for the last six years?" Lothar asked.

Llane was torn. What Lothar said was true. They had, indeed, not been able to rely upon Medivh. But he looked so much better now. So much stronger, more like his old self. Obviously, whatever had been draining him had been addressed. And surely, Lothar could not forget how the Guardian had "magically saved their backsides" when the trolls had been a heartbeat away from taking the kingdom. Medivh had earned their trust in the past, and he had come through even recently, exhausted as he had been.

"Please, Anduin," Llane began, "Medivh is the Guardian—"

But Anduin didn't allow him to finish. "Not the one you remember! He's lost it! He's unstable! And he won't be there when you really need him."

Llane pressed his lips together tightly. He needed

his commander at the top of his game more than ever before. Quickly, he strode to Lothar. "Find your bearings, Anduin." His voice was firm and controlled, but brooked no disobedience.

Lothar's eyes were wild, despairing, but full of concern. "I'd march into hell for you, Llane, if I felt there was even the slightest chance of victory! You *know* that! But this is *suicide*!"

"Is this about Callan?" Medivh's voice was calm, with a trace of sorrow in it. Lothar's face froze and his body went rigid. Slowly, he turned to look at the Guardian.

"It was a tragedy—"

Lothar's face went ashen, and then he flushed. "Don't. You. *Dare*."

It had to be awful for both of them, Llane thought. Medivh had clearly been unwell, and his act of bringing down lightning to separate the warring parties had saved many lives, almost at the cost of his own. It had indeed been a tragedy that poor Callan had been caught on the wrong side of that defensive action. It would, Llane thought sadly, be only natural for Lothar to harbor resentment toward Medivh, perhaps even blame him entirely for Callan's death. But there wasn't time for this. There was barely time left for anything.

"If he hadn't been trying so hard to win your approval, he might still be with us today," Medivh said. Lothar was trembling violently. Sweat beaded his brow.

"Medivh—" Llane began.

"Callan wasn't ready. You knew it, but you let him play soldier anyway."

The words were unkind, and Llane opened his mouth to chide the Guardian, to ask him for an apology so they could focus on the dire situation at hand, but it was too late.

Lothar exploded, bellowing in incoherent rage, lunging for Medivh. Llane, Karos, all those assembled surged forward trying to break them apart. Medivh stepped back, his hands raised, defensive magic roiling in the palms of his hands, but he restrained himself—unlike Anduin—and did not loose the spell.

"Stop!" Llane commanded, shouting at the top of his voice. "Anduin—"

"*You* killed him!" Five men had the Lion of Azeroth now, and even they seemed to be having a hard time holding Lothar back as he struggled against them. His eyes were locked on Medivh, who maintained his composure despite Lothar's almost rabid behavior. "My friend, are you?" Lothar snarled. "*My good, old friend…*"

Llane looked over at Medivh, who regarded him sadly. It killed him, but the king knew what he had to do.

"Varis," Llane said, reluctance coloring his words, "Take Commander Lothar to a cell and let him calm down." He swallowed hard. How had it come to this?

Varis hesitated, and Llane understood why all too well. This was Anduin Lothar. The Lion of Azeroth. Varis's commander, who led by example and inspired respect. And yet, it seemed even heroes had breaking points.

Llane's heart ached for his friend. But although he loved Anduin like a brother, the safety of the kingdom, always, had to come before Llane's personal affections. Reluctantly, Llane said, "You are no use to us like this." Lothar, to his credit, left under his own power, although the look he shot the Guardian of Azeroth was pure venom.

Medivh stepped beside the table, looking down at the map. He lifted the figurines that represented three legions and placed them in front of the small model of the Great Gate.

"We'll save the kingdom, my lord," Medivh reassured him. "You and I."

Only a few days earlier, Lothar mused with a bitter humor, he had visited the Guardian Novitiate in a cell. Now, he was on the wrong side of the bars. *How the world turns*, he thought.

What had happened? Yes, of course he was still aching and hollow over the loss of his boy. Any father would be. And there was more to his pain. Guilt ate at him, and it had been that guilt that Medivh had played upon, goading Anduin to attack him. But in the name of the Light, why? Medivh was his friend— or he had thought so, anyway. And how had Llane not seen what the Guardian was doing?

He buried his face in his hands, wanting everything to go back to before he had ever met

Khadgar, when Medivh was a part of his past and Callan a part of his present, when everything was normal. *No*, Lothar corrected himself. *Not everything*. He did not want to lose Garona.

He heard the key turn in the lock and the door swing open. Hoping against hope that Llane had changed his mind, Lothar looked up. But it was Garona who stood there, as if he had summoned her with his thoughts.

In the midst of all the white-hot pain and fear and despair of this moment, there was a place of calm warmth inside him as their eyes met.

"Why are you here?" he asked her.

She was an orc, to the point, and focused on fighting. "The king. He goes to fight the Horde. With your Guardian's help, Durotan will kill Gul'dan."

His stomach clenched. "Don't trust him."

Garona frowned at him. "I have told you. Orcs do not lie. "

"Not Durotan." Lothar rose and went to the bars of his cell as she strode toward him. "Don't trust Medivh." She looked at him, confused. There were a thousand things he wanted to say, to warn her about, but Varis waited at the door. He would not have long with her.

She did not need explanations. "I will try to protect your king," was all she said.

Impulsively, he said, "Don't go with them."

"Why?" She stepped closer as he moved to the bars and gripped them. She placed her hand over his; warm, strong, comforting. She, who knew so much of pain, somehow understood gentleness better than anyone he had ever known.

He thought of last night, of her hands on him, and reached his own hand through the bar to caress her cheek.

"I don't want you to get hurt," he said, softly. Two decades since Callan's birth. Since Cally's death. And for the first time, her sweet, gentle face was not the one foremost in his thoughts—or his heart. It was stupid, it was reckless, it was unbelievable—and it was undeniably real.

Emotions flitted over her face. She reached to her slender throat, snapping the leather thong that encircled it. She held the pendant for a moment, then took his hand. He felt the tusk of her mother, warm from having nestled against her heart, settle in his palm. Garona folded his fingers tightly over the most precious thing she had to give.

"Come back alive," Lothar whispered. He squeezed her hand tightly. *I couldn't bear it if this war takes you, too.*

Garona nodded, but he knew what she meant by it. It was an acknowledgement of his words, not a surety. She was too honorable to make promises she could not keep. Instead, she lifted the concealing hood over her head, regarded him with those dark eyes, and went to war.

18

The humans could not take their terrified eyes off of Durotan. They peered at him through the bars of their own cages, doubtless wondering what he had done to warrant being imprisoned alongside them. Or perhaps they feared he was there to trick them and torture them more, somehow. Durotan regarded them sadly. He had tried to help, but his attempt had failed. *He* had failed, and now he was here, with his own fears regarding the cruel things with which Gul'dan's orcs had threatened his clan.

"Hey! Frostwolf!" shouted his guard. Durotan took his gaze away from the humans and frowned. Orgrim Doomhammer was striding up to Durotan's cage. The Frostwolf chieftain tensed. What new horror had his once-brother come to inflict? The guard stepped into Orgrim's path. Orgrim's steady pace did not falter. He merely raised the Doomhammer and casually swung it down to crunch the startled guard's head.

He did not rise.

Orgrim bent to pick up the guard's key and his eyes met Durotan's. With the same casualness Orgrim had just displayed in killing the guard, Durotan said, "Now you are enemies with all sides."

"I'll tell them it was you," Orgrim responded. Durotan, with the knowledge of years of friendship, noticed that Orgrim's hands trembled ever so slightly as he unlocked the cage. He glanced at Durotan, who sat quietly while Orgrim unfastened the shackles about neck, feet, and hands. He extended a hand to his chieftain, and Durotan took it. Slowly, wincing with feigned stiffness, Durotan let Orgrim help him to his feet. The two regarded one another for a moment, then Durotan struck his old friend savagely in the chest. Orgrim stumbed back against the twisted wood of the cage, falling. Instead of striking back, he simply sat there, his head lowered.

Finally, Durotan spoke.

"What happened?"

Orgrim looked him full in the face. "I am sorry, Durotan. I did not see how we could side with the humans against our own kind. I was wrong, my chief. Gul'dan's fel magic is destroying us."

Durotan closed his eyes, wanting the last few suns back, wishing things were other than as they were. But that way lay madness. He extended a hand to Orgrim. Orgrim took it and rose. Forcing himself to speak calmly, Durotan asked the question that was uppermost in his heart.

"Where is Draka?"

"Safe. She and the baby, both. But the rest... Most of them..." Orgrim's pain and regret was naked on his face, and in the gray dawn light, Durotan could see tears in his eyes.

It was too late for tears. Too late for apologies, regrets, forgiveness. Pain, grief, rage surged inside Durotan, but he quelled them ruthlessly. He would be stone. It was the only way he would survive long enough to do what he needed to. He turned away from Orgrim, the betrayer. But Orgrim's voice called after him.

"They wouldn't follow him if they could see what he has become."

"Then I'll show them."

Gul'dan's orcs had set the Frostwolf camp on fire, in an attempt to burn all that remained of Frostwolf culture. Most of it had burned out, but here and there flames still climbed into the night. The awful light revealed without remorse a camp in shambles, and the wall Durotan had built about his heart threatened to crumble. He had to force himself to walk forward, to see what Gul'dan had done to his people in return for what Durotan had done to him.

There were far fewer bodies than he had expected. Durotan did not dare allow himself to hope that this meant that his people had succeeded in fleeing unharmed. No, more likely Durotan had taken them alive to use as fuel for the fel. The corpses he did discover lay where they had fallen— the ultimate disrespect. Some of them were charred by the fire. Here lay Kagra, Zarka, Dekgrul... even Shaksa and her siblings, the ebullient Nizka and the toddler Kelgur.

He had made his choice to protect not just them, but all the orcs. This very world. Durotan knew in his bones that it had been Gul'dan's death magic, the fel, that had destroyed Draenor, and would eventually destroy this world, this Azeroth, as well. And the orc people along with it.

But he had underestimated the bitterness of the cost. Never thought that Gul'dan would give the word to obliterate an entire clan, including its children.

There were brief flares of gratitude. Orgrim had spoken the truth about Draka and little Go'el, at least. While all their food, clothing, furnishing and weapons—including Thunderstrike and Sever—had been taken to serve the needs of more loyal orcs, there were no mutilated bodies lying on the bare earth. Nor did he see any sign of the aged, blind Drek'Thar or his attendant, Palkar—or of their ritual items. Had they been taken, fuel for the fel? Or had they escaped?

Durotan's eyes fell on a Frostwolf banner. It had survived the fire, though it was singed at the edges. There was a bloody handprint on it. Someone had tried to save it.

The walls around him came down then, but not

for grief. For fury. Durotan reached to pick up the banner and clutched it tightly while he let white-hot rage run unfettered through him.

He had lost everything. But he was not yet done.

They wouldn't follow him if they could see what he has become.

Then I'll show them.

Hope, thought Llane as he rode through the torchlit night streets of Stormwind, was perhaps the most powerful weapon of all. And sometimes, it was the only weapon. He had feared it would be their only weapon in truth, but Medivh had returned, even if Lothar had... temporarily... been overwhelmed by the mindlessness of grief. Hope had returned to him, and he saw it reflected back at him on the faces of the citizens of the capital city, as they thronged the streets, even as that hope was tempered with the worry that all thought of war evoked, despite the hour.

The river of horses and armored soldiers forked around the towering statue of the Guardian, then rejoined as they approached the city's gates, where his family stood on a hastily erected dais waiting to send him on his way. His daughter, almost as tall as her mother and looking more like Taria every day, stood with her hands clasped, perfectly mimicking the gesture of the queen. Except Adariall trembled more than her mother did. *The burden of a princess,* Llane thought. Llane gave her a reassuring nod, then his gaze fell on Varian. The boy was splendid in his formal tunic, breeches, and cape, but he leaned on the balcony as if he wanted to climb over it and into his father's arms. His prince's circlet rested atop his dark head, and his lips were pressed tightly together. The expression made him look stern, but it tugged at Llane's heart. He knew it meant the boy was struggling to hold back the tears that made his eyes shiny. Too smart for his own good, that one. Llane and Taria had said all the reassuring things to their children, and truly, with Medivh restored and at his side, Llane felt more confident than he had since the whole horrifying ordeal had begun. But Varian picked up on the subtle glances, on the things unspoken. He would be a good king one day. But, hopefully, not too soon.

Llane longed to embrace the boy, but he was almost a man now, and would not appreciate a public display. So Llane granted the boy the gravitas he deserved. "There is no other man I would entrust my family's welfare to, Varian. Keep them safe until I return."

Varian's chin quivered, ever so slightly, but he nodded

Taria regarded her husband now, slender and regal, her dark eyes on his. Taria, his best friend's sister, who balanced a kind heart with a level head better than he ever could. Who had seen him ride off to possible death more times than he could count. Who had seen him uncertain, and determined, and joyful, and battered, and who loved him through all of those seasons.

They had said their goodbyes earlier, in private. They needed no more. They knew.

"Ready?" It was Medivh who broke the moment, sooner than Llane would have wished. The king nodded, and without another word he squeezed his horse into a trot as they headed for the open gates of the city.

"I'd feel better if Anduin was riding with us," Llane admitted to the Guardian.

"We'll do fine," his old friend assured him. "I'll return to Karazhan and ready myself for the battle. The Frostwolves will meet you on the way. Find me at the portal." He turned his horse around and cantered off, doubtless to find a quiet spot to create a portal of his own. Outside the gates, the three legions, all that they would need, according to Medivh, awaited their commander.

Garona brought her horse up to fill the vacant spot next to her king. Her eyes met his for a moment, then both of them looked straight ahead. Llane knew their minds should be focused on the upcoming battle, but he suspected that Garona's thoughts, like his, were with Anduin Lothar in his prison cell.

Anduin Lothar wanted out of his prison cell.

Immediately.

He stared at his knuckles, raw and bloody from his futile attempts to beat down the door. He sucked at the blood for a moment, calming himself, then tried again.

"Guard?" He smiled and spread his hands. "It's clear this door is solidly built. I'll save my fighting for defending the realm. I know you're just doing your job. And a good one, at that. But I've cooled down now. So, if you'd just come and open this cage... so I can protect the king."

The smile hurt his face, and he could still taste the coppery blood. The armored guard holding a poleaxe at the end of the hallway was having none of it, however.

The guard didn't move.

Lothar snarled and punched the door again, making it clang in protest, and the soldier cringed. "*Open the cage!*" he screamed.

The guard stepped forward, mindful to keep a safe distance between him and the enraged warrior in the cell. "Commander, please! I'm just following my—"

Lothar hurled his tankard at the frustrating man, completed the phrase, muttering "orders" when the guard suddenly disappeared in white smoke and a crackle of blue lightning. In his place stood a terribly perplexed-looking sheep. It bleated unhappily as Lothar, also terribly perplexed, looked at the hand that had hurled the tankard and wondered what he'd done.

All became clear when Khadgar emerged from the shadows, snatched up the sheep-guard's keys from the floor, and hurried to unlock Lothar's door.

"Where the hell have you been?" *Ungrateful*, Lothar thought, *but sincere*.

Khadgar turned the key and the door swung open. The boy looked like he had aged ten years.

"The Kirin Tor," the mage said. Following Lothar's gaze on the sheep, he added, "It only works on the simple-minded." He dropped a bag containing Lothar's sword and armor on the floor. "Your armor, Commander," he said to Lothar, and to the sheep, "Sorry."

He looked about and spied a cold brazier. "We've got a full day ahead of us," he told Lothar, sticking his hand in the brazier and grasping a piece of burned wood while Lothar threw on his armor. Bending, he began to sketch a circle.

"I just hope we're not too late," Lothar said.

Khadgar looked up. "We can't go after them. Not if you want to save Azeroth." Lothar, already at the door, whirled around.

"My king needs me!"

"Azeroth needs you more," Khadgar shot back. "If you want to save your king, we have to stop Medivh first."

Lothar had never been more torn in his life. His dearest friend was even now in the process of being betrayed by their other dearest friend. About to be run over by a flood of power-crazed, green-tinted monsters. Azeroth seemed very much an abstract idea when set against that image.

But he knew what Llane would want him to do.

Khadgar had begun the teleportation incantation. White-blue magic was starting to form the familiar bubble. Lothar took a deep breath and returned, stepping inside the circle. Khadgar rose, summoning the magic to his grip as if he were gathering the reins of a horse.

"Where is Medivh?" Lothar asked.

Khadgar looked him right in the eye. "We've got a demon to kill."

19

She had been running all night, with her child strapped to her back, and even she, Draka, daughter of Kelkar, son of Rhakish, was exhausted. She had not dared to stop, knowing that Gul'dan's orcs were following her. Had she been an ordinary orc female, with an ordinary orc child, they might have looked the other way. But she was the wife of one chieftain—and the mother of another, she was certain of it. Gul'dan had not ordered the destruction of her clan because he was angry. That would not worry her. Anger burned out, refocused. Gul'dan was afraid of the Frostwolves, and fear lingered long.

He had all but begged them to join his Horde, and now that Durotan comprehended the depths of the danger, Gul'dan could not let him live. As soon as Blackhand had come to take her heart away, Durotan was dead. Even if he walked and breathed now, he would not live long. Nor would she, nor their child. Orgrim's change of heart had come too late for them both. She wanted to sob, to rail against fate, to hold her baby—and die with him at her breast. Draka loved Durotan passionately, but what she felt for this little life was as an inferno to a cook fire.

She would live for him. She would die for him.

Draka could go no further. She was too weary, and they were not far behind. When her flight took her to a stream, with nowhere else to run, she made a decision. The water caught the light of the new sun, sparkling brightly, bringing tears to her eyes.

"Spirit of Water," Draka said, panting. "I can bear my child no further. They will never stop hunting us. They will find us, and kill us, if he stays with me. Will you take my baby? Will you keep him safe?"

Draka was no shaman. The Spirits did not speak to her, as they did to Drek'Thar. But she could hear the murmur of the water, and as she watched, a fish leaped, and fell back into its depths. Her heart suddenly stopped aching, and, quickly, she removed the carrying basket from her back and waded into the stream. She kissed the soft, green cheek, gently, tasting the salt of her own tears, and placed the basket into water. Draka tucked the blanket around him tenderly, a white square of cloth embroidered with the Frostwolf emblem.

Perhaps some human will remember, she thought. *That the Frostwolves tried to help them. That… that we died because of that choice. All but you, my precious Go'el.*

Water filled her eyes. Water, the element of love. Love for a mate. Love for a child. Love for a clan. Love for a dream of something better, in the midst of darkness, and dust, and despair.

The baby seemed confused, and raised his tiny, soft green arms to her. She caught one of the little fists and held it. "Remember," Draka told him. "You are the son of Durotan and Draka, an unbroken line of chieftains."

And then, her heart breaking for the thousandth time in a handful of hours, she sent him on his way. "Water," she said, "keep my baby safe!"

A roar caused her to turn. A Bleeding Hollow orc emerged from the forest, but his eyes were not on her. He was looking at the baby. He snatched up the knife Draka had left on the bank, and raced down to go after him.

But Draka was there.

He had her dagger. But that did not mean she was unarmed. She hurled herself upon the would-be killer of her child, driven by love and devoid of fear, seizing his flesh with her nails, carving out chunks with them, and, like a frost wolf herself, opening her jaw as wide as she could and burying her teeth in his throat.

He went down, startled; stupid, to think a Frostwolf without a weapon was a Frostwolf without defense. His tainted green blood, acrid as ashes, spurted into her mouth even as a horrible, cold-hot pain sliced through her. He had plunged her own dagger into her gut.

All the strength left Draka's body as she

collapsed atop her fallen enemy. She was dying, but she was at peace. As her life bled onto the sand, she remembered the words she had said to Durotan when she had returned from her Exile: *When all is done, when the sun of my life sets, I would see it do so here, in Frostfire Ridge.*

She would not die on Frostfire Ridge. She was dying here, now, in an alien land, with a husband who would soon join her in death, if he did not await her already. The last image that filled her eyes was that of her baby's vessel, bobbing on the water. And as her vision darkened, Draka, daughter of Kelkar, son of Rhakish, thought she saw the river's gentle waves turn into embracing arms.

Water, take my baby.

Her eyes closed.

Water, take...

All the chieftains of the Horde and most of their warriors had gathered outside Gul'dan's tent. They were stunned to see the Frostwolf as he marched forward. Durotan wore a wolf pelt over his broad shoulders, the beast's head serving him for a helm. He had already killed three guards before they could warn their vile leader, and now the others parted to admit him, regarding him with loathing, arrogance, and curiosity as he tossed the singed banner to the dusty earth in front of the warlock's tent.

"I am Durotan, son of Garad, chieftain of the Frostwolf clan," he cried, letting his fury fuel his voice. "And I am here to kill Gul'dan."

As he watched them, their postures shifted. The arrogance left them as they realized that he came without a weapon, yet had just challenged the most powerful one of them all to an honor battle.

The defiant, insane declaration brought forth Blackhand, at least, from the tent. He looked Durotan up and down. "A ghost cannot invoke mak'gora," Blackhand declared. "You are chieftain to no clan. Your people are food for worms."

Durotan choked back his rage. This orc before him was not the target of it. He opened his mouth to speak, but before he could, he heard a familiar voice beside him.

"Some of us still live, warchief," said Orgrim Doomhammer.

Durotan, surprised, turned to look at him. Orgrim had destroyed their friendship, but it was not too late for the son of Telkar to rediscover honor.

Now, at last, Gul'dan emerged. His glowing gaze fell upon Durotan, then on Orgrim, and his frown deepened. Durotan barely caught the words the warchief and the warlock exchanged.

"Shall I make a quick end of them?" Blackhand offered.

"I always thought you were one for tradition, Blackhand," the warlock replied. "Durotan," he said, more loudly so that all could hear. "Your clan was weak, and you are a traitor. I accept your challenge, if only to personally rip the heart out of your pathetic body."

"What of the portal?" Blackhand spoke to Gul'dan, but his gaze was fixed on Durotan. "You must be ready when the incantation begins."

The incantation... Durotan did not know much about the details of how the portal would open. Gul'dan had hoarded such knowledge. But if Durotan could survive long enough, perhaps his death could, at least, aid the humans who had been so willing to trust him.

"This won't take long." Gul'dan's thick, green lips curved around his yellowed tusks in a cruel, savoring smile. He handed his staff to Blackhand, and reached for his cloak. He pulled out the sharp pin that served for a clasp, and the cloak fell to the ground. Everyone present stared.

Gul'dan had always appeared to Durotan stooped and old, with a white beard and seamed face. But as the cloak fell away from his frame, leaving his torso bare in the growing morning light, it revealed a physique that made Blackhand look like a child. Muscles strained against the taut green skin of an orc who looked, as Grom Hellscream had said, as if he had the strength of five.

But that was not what had Durotan and all the others gaping in shocked silence. Durotan remembered when Gul'dan had come to the Frostwolves for the first time. He had worn this same cloak then. At the time, Durotan had been confused, unable to determine how the spines with the tiny skulls fixed atop them had been sewn into the fabric. Now, he understood.

The spines had not been attached to the cloak. They were protruding *through* it.

They and their macabre decorations were growing from Gul'dan's body.

Gul'dan basked in the awe and horror his appearance inspired, and Durotan knew with a sick feeling that the fel-distorted monstrosity in front of him was more than likely right. This would not take long.

But Durotan resolved to make Gul'dan's inevitable victory dearly bought. He stepped forward into the ring, shrugging off his own wolf-fur cloak and letting it slip to the ground. He stood, calculating, waiting, letting Gul'dan circle him.

And with a bellow, he sprang.

Moroes was dead, a withered, papery husk, sucked dry like the remnants of an insect when the spider has gorged. So poised and dignified in life, he now sprawled, legs akimbo, in front of a font gone sickly green which bubbled and emitted evil wisps of misty fel.

Lothar lifted his gaze from the dead castellan to the upper platform. He was both relieved and aghast to see his old friend standing there. He could not see the Guardian's face, but his form was unnaturally erect, and his arms were held up to the sky.

Lothar caught the young mage's eye. Khadgar nodded, moving slowly to the left, toward the scaffolding that supported the golem Medivh had been working on when they had first arrived. Lothar stepped to the right. With luck, they could pin the Guardian between them.

And do what? his sad, sick soul asked.

Something. Anything, his mind replied.

He had thought he would be angry, but instead he was more sorrowful than anything else. "Medivh," he called, calmly, carefully.

Now, Medivh lifted his head, and horror spurted through Lothar. His face was still recognizable—but only barely. It was covered with lines that were like cracks in marble. His beard had been replaced by a line of small, downward-jutting horns. And the Guardian's eyes were pitch black.

Casually, Medivh raised his arm. Energy pulsed, and Lothar was seized by the shape of a huge, sickly yellow hand and lifted into the air. The Guardian's eyes flared, like a small eruption of green magma, and the magical hand tightened. Lothar's breastplate began to crumple, as if he were a toy soldier squeezed too hard by a bored child.

From below and behind Khadgar hurled a blast of energy at Medivh's back. Without even turning, Medivh countered the spell with his right hand, turning the blue missle back on its sender. He released his grip on Lothar, letting his old friend drop and turning his attention to Khadgar.

But Khadgar wasn't there. Lothar lay still where he had fallen, feigning death for a long, tense moment. Then, Medivh begin to chant. He had listened to the Guardian summoning spells for years, but he had never heard anything like this. It made his throat turn dry, his skin crawl, and he would have known without being told that what was being spoken was the darkest evil that could be imagined.

Lothar used Medivh's distraction to crawl to Khadgar in the mage's hiding place—beneath the golem's thick clay body.

Khadgar looked pale. "It's the incantation to the orc home world. He's opening the portal. We need to shut him up!"

The mage nodded, then froze. Lothar strained to listen. Medivh, no doubt having realized that the "dead" Lothar was no longer where he had been dropped, was moving overhead. Looking for them.

"Ideas?" hissed Lothar. Khadgar licked his lips, then leaped to his feet, shouting an incantation. Blue orbs of cracking fire exploded from his fingertips in the direction of the chanting. Chunks of stone were blasted from the pillars, toppling down in a dusty pile. But Medivh was nowhere to be seen.

"Very impressive," and the voice seemed to come from everywhere. "Now try shutting *him* up."

A green glow came from directly above them. The chanting had resumed, but the voice was no longer coming from the Guardian. It issued from the featureless clay face that now sported eyes of emerald fire, and a green slash of a mouth.

"Well," Lothar quipped, "*That* went well."

Not content with simply being a vessel for Medivh's unholy chanting, the golem began to move, shrugging its gargantuan shoulders as if waking up.

Pieces of scaffolding and various tools toppled to the floor. "Do something!" Lothar shouted. Khadgar gave him look that said plainly, *what do you expect me to do?* "Fine," Lothar muttered, "I'll handle him, you take care of Medivh."

Khadgar swallowed, nodded, and started to scramble up the golem's scaffolding. The golem straightened, infused with strength, shattering the remnants of his scaffolding like a prisoner casting off shackles. Khadgar leaped upward to the circular platform just in time.

"Hey!" Lothar called, trying to draw its attention. "Over here! Clay face!" He hurled a carving tool at its lumpy brown head. Faster than Lothar had anticipated from something so gargantuan, it turned its head and fixed its sickly green gaze on him. Then it lunged, lurching forward like a great ape.

Its left fist slammed down. Lothar leaped away, tumbling to the floor, as the creature struck where he had been seconds earlier. It followed up with a second swipe, dragging its right fist through the sickly green magic of the font. The hand emerged, dripping, glowing, and no longer clay, but solid black stone. This time, when the golem punched down, the stone fist smashed right through the floor, and Lothar tumbled down to the next story below.

Khadgar, meanwhile, fired a bolt at Medivh, but the Guardian deflected it, warping it so that it plunged into the pool of fel.

He began to bombard the younger mage with missiles, fireballs, and bolts. Khadgar somehow managed to block them, trying to get them to ricochet back to Medivh. But instead of returning to their sender, the magical attacks were caught by the power of the fel and began to whirl around the tainted font in a blur. Seemingly without effort, Medivh stepped up his offense.

Khadgar summoned all his magical energy, gathered up the whirling wisps orbiting the pool, and hurled the accumulation at Medivh. At the last second, the Guardian dove for cover as everything around him shattered.

All was quiet. Had Khadgar managed to—

Slowly, carefully, Khadgar moved toward where Medivh had hidden.

There was nothing there. The Guardian was gone.

20

With a bellow, Durotan closed the distance between himself and Gul'dan, swift as one of Draka's arrows, landing a clean punch across Gul'dan's jaw with all his strength behind it. Taken utterly by surprise, the warlock stumbled and fell. But before Durotan could press his advantage, he was on his feet, seizing the Frostwolf by his throat and lifting him up. Gul'dan began to squeeze.

Durotan's vision swam, but he kept fighting. He would keep fighting until he was dead. He didn't need to live through this. All he needed to do was what he had promised Orgrim he would—show the Horde the true face of the thing that led them. He shoved ineffectually at Gul'dan's twisted, green face, then his questing hands clutched two of the warlock's hideous horns. Even as Gul'dan's fingers tightened around Durotan's throat, the Frostwolf pulled the spikes with all his strength until one snapped off in his hand. He used the sharp end as a dagger, stabbing Gul'dan with his own unnatural horn.

Gul'dan roared, in pain, not anger, this time. He hurled Durotan several yards. Durotan hit the earth hard, gasping. Snarling, Gul'dan charged his enemy. He was huge, his body bristling with unnatural spikes and horns, his muscles stronger than Durotan's. He pummeled his enemy with punches, each landing hard. Durotan rallied. He deflected the warlock's next powerful swing with a kick, and dodged. Again Gul'dan struck, and again Durotan evaded it, landing a punch of his own.

But this time, Gul'dan caught his opponent's arm and pulled him in. His splayed his hand and pressed it to Durotan's chest. Green light sparked around his fingers as Gul'dan looked about furtively.

Suddenly, Durotan's legs quivered, threatening to buckle. Weakness seeped through him as he saw a thin, white trail pass from his body into Gul'dan's hand. Before his shocked eyes, the warlock's body grew even larger, the muscles swelling. Chuckling, Gul'dan seized Durotan's arm and wrenched it out of its socket. There was white-hot pain, and then a snapping sound, and then Durotan's arm dangled, useless.

He dropped to his knees. Gul'dan pulled back, leering triumphantly, then lifted his gargantuan green fist for the death blow.

Durotan shouted and abruptly lunged upward.

His head slammed into Gul'dan's chest, sending the other staggering backward a few steps. He did not give the warlock a chance to recover. He clenched his good fist and landed blow after blow. Each time his fist struck unnatural flesh, he held the face of a Frostwolf in his mind, fueling it with passion and righteousness. Kurvorsh. Shaska. Kagra. Zakra. Nizka.

Draka.

Go'el.

A sound penetrated his ears that was not the singing of his blood in his own veins, or the cries of the watching crowd. The voice was human, and yet not, and it was chanting. Hope surged inside Durotan. Gul'dan needed to be at the portal, draining innocent human lives to open the Great Gate and bring in the rest of the Horde. Instead, he was here—fighting Durotan.

But Gul'dan heard it, too, and slammed his clenched fist into Durotan's wounded arm. The Frostwolf bellowed in agony, but held onto consciousness by sheer will as he staggered back and fell to his hands and knees.

Gul'dan cursed, not pressing the attack. "I have no time for this," he muttered. "Blackhand!"

The warchief looked over at Durotan appraisingly, taking note of the useless, dangling arm, the blood on his face and body, his shuddering breaths. Then his gaze traveled to Orgrim, and the banner Durotan had so defiantly sunk into the earth. Finally, he looked at Gul'dan.

And grinned.

"This is the mak'gora," Blackhand said. "We will respect our traditions. Keep fighting!"

Gul'dan gave his warchief a furious look, and a fresh sense of hope flooded Durotan. If the warchief was beginning to see how vile, how dishonorable Gul'dan was, then surely the others would as well. The warlock charged now, with not a sneering arrogance, but an urgency and desperation. It made his blows harder when they landed, but it also made him careless. Again, and yet again, Durotan was able to evade a blow that could break his skull and deliver a powerful attack of his own, even with but one good hand. But when they connected, Gul'dan's blows were vicious. More than once, Durotan felt a rib snap beneath the warlock's clenched fist, but he refused to cease.

Keep going. For your clan. For the orcs who yet live. For their children.

A blow to the gut that had him doubled over and barely able to stumble out of the way. A sliding punch that cost him his sight in one eye. He endured it all.

He kept fighting. And he felt the tide start to turn.

What had once been jeers had turned to first silence, then murmurs of admiration. Gul'dan's head whipped up and he stared at the orcs. "His" Horde.

Then, his lip curled with pure loathing, he slammed his hand against Durotan's chest, and began to drain him.

A gasp rose up among the crowd. "Gul'dan cheats!" came an outraged voice. Even as Durotan felt his life being siphoned to further Gul'dan's grotesqueness, he felt joy. He had done it. It was impossible for the warlock to conceal his handiwork; Durotan knew he now resembled the draenei prisoners, their lives sucked from them until their bodies were misshapen and dessicated. He had forced Gul'dan to show the Horde exactly what he was.

Gul'dan drew back his hand, wreathed in the white mist of Durotan's life, clenched his fist, and slammed it full force into the Frostwolf's chest. The pain was unbearable. Durotan flew through the air, landing hard. His connection to the living now was but the finest thread.

Cries were going up, now. "You cheat, Gul'dan!" "Shame on you!" "This is not our way!"

Durotan had to rise, once more. Every sinew and muscle, every drop of blood was fiery agony. He fought it through sheer force of will, climbing to his feet and swaying. He could barely draw breath, but he filled his lungs and cried, "Gul'dan! You have no honor!"

With a low growl that grew louder with each step, Gul'dan bore down on Durotan, not swinging his arms this time, but holding them open, reaching for his enemy. Durotan struggled, but the arms around him were as strong as bands of iron, and he had no strength left. Gul'dan clutched him close in a travesty of an embrace, utterly heedless now of what the Horde saw. He crushed Durotan's rapidly deteriorating body to his, so that more of his skin could pull forth the Frostwolf's life energy. Durotan felt his spine snap. Through the haze of agony

Durotan could see strange golden light pouring off his body, as his life—his soul? He did not know—went to feed the warlock's ravenous, fel-driven hunger. Gul'dan smiled up at him ferally, triumphantly, as he paraded about the ring displaying Durotan's dying body. Then, at last, when he could get no more from the Frostwolf, he threw Durotan down in disgust.

There would be no more rising for Durotan.

He found himself gazing up at Orgrim, but could not speak. He tried to lift a hand imploringly, but he could only twitch his fingers. But Orgrim understood. His eyes filled with tears, and he nodded. He, who had betrayed the Frostwolves, would now speak for them.

And that was all right.

The orcs had seen. Durotan had done what he had come to do.

It was enough.

Orgrim looked around at the assembled orcs. "You will follow this *thing*?" he cried, putting all his hatred and contempt into the word. "Will you? You will follow this *demon*? I will not. I follow a *true* orc. A chieftain!"

The crowd stared, murmuring. "He does not even look orc now," Orgrim heard. Gul'dan stood, panting, daring them to defy him. Orgrim saw several orcs turn to leave. Some of them, he noticed, had the green tinge to their skin. They had seen their fate played out before them should they continue to use the fel, and were choosing to have no part in it.

Orgrim turned back to his friend and chieftain, whom he had betrayed. Durotan, son of Garad, son of Durkosh, was still. But he had died as he had lived, with courage, and conviction, and in a righteous battle against a terrible foe.

He recalled Durotan's words, before the Frostwolves had marched south to join the Horde: *There is one law, one tradition, which must not be violated. And that is that a chieftain must do whatever is truly best for the clan.*

Today, Durotan's clan had not been Frostwolves. His clan had consisted of the entire Horde.

Orgrim knelt beside his fallen chieftain and grasped one of Durotan's tusks. He twisted it free. "For your son," he told Durotan. "So your spirit can teach him."

"I will deal with you later, Orgrim Doomhammer," Gul'dan threatened. Several orcs were striding away in disgust after the offensive spectacle they had just witnessed. One of them spat, "Your power is not worth the price, warlock!" Orgrim paused, wanting to see this play out. Gul'dan, all but frothing at the mouth in his rage, reached out his hand. Three orcs who had the misfortune to stand near him—including, Orgrim saw, many who had been faithful to the warlock—arched in agony as their life essences were not siphoned, not extracted, but savagely ripped from them. The white energy flowed into Gul'dan's outstretched hand. The warlock raised his other hand, and from it streamed the sickly, all-too-familiar color of fel energy.

"Anyone else?" Gul'dan challenged. Those who had not already moved out of reach of the angry warlock stood, shuffling their feet. They did not not want to stay, but neither did they wish to die as their comrades had. As Durotan had.

"And you, warchief!" Brimming with fel energy, Gul'dan whirled, his hand shooting out as he funneled everything straight into Blackhand. The warchief fell to the dead ground, screaming and writhing as his body was twisted and contorted. "You will take the fel," Gul'dan shouted over Blackhand's tormented cries, "and you will become stronger than any orc has ever been! And when the fel has remade you, you will crush the smallteeth!"

The green washed over and through Blackhand. Muscles swelled so large his armor popped off his body in places. Tendrils looking like veins pumping green blood twined along him, even down his metallic, claw-like appendage. Blackhand looked up, his eyes so bright with the fel that mist roiled from them. Orgrim turned away, sickened in body and spirit. It was too late for Durotan, and it was too late for Blackhand. But it was not too late for him, and the the few others who had been forced to see with fresh eyes thanks to the sacrifice of the Frostwolf chieftain.

As he strode into the forest, away from the fel and its false promises, he heard Gul'dan screaming, "Now—*claim my new world!*"

* * *

The Black Morass, the enemy, and innocent prisoners awaited King Llane and his troops over the next rise. Beside Llane rode Garona, who had been casting concerned glances at him.

In silence, the small group crested this final rise, and Llane's stomach turned to ice.

The Frostwolves will meet you on the way, Medivh had told him.

And so they had. Impaled Frostwolves lined the road, an obscene invitation to enter the vast encampment of orcs. Horror closed Llane's throat as he looked from body to body. Some had pendants with the clan's symbol dangling from their necks. Others had had the Frostwolf banner stuffed into their mouths. There were so many…

Medivh had been wrong. The rebellion had been snuffed out. Their would-be allies had been reduced to gore-encrusted, stiffening corpses… or worse.

Llane took a long, deep breath. He forced himself to look past the horrifying spectacle, past the sea of orc tents, to the cages filled with prisoners. His people—still alive, for now. And beyond them— the Great Gate. The dark portal, which would shortly birth a flood of ravaging orc warriors. The Horde would descend upon Azeroth, slaughtering his people. The fel used to make them fierce would suck the life out of Azeroth, leaving it as dry and desiccated as the orcs' own world. It was already happening. The Black Morass had been a swamp, but in the area around the portal, there was only parched earth, a grim preview of what was to come.

Unless, somehow, they were stopped.

"We few, then," he said. Suddenly, a rain of fire and stone fell upon them, launched from hidden catapults. They had walked right into a trap—baited with hope, sprung with horror, and promising soon death for likely every member of the three legions who had followed Llane in this wretched folly.

Anger chased out despair. Anger, and awe at the courage his troops were displaying. Llane pulled out his sword. "Trust in your training! Trust in your arms! Ride with me! The Frostwolves have fallen, but with the Guardian's help, we can still destroy the gate and bring our people *home*!"

A cry of defiance rose up. Though it issued through a pitiful handful of throats, it was passionate and defiant. The king of Stormwind and his three legions charged forward, shouting their battle cry. They were met with an answering bellow, deeper, darker, and the orcish army met them halfway.

Gul'dan disliked how he had been played. Pushed to his wit's end by the Frostwolf's stubborn refusal to simply die, he had unwisely revealed his usage of the fel. He had lost some of his best warriors, Orgrim included. *I should have known better than to trust a Frostwolf*, the warlock thought bitterly. But they were gone, and soon enough, many times their number would surge through the great gate. His Horde.

More than once over the last several moments,

Medivh's chanting had been interrupted somehow, but interruptions did not matter. Every time the chant had resumed, and from his platform overlooking the battle below, Gul'dan could see that all was still going according to plan. Blackhand, fel-bloated and undefeatable, was down there now. As Medivh had promised Gul'dan, only a feeble three legions had arrived with the human king. Armed with weapons Gul'dan had never seen, yes, but they were outnumbered, and outmatched, and what did weapons matter when there were no hands to wield them?

And farther away still, the gate.

Earlier, before the ritual had begun in earnest, orcs could, and had, walked through it as if it were nothing other than an ordinary archway. But now… now, he could see Draenor. See shapes moving. Orcs. Ready, more than ready, to come through, to become engorged with fel, to take, to devour, and take more still.

It was time. Exultation flowed through Gul'dan. This was the moment Medivh had promised. This was the triumph of the so-called Guardian of Azeroth, of the fel… the triumph of Gul'dan. He marched to the cage of terrified humans, enjoying their fear for a few heartbeats before he splayed his hand hard and began to pull out their precious, sweet life energy. Their screams were music to his ears, and, grinning, he lifted his other hand.

"Come, my orcs," he said, in a tone laced with affection, as of a parent to a beloved child. "Let the fel unleash the full power of the Horde!" His other hand shot out, in the direction of the distant portal. A flood of emerald energy, routed through him, exploded out in the direction of the gate. It raced over the ground, heedless of the fighting going on beneath it, of lives lost and blood spilled. Sped along by the chanting, it wanted only to reach the gate, to open a pathway so that more fel could enter, to claim more victims.

And the first small figures, shouting for blood and brandishing weapons, came through.

Medivh's voice still sounded from the mouth of the clay man. It stretched out a massive, tree-trunk leg, stepping down to where Lothar stood on the story below, and Lothar hacked at it wildly. His sword bit deep, dragging through the heavy clay and he managed to sever the limb at the knee. The golem jolted. Lothar dove out of the way, but the cursed thing would not fall! He glared furiously up at it, frantically wondering how he could muzzle the monstrosity, and spotted something dangling from the golem's shoulder: the tool that Medivh had used to shave off curls of clay—a length of wire held between two wooden handles.

Not muzzle. Bridle. Even better.

Lothar abandoned the sword. He climbed up the creature, digging in feet and fingers, until he had reached the thing's shoulders. Seizing the wire garrote-like apparatus, he slung it over the golem's misshapen head and yanked it into where its mouth was. Immediately it lurched, turning around and trying to strike the pesky thing perched atop it with its huge, obsidian hand. Lothar scrambled out of the way and the stone fist smashed through the wall of the Guardian's chamber. The golem followed the movement, bending over and trying to shake Lothar from its back.

Lothar looked up in time to see Khadgar on the lower level, sprawled face down, covered in rubble. He didn't move. Lothar had no time to fear for the mage, though. Medivh had turned and impaled his old friend with his glowing green gaze, and was drawing back his hand for an attack.

Lothar yanked violently on the wire. The golem was hauled backward by the motion just in time to take the Guardian's attack spell full in its chest. It toppled backward, hurtling downward to smash through the lower-floor window. Half of the clay being remained inside, the other half—with Anduin Lothar clinging to it—dangled out the window. Lothar hung on grimly to the wire, then realized to his horror that the wire was now doing what it had been designed to do. It was cutting, slowly but inexorably, through the clay.

A second later, a huge chunk of the golem's head was severed, hurtling down past Lothar's own head to splat onto the earth below. Lothar scrambled to hang on, shoving his feet into the golem's still-soft earthen back to secure his purchase. Dangling upside down, up to his calves in clay, he registered, barely, that the chanting had stopped.

But even with half its head and one leg sheared off, the golem still moved. It reached out a hand to the ledge, hauling itself and its unwanted rider back inside to the safety of the lower level. It leaned against the wall, and then attempted to reposition itself. It was about to pin Lothar between itself and the curving wall of the tower. For a moment, Lothar thought it would succeed. He unfastened his boots, freed himself, dropped to the floor, and rolled out of the way as the thing slammed itself into the wall.

When it did so a second time, Lothar realized that the creature was as of yet unaware that it no longer hosted a human parasite. He swore as he suddenly noticed that the chanting had resumed. He took advantage of the golem's distraction to hasten to Khadgar, lifting books and debris off the body. To his relief, Khadgar looked shaken, battered, and bruised, but intact.

"Hey, kid," he said. "Wake up!" Khadgar did not move. Lothar slapped his face. Khadgar jerked, eyes flying open, and his hand grasped Lothar's wrist. "You all right?"

Khadgar nodded, blinking dazedly. He looked past Lothar at the golem. "Quick thinking, slicing its head off like that."

"Yeah," Lothar deadpanned, having no intention of disabusing the young mage of the notion. "Just how I planned it." He hauled Khadgar to his feet. "What now?"

"The Guardian has to speak the incantation himself. As long as he's doing that, we can get in close. Distract him." Khadgar strode purposefully toward the lumbering clay creation.

"And then?" Lothar asked.

"Get Medivh into the font," Khadgar replied. He took off after the golem.

"Is that all?" Lothar asked sarcastically, but even as he spoke the words he realized that this was the precise moment when he fully trusted Khadgar, as he began to climb up to the font level where Medivh stood, still chanting the horrible spell that would permit—perhaps was already permitting—thousands of bloodlust-enraged orcs to spill into Azeroth.

He moved slowly, taking his time although everything in him urged him to *hurry, hurry*. He paused, but the Guardian seemed far too caught up in his incantation to have noticed Lothar closing in on him from behind. Impulsively, Lothar spoke, still carefully closing the distance between them.

"Medivh... if there is something of you still in there, old friend... come back to us." There was no response. Medivh seemed utterly oblivious to Lothar's presence. Sorrowfully, Lothar reached with one hand to cover Medivh's mouth.

Without even pausing in his chant, Medivh shot out his hand, seized Lothar by the throat, and lifted him up. Lothar's hands went to his neck, trying desperately to pry Medivh's fel-strong fingers from it. Effortlessly, Medivh moved him until Lothar dangled directly in front of him—and directly above the sickly green font.

The grip on his throat was tight, the fingers

digging in, but Lothar could still breathe. Still speak.

Why? Why not just crush his windpipe and be done with it?

"Medivh," he rasped, his eyes pleading.

Medivh hurled him away. Lothar sailed clear across the font to land hard on the other side of it.

Lothar gasped for air, fishlike, his lungs initially refusing to cooperate. Gritting his teeth against the fresh pain, he clambered to his feet, swaying drunkenly. Below him, Khadgar was attempting to trap the lumbering, half-headed golem. Lothar didn't know why. He didn't know much right now, only that he had to—*had* to—keep trying.

"Come on! Kill me. I've got nothing left to live for now, anyway," he shouted once breath had returned to him. Medivh ignored him. He simply stood, implacable, continuing that damnable chanting. "After all, life is just fuel to you, isn't it?" He was trying to goad the fel-thing into losing its focus, into attacking him. Killing him, if need be, if it would silence the chant. His voice was raw with pain as he thought of his boy, dying so brutally, shredded by the monster's claws while his father had been forced to watch.

And then he thought of Llane. His friend. His brother, truth be told, by law and in his heart. "But Llane," Lothar said to Medivh from across the pool of fel, "he believed in you. Don't kill your king. Don't kill your friend."

Medivh paused in his chanting. His eyes changed color, from sickly green to coal black. A cold fear twisted Lothar's gut. "Whatever is you plan to do, kid," he called to the unseen Khadgar, "do it now!" Even as he spoke Medivh stepped into the font.

It was exactly what Khadgar had instructed Lothar to attempt to do. Lothar sagged in relief. They'd done it. He'd reached Medivh. The Guardian had stepped into the powerful magical font, and—

—began to *grow*.

21

Taller, bigger, wider—everything about Medivh grew larger. Muscles layered themselves upon him, taking his fit but ordinary build and transforming it into something that looked more like an orc than a human, and more like a demon than either. His skin took on a green tint, and green mist began to pour from his eyes. With each step, some new horror twisted Lothar's old friend into a walking nightmare. Twin sets of horns sprouted from Medivh's forehead. Jagged shards of what looked like obsidian daggers speared upward from his shoulders, for all the world as if the raven feathers that had trimmed Medivh's cloak had turned to black crystals.

"Now," Lothar said, horror swallowing the words. The thing that had once been the Guardian of Azeroth continued to advance, continued to grow, to reshape itself, and its terrible gaze was fixed on Lothar.

"Now!" he shouted to Khadgar. "Now, *now*!"

There was a shimmer of pale blue energy directly above Medivh's head, and then the massive clay golem, all eighteen feet and countless pounds of it, came crashing down onto the demonic figure in the felpool.

It was as beautiful as Gul'dan could have imagined. The orcs charged through, from a dead world into verdant one, and the Horde bellowed a welcome. The humans despaired, and died, and Gul'dan was glad. Then his smile faded.

The green glow around the interior of the portal flickered. The image of the rest of the Horde on Draenor, waiting to come join their brethren. Such had happened before, but his great ally had always resumed. So Gul'dan waited.

Silence.

The images continued to fade even more. Still, the chant did not resume. "No," murmured Gul'dan. "No, *no*…!"

A final flicker, an image of orcish silhouettes that would remain burned into his mind's eye, and then they were gone. For a long moment, Gul'dan stared, aghast, and then he cried out till his voice was raw with rage. He whirled on the nearest cage, crammed with shrieking humans, and grasped the bars with his hands. He looked at their ugly, soft faces, then with a mighty wrench, shoved the entire cage off the platform, taking only the faintest pleasure in watching it smash to pieces and pulp far below.

"So be it!" he growled. "Our might alone will take this world!"

Khadgar hurtled down along with the golem he had teleported, landing in the font and looking tiny beside the two unnaturally sized figures. The boy gasped, and Lothar saw with horror that the fel was beginning to work its dark magic upon Khadgar as well.

Green energy crackled around Khadgar as he turned to face Lothar. He extended a hand in the commander's direction, fingers spread wide, and Lothar braced himself for a ball of fel magic to hurtle toward him, to drain him of life and leave only a contorted shell. Instead, the air around Lothar shimmered, then formed a blue-white dome. Through the green mist that surrounded the boy, he smiled, reassuringly. And Lothar realized that far from attacking him, Khadgar had cast a shield spell around him.

The youth moved forward, kneeling beside Medivh's enormous, horned head. He reached out a trembling hand and clamped it down on the demon's forehead.

"You're stronger than he is," Lothar said, and realized that he believed every word. Khadgar had not faltered, and was not doing so now. "Get rid of it, kid!"

But Khadgar wasn't getting rid of it. He was harvesting it. The fel whipped around Khadgar and Medivh, a storm of livid, sickly green. He was siphoning it from Medivh, pinned under the broken golem and bellowing as he tossed his horned head. He was pulling it from the font, draining it dry. All of it was funneling directly into Khadgar. Green energy roiled off Medivh in waves. Lothar realized that Khadgar, that wet-eared boy, was using himself as a living conduit to expel the fel taint from Medivh.

And it was working.

As Lothar stared, rivited, both horrified and hopeful, Medivh's demonic form began to shrink, slowly returning to its original size and shape. The tossing head lost its horns, and Medivh's long hair once again flowed from his scalp. Khadgar released him and turned his attention to the font itself, plunging his hands in it, his face, drawn and tight, screwed up in concentration.

Lothar felt the very walls of Karazhan itself groaning from the strain.

The boy's tight face had gone slack. The green eyes widened, as if seeing something that was not there. His mouth opened in a silent O of awe at whatever it was the fel was showing him.

No. Not Khadgar. Not the boy who had broken into the barracks in search of answers, who had issued the first warning of the very substance that was now threatening to destroy him. Lothar had seen what the fel could do. The thought of that happening to Khadgar, and the horrors that the mage could inflict on the world—

Khadgar closed his eyes. And when he opened

them again, Lothar saw that they glowed not green...
but *blue*. "From light comes darkness," Khadgar
said, his voice raspy, "and from darkness... *light*...!"

Khadgar flung his arms out and arched his back.
He screamed, a raw, ragged, yet determined sound,
and blasted the fel *out* of him, *out* of the font, *out* of
Karazhan. The very air itself was rent with a horrible
boom as a wave of chartreuse energy surged from
the boy, washing over Lothar's magical shield like
water over a glass container.

Khadgar stood, weaving, then collapsed,
coughing and retching.

The Guardian's font was empty.

The shield around Lothar disappeared, and he
raced over to Khadgar. He was propped up on his
hands, his head bowed, still hacking as small bits of
fel wafted up around him and then vanished

Would Lothar have to deal with Khadgar, or had
the boy won his own battle? "Show me your eyes,"
Lothar whispered intensely.

Khadgar took in a great gulp of air and turned
his face up. His eyes were clear and brown. Lothar
slapped him heartily on the back. Lothar sagged in
relief, and for a moment the two simply grinned at
one another, marveling that they were still here. Still
alive.

A familiar cawing sound came from outside.
Lothar looked at Khadgar quizzically. "I sent her
here, when I came to get you," Khadgar said, still
panting. "I thought we might need her."

"You were right," Lothar said, sobering. They

might have stopped Medivh, but they were far from done. "I have to go."

Medivh. Lothar glanced at his old friend. He was pale, and still. But he was Medivh, again. Khadgar had given him that.

"I'm proud of you," Lothar said to the young mage. Words he should have said to Callan. It was too late for Medivh, too late for his son. But not too late for Khadgar—or for him. The boy lit up, and Lothar touseled his hair. He rose, barefoot; his boots were still embedded in the golem. He raced across the sharp shards of stone heedlessly, seizing his sword and heading for one of the open windows. The gryphon saw him, and flew beneath him as, not breaking stride, he leaped with full trust atop her furred and feathered back, and went to the aid of his king.

Khadgar sat for a moment, collecting himself. He deeply regretted that he had been forced to kill the Guardian. It had not, ever, been what he had wanted. But he was glad he had stopped Medivh from opening the portal. Slowly, he got to his feet, hoping Lothar would be in time to make a difference. He shook his head, trying to focus on what he could do from here to help.

The font would be of no use. It was empty—of both true magic, and fel. He—

Khadgar blinked. A soft voice, murmuring an incantation. Medivh was alive—and still trying to open a portal to let the orcs—

No. No, Khadgar had been listening to that incantation repeating itself for what felt like forever. He had memorized the words, and these were slightly different. And there was one word that made his heart leap.

Llane had nothing to lose, and all to gain, and he made the most of it. Thanking Magni's ingenuity and generosity, he rode among the men, cheering them on as they used the boomsticks against orcs seemingly as large as trees to, quite literally, stop them dead in their tracks. The numbers against them were vast, but with these weapons, these "mechanical marvels," the odds were becoming less uneven with every cracking, echoing sound.

Those like him, who chose more traditional weapons, rode around those orcs who were injured but still a threat, spearing broad green chests, stabbing exposed throats, slicing off limbs with weapons that had been sharpened to perfect keenness. They were cutting a swathe through the tide of orcs, bearing straight for the portal and the human prisoners who were waiting for rescue—or a fate Llane would not wish upon anyone. Not even the orcs themselves.

When he could spare a glance, Llane had watched the image of the army in the portal's interior grow clear, and fade, and clear to terrible purpose. He recalled his argument with Lothar, about how there were so many of the orcs. How he had argued for containment. Foolish, now. He had been so busy trying to stem a river, he had not fully appreciated that there was an ocean's tidal wave behind him.

He brought his charger forward toward a savage orc female who was locked in combat with one of his men. Llane bore down on the enemy with three feet of steel, slicing a long, bloody slash through the leather armor she wore. She threw him a furious glance. Her teeth snapped ferally and she launched herself at him, hands extended, and grabbed his leg to pull him off his mount. Then her head toppled from her shoulders, and Llane met the eyes of the man who had saved him. He nodded, then turned to find another opponent.

Sucking in air, Llane looked again at the gate, and his eyes widened.

There was no more sign of the Horde gathered on the other side, shouldering for which one would pass through first to Azeroth. There was only a view of the Black Morass. Then, even as he felt gratitude bubbling up inside him, the center of the portal began to move. Except this time, the light limning it was not sickly green, but a fresh, clean blue, and Llane was not looking at Draenor.

He was looking at Stormwind.

A shout of laughter, genuine and joyful, burst from him. His old friend had not forsaken them! "Thank you, Guardian!"

Llane looked around and spied Karos, his armor spattered with dark brown blood. "Karos!" he shouted, and when the soldier acknowledged him, Llane looked for Varis, crying out his name as well.

Varis had lost his helm at some point in the battle. His brown face brightened as he turned and saw the glimmering image of the Stormwind Cathedral which had replaced the grim ugliness of Draenor.

"Forward!" he shouted, and his troops rushed to obey, revitalized by the sight.

Llane looked around for Garona. She had just dragged a broadsword through the thick green torso of an orc. He had lost track of how many he had watched her kill. "Garona!" he shouted. "Ride with me!"

Without hesitating, she raced toward him and sprang up behind him on the horse. They set off at a mad gallop for the portal, now a symbol of hope rather than despair. They fought their way through, but it was easier than they had expected. The orcs had been shocked when the portal had been redirected, and the soldiers had rallied. Llane and Garona passed dozens of cages, some of which were already being hacked open.

"Varis! Set the men in a perimeter. Garona, Karos, take as many as we can spare to free the prisoners. Send them through! We will hold the line as long as we can!"

Khadgar's eyes widened. He stumbled over to where the Guardian lay, his body trapped and partially crushed beneath the massive weight of his clay man. His eyes glowed blue, the color of mage's magic, not warlock's. And as Khadgar watched, a radiant, sky-blue tear trickled down Meidvh's face.

When Khadgar spoke, his own voice was thick. "You're redirecting the portal to Stormwind!" Medivh blinked. The blank eyes refocused, retrained themselves on Khadgar's face. He reached up a hand feebly to Khadgar, then let it fall.

"It's the loneliness that makes us weak, Khadgar," he said in a voice tinged with regret. As Alodi had told Khadgar, the boy recalled. Something so simple, so human, had destroyed a Guardian, and nearly the whole world along with him. "I'm sorry. I'm sorry. I wanted to save us all. I always did."

His eyes unfocused, and he was still.

22

The ocean of orcs was closing in, but Llane still felt confident. While he could have wished that the Guardian had redirected the portal sooner, he was nonetheless profoundly grateful. He and the remnants of the three legions had fought their way to the gate. While Llane, Garona, Varis and a line of Stormwind's finest knights continued to stave off the waves of the enemy as best they could, Karos and others had freed the human prisoners and were protecting them as they fled through the gates to safety.

But the orcs kept coming. *Sweet Light,* Llane thought, still almost dizzy with relief at the turn of the tide, *we would have had no chance at all had Gul'dan brought in the rest of the Horde. Humanity might not have survived.*

"My lord, we must retreat!" The cry came from

Varis. The man was as brave as they came, but he was right. The orcs were starting to win this fight here, at the base of the portal. More and more of his soldiers were falling; more and more huge brown and green-skinned orcs were shouldering each other aside, eager to fill the void.

"We should leave," Garona agreed.

"Shortly," Llane said. "There are only a few more cages left. We'll save as many of our people as we can first."

"My lord," Varis said again, "I do not think—"

From behind Llane, a cry of horror and fear arose. He turned in his saddle, and felt the blood drain from his face.

The blue light that outlined the center of the portal, and the sight of Stormwind within it, was sputtering. Before Llane's shocked gaze, the image of his city melted like wax, as if it had never been. All that was visible now in the center of the portal was the desiccation that had once been the Black Morass—and the group of orcs that had run around the gate's back.

The gate had closed.

The orcs had seen it, too. And they roared as well, but with bloodlust and a hunger that would soon be sated. Llane was reeling. What had happened? Why had Medivh stopped? Then he knew.

"We've lost the Guardian," he murmured.

He looked out over the sea of orcs, then at his comrades. They all bore the same shocked, stunned expressions. They had been so close...

It did not matter. "We've done what we came to do," he said to them, looking at each in turn. An odd peace settled upon him. "No one could do more. All is as the Light wills it, my brothers and sisters."

He turned to look at Garona, and gave her a smile. Expressions warred on her beautiful green face. She had wanted victory, of course. They all had. In the end, a victory would have saved the orcs as much as if would have saved the humans, but that could not be helped, not now.

Or could it?

An idea, wonderful and terrible, began to blossom in his mind. Llane turned his attention to his enemy. Fighting was still going on at the ends of the line of defenders, but here, in the center, things had, oddly, lessened. Now, Llane saw why.

Blackhand was coming.

He stood head and shoulders above the tallest of the orcs, his skin boldly green, his muscles bulging and powerful and veined. Was it blood that pumped through his veins, Llane wondered, or green fire? No matter. Blackhand was coming, shoving aside orcs and humans alike who blocked his path, and he was coming for Llane.

"Garona," Llane said, and was surprised at how calm, how certain, he sounded, "we're outnumbered. We can't retreat. We're going to fall. But *you* don't have to. No good will come from us both dying." Slowly, with hands that trembled, he removed his helm and let it fall to the earth. The cool rush of air on his face and sweat-soaked hair felt good.

Her jaw set. "I will die with you. I have chosen my side."

"You don't understand." He turned his full attention upon her, his dark eyes boring into hers. "Your killing me is the only hope we have for peace. You once told Lady Taria that killing her would bring you honor. Killing me would make you a hero."

Her eyes flew wide in comprehension. "No!" Garona spat.

The very thought of such betrayal was wounding her. Llane saw it. But he would have asked this same favor of Lothar, had the position been the same. Even of Taria.

"You were a slave," he continued mercilessly. "You could be a leader. I'm not leaving here alive, Garona. That *thing* is going to kill me. But if you did so first—if you could claim killing the human's *warchief*... You know us, Garona. You *know* us— and you care for us."

He reached for her hand that clutched the small knife Taria had given her, grasping her wrist. "Survive. Bring peace between orcs and humans. He paused. "I can't save my people, not now. But *you* can."

"By slaying the king, my friend." She was angry, insulted... hurt.

"You must."

It was blunt, and it was true, and it was very orcish of him to say it. Llane knew that; knew that if she had learned to see the good in humans, he and others had learned to see the good in orcs. But Lothar, Khadgar... Taria... they would not know, not at first, about this dreadful bargain. About a possible future for humanity bought with the blood of a king. Garona knew this, too. She would be throwing away true acceptance for false honor.

Llane saw in her eyes that she could not do it. He felt a surge of despair and turned away. The battle still raged. His people were still dying. And the monstrous thing that had once been an orc lumbered inexorably toward him, his eyes glowing green with fel energy.

Llane didn't want to die. He wanted to live, to be with his wife and children, celebrate weddings, and births, to drink a pint with Lothar and Medivh, to see harmony in his realm. To discover how beautiful his Taria would look with laugh lines and the white hair of wisdom.

But Death was coming, and he would meet it bravely. It was all that was left to him. He drew his sword and stood facing the orc they called Blackhand.

It was then that he felt the touch against his bare throat. Cool fingers, their brush feather-light, the calluses of years scratching gently at his skin. Almost tenderly, those fingers slipped under his chin and tilted his head back.

Yes.

Llane exhaled a sigh of relief and gratitude, closing his eyes and yielding to that touch, willingly offering his throat to the woman standing behind him. If killing was ever an act of love, he knew this was one such. Garona would do as he had asked her, although he knew it broke her heart. His only regret was for the hatred she would be forced to endure until the time came to set things right.

His death would not be in vain—nor would, he prayed to the Light, Garona's torment be.

He was thinking of Taria, her wide, gentle eyes, the sweet, secret smile that was only for him, as his queen's own dagger, held in the hand of the truest of friends, ended his life.

As his gryphon dove, her body responding to the urgency she could feel in her rider, Lothar saw a scene of madness. There was the gate, closed now, thanks to his efforts and, more importantly, Khadgar's. Most of the cages were open and empty of prisoners.

But in the panorama beneath him, of moving bodies and the orange glow of fires, Lothar saw very few glints of Stormwind armor in a sea of green and brown skin. He scanned frantically for the king's banner, but did not spy it. What was left of three legions was a pathetic handful of soldiers and horses, forming a final and impossible defense at the base of the portal that now opened onto nothing at all.

Where was Llane? Where was his king?

The gryphon dropped like a stone. Lothar clutched his sword with his right hand, and clung like a burr with the other. His eyes swept the scene, searching for the best place to attack.

There.

Blackhand was the warchief's name. The one whose hand Lothar had taken—and the one who, in return, had taken Lothar's child. He was even more abominable than before, huge, unnatural, swinging his weapon almost leisurely. The few who were left of Stormwind's finest were falling before him at a rate that would have been comical if it hadn't been so galvanically terrifying.

There came a glint of color as Blackhand hoisted a fallen soldier. The knight was passed along from one orc to another like a wineskin at a festival, the orcs laughing and jostling it. Lothar caught a flash of blue and yellow, and armor that was decorated and exquisitely carved—

Red sheeted over Lothar's vision. He must have screamed, because his throat hurt suddenly, and there was a terrible sound in his ears over the din of battle.

The gryphon landed directly on top of a green-skinned orc, and began shredding him with her beak, talons, and hind legs. Lothar sprang from her back, stabbed at an orc too shocked to respond in time, and seized his mace as the greenskin fell.

Llane. Llane.

They had dropped him, his king, his brother, to turn and fight the strange death that had appeared so unexpectedly from the sky. Heedless of his own injuries from the fight with Medivh, indeed of anything other than the swing of his sword and where his friend lay on the hard, dry ground, Lothar fought his way toward the crumpled figure.

Llane—

He was sprawled on the ground, face down, but his armor was unmistakable. He wore no helm, and

Lothar's body turned to ice as he saw the dagger protruding from Llane's throat.

He had ordered this dagger made when his sister had turned thirteen. He knew every line of it. And he knew to whom Taria had chosen to bestow it, as a gesture of trust.

Lothar continued to kneel, to stare, to question the evidence of his eyes. Strangely, in this awful moment of loss and failure, of betrayal and broken hearts and devastation, all he could think was *why did you take off your helm, Llane? Why did you take off your helm?*

Slowly, as his traitorous heart continued to beat instead of stopping and hurtling him into death alongside his brother, Lothar again became aware of his surroundings. A few feet away, the gryphon was screaming, defending him as he crouched, shocked almost beyond reason, over the body of his assassinated liege.

He could fight. He could die too, here, taking more than a few of them with him. But all Lothar wanted was to take Llane home. He would not leave him here, to be tossed about by laughing orcs, to be the center of some barbaric display of triumph. Llane was going home. Lothar had failed to save him. He owed him this, at least.

He heaved Llane's body, armor and all, over his shoulder, staggering just a little before marching toward the still-combative gryphon. The orcs near him were so astonished at his behavior that they failed to challenge him.

"Stormwind!" he shouted to the gryphon as he put one foot in the stirrup and flung himself the rest of the way. With the effortlessness of a beast that had been trained for just such demands, the gryphon ducked and twisted her body, propelling Lothar and his precious cargo safely onto her back.

She had leaped upwards when suddenly she came to a jerking, violent halt. Lothar whirled to see Blackhand's hideous face leering up at him. His remaining natural hand had closed firmly around the gryphon's hock, and although her wings beat frantically, the warchief hauled her back down to earth.

Lothar must have fallen, for the next thing he knew, he was flat on his back, staring up at a ring of ugly faces peering down at him. Slowly, painfully, he turned his head just in time to see Llane's sword hurtling end over end toward him. It impaled itself in the dirt two feet from Lothar's head, gleaming unbearably brightly in the sun.

He was surprised he had not been swarmed by bellowing orcs hungry for his blood. As he got slowly to his feet, he heard them murmuring a single word: *Mak'gora*.

They had all stepped backward, leaving the area clear for two opponents: their warchief, and Anduin Lothar. One of the orcs had the gryphon's head under his arm. Another held her squirming torso. They would not hurt her; she was useful to them. Llane's body had toppled off and lay at an unnatural angle in the dust.

The sight rekindled Lothar's fury. He stood, steadying himself, looking at the crowd of silent, expectant orcs, and then at Blackhand, pacing a few yards away.

Blackhand held no weapon in his good hand. He was armed solely with the metallic claw hand; the five blades with which he had gutted Callan. Lothar willed the red haze of bloodlust to clear. He would not die under its obscuration.

Slowly, he picked up his brother's sword, never taking his eyes from Blackhand's glowing green ones. The orc stood still as a statue save for breathing that lifted, then let fall, his obscenely broad green chest. He recalled the silent vow he had made Blackhand—that he would take his life. No matter what it took.

Whatever Lothar did now, he was meat. Garona had spoken glowingly of the "honor" of orcs; honor that, it seemed, allowed them to betray those who had trusted them, and drive a knife into the throat of one of the finest men Lothar had ever known. They had no honor. They had only bloodlust, and conquest, and death.

Still, the orcs did not charge.

Lothar arranged his fingers about the hilt, remembering how often he had seen it in Llane's hands as they sparred, or fought in earnest. Against trolls. Against uprisings.

But it had fallen from his grip against orcs.

Still. Steady.

And then Blackhand charged.

He moved swiftly for such a mountain of a

monster. Lifting his enormous clawed hand, the fel twining about it like snakes, he screamed his victory cry as he bore down upon the human, so much smaller than he and armed with a single sword.

Lothar surrendered to his training, into the trust of his brother's spirit to guide his hand. There was no justice that could be bought here today. But at least his son's killer could fall, could threaten no other parents with the loss of their beloved child. This, he could have.

He stood, waiting, then ran straight at his enemy. At the last moment, he dropped, sliding beneath the running orc, his bare feet ripped to shreds by the stony earth as he slashed upwards, using Blackhand's own momentum against him.

Blackhand cried out in pain, stumbling to a halt. He kept his feet for a heartbeat, then dropped to his knees. Lothar came up behind him, and using the full force of his body, thrust the sword deep into Blackhand's torso.

"For my son," he said, quietly. He kicked the warchief, and Blackhand pitched forward. Green blood pooled beneath him. He did not rise.

There was stunned silence. Lothar lowered his sword, glancing around at the crowd. From the distance, he heard an angry roar and orders uttered in a raspy, furious voice. Heads turned toward the sound of the voice, then back to Lothar. Doubtless, they had been given the order to kill.

He tightened his grip on the sword, ready to take as many of them with him as he could. But they stayed where they were, staring at him, their tiny, oddly intelligent eyes unreadable. One orc started to move forward, lifting an axe. Another's hand came out and touched his chest, stopping him. The first orc frowned, but lowered his weapon.

Their chieftain had wanted a duel. Lothar had given it to him, and the orcs would honor the rules of such a thing.

Lothar wished they would not.

His gaze traveled to the fallen body of his king. The orcs on the field of battle remained motionless. And then a terrible bellow rent the air. Lothar turned to see two of the ugliest things he had ever beheld approaching him. One was a hunched orc, bright green, with a long gray beard. His eyes glowed brightly with the fel—as brightly as Medivh's had done. He marched forward, leaning on his staff, horns bristling where they poked through the cloak that covered his back.

It could be none other than Gul'dan.

The other orc who stood beside him Lothar had once considered beautiful. But to him, now, Garona was more abominable than the fel-twisted creature she stood beside. Their eyes met.

Garona had to use every ounce of her strong will not to break down weeping as Lothar stared at her. How she had not done so before now, she did not know, but she needed to be stronger than she had ever been. Lothar's eyes glittered like those of a feral creature.

She could see in them his broken heart, for Llane's death, for her betrayal. He looked like he would welcome his death. But Garona would not.

"Kill him!" Gul'dan ordered, pointing a sharp-nailed finger at Lothar.

The human looked at the orc warlock for a moment, then hoisted the body of his fallen king across his shoulders—armor and all. His knees buckled, but only slightly, then Lothar turned his back on his enemy, walking steadily toward the gryphon. To safety.

"*Kill him!*" shrieked Gul'dan, froth on his green, withered lips.

The other orcs shifted their weight, but still did not move. Lothar did not slow. They were uneasy with their leader now, where once before they had followed him with something akin to worship. Something had changed, something more than the simple failure of the gate. Anduin Lothar had defeated the mightiest warrior the Horde had ever known in a fair and honorable mak'gora. The orcs would not turn against him now.

"The mak'gora is sacred, and the human has won his duel," Garona said to her former master. Her heart raced in her chest, but she kept her voice calm. She would betray nothing to either Gul'dan or Lothar. She gestured to Blackhand's fallen, gargantuan body. "Let them pay respect to their dead war chief. Let your warriors have their tradition."

But the warlock would not let it go. He turned his attention from the retreating form of the human to his Horde. "What are you waiting for?" he demanded. "I save your miserable lives and you thank me like this? Do as I say!"

His words were not having the effect he intended. In fact, Garona realized, they had just the opposite. Orcs who had looked uneasy just a moment ago now had their jaws set. Gul'dan saw it too.

"Traitors!" he spat. "Obey my orders!"

One of them, pushed too far by Gul'dan's insult, shouted back defiantly, "You would not be alive to *give* orders if you had fought Durotan fairly!"

Garona thought Gul'dan would strike down the insolent orc. But though he seemed maddened by rage, he was not yet that unwise. He sneered at them, then turned toward Lothar, who was nearly to the gryphon—and safety—by this point. "Get out of my way," he said to his defiant Horde. "I'll do it myself!"

So the noble Durotan was gone, as well. The news was expected, but it still hurt Garona, but not as much as Gul'dan's last words. Lothar might have been able to defeat Blackhand, fel-bloated though that orc had been. But he could not stand against the full might of Gul'dan's fel. He would die.

Garona knew she should let that happen. The Horde was already unhappy with their leader. If he were to kill Lothar now, there was a very good chance that they would turn on him. And if she became their leader, she could broker peace.

But Lothar would die. And Garona couldn't bear it. A peace would come, perhaps. But it would not be today. There was no hesitation in her heart or her body as she darted forward, placing herself between the man she loved, who believed her a betrayer, and the Horde leader, who believed her true.

May Gul'dan still think so, she thought, then spoke, harnessing her anger and rage into hard words. "Who will obey you if you go to war with your own kind?"

He stared at her, his green eyes venomous, her life in his hands. Calculatedly, Garona let her voice quiet to tones of reason. Earlier, Gul'dan had given her a title she had dreamed of all her life: orc. She had honor in the Horde's eyes, exactly as Llane had anticipated. The warlock could not attack her outright, but her words had to be exactly right—or she and Lothar both would die.

"You saved us, Gul'dan. Brought us to this new world. But we cannot abandon our ways. If you do this, you will lose the Horde. You are our chieftain. We already know you are strong with the fel. Now, it is time to show us a different kind of power. A chieftain puts the needs of his people first."

Unbidden, and unwanted, the memory rushed back. Standing with Taria, speaking of Durotan. *He freed me... and he is loved by his clan. He puts their needs first. Always. He is a strong chieftain.*

Strong chiefs must earn their clans' trust.

Taria, giving Garona her dagger, which Garona had returned embedded in Llane's throat.

Furiously, Garona pushed aside the image of the widowed queen, focusing only on Gul'dan. She had the power of the truth behind her, and he knew it. His eyes darted to the one orc who had spoken out, then back to her. Garona forced herself to sneer as if in anticipation as she added, "There will be other days to kill humans."

I have lost so much today. Llane. Varis and Karos. The trust of good people. You will not take Lothar, too. You will have to go through me to do so.

Lothar had paused, stiff, when Garona had placed herself between him and Gul'dan. For a horrible, wonderful moment, he thought she would explain what had happened—that she was no traitor. But no. She argued for his life, he could see that. But only for her own reasons.

The orcs who held the gryphon released her to him. He laid his friend across the creature's back and, suddenly feeling every one of his injuries, climbed up behind him.

The gryphon rose, carefully, as if she understood what she bore. As she climbed skyward, Lothar, unable to help himself, took a last look at Garona.

Their eyes met. He could not read her expression. Then, mercifully, the gryphon leaned into the wind, and her strong wings bore him away from the battlefield, away from the Horde, away from the green-skinned woman he had once held in his arms, and thought true.

23

Khadgar leaned out the window of the inn, gazing at Stormwind as it unfolded itself below him. He'd spent many hours in this room, but his gaze had been focused elsewhere: on books, on puzzles. He'd read by candlelight more than daylight. Now, his gaze roamed over the blue roofs, the beautiful white stone cathedral, and lingered on the statue to the Guardian of Azeroth.

A role that could have been his, had things been different.

"It's just as well," came a voice. Khadgar jumped slightly and looked up to see Anduin Lothar leaning against the doorframe. The older man grinned. "You would have made a terrible Guardian."

Khadgar laughed a little. "Saving the world isn't a one-man job. Never has been."

Lothar said, with unwonted kindness, "I would have helped out." He closed the door behind him and pulled out something from beneath his shirt, tossing it onto the table. It was a small dagger, exquisitely wrought, its jeweled hilt winking.

Khadgar's breath caught. "Garona's dagger."

"I pulled it from Llane's neck."

It wasn't possible. Garona would not have done such a thing. She *couldn't* have. Khadgar stared at the blade, then up at Lothar, and stated, firmly, "There has to be an explanation."

"Yes. She made her choice." Lothar's blue eyes were hard as chips of ice, but there was a tightness at their edges that spoke more of pain than of anger.

No. Khadgar didn't know how he knew it, but he did. "I don't believe that."

He didn't shrink from Lothar's perusal. At last, the commander said only, "Maybe you and I didn't know her as well as we think we did." Lothar nodded toward the dagger. "I just thought you deserved to know."

And he was gone. Khadgar stared at the blade, given by a queen to someone she had trusted, but that had, somehow, ended up in her husband's throat.

He stared at it for a long time.

Taria had dressed with great care. Her hair had been styled, her crown set upon it. Cosmetics gave her artificial color, but did nothing to conceal the pain in her eyes and exhaustion that caused her cheeks to appear hollow. And that was all to the good.

She had dressed this carefully on her wedding day, when she had formally entered her husband's life and world. She had done so then with joy, willing to share that joy with her people, as royalty should. Now, as royalty, she would be saying farewell to her husband's presence in her life, and would do so publically. Such, also, was royalty's duty.

The news had crushed her—particularly when the anguishing details of how her husband had died had been revealed to her. Lothar had not wished to disclose them, but he knew, as she did, that as queen, and the regent of the future king, she needed to know the wrenching truth.

Tears leaked out from under her lids, but she blinked them away. Yes, they were all grieving, she foremost among them. But the people of Stormwind needed her strength today, and that, Taria would give them.

Thousands were assembled, a great sea of upturned faces, stretching back to reach all the way down to the harbor itself. They did not cheer when she strode out to greet them. She had not expected them to.

Llane lay in the center, on a raised funeral pyre. Men were buried. Kings were burned. In front of him was his sword and his battered shield.

Taria stood straight as a ramrod the dwarves used for their rifles. She strode without hesitating toward her husband's body. The priests of the Light had bathed his body with care, dressed him in fine clothing, and strapped on armor that had been carefully polished. They had washed and mended the magnificent cloak which had been sullied and torn in the battle; rent by swords, and also stained where it had been fastened by a brooch about his...

She swallowed hard, leaned forward, and kissed his pale cheek. Looking out at the subdued crowd, she could see so many different types of faces. Store owners, and refugees. Humans who had come from Lordaeron and Kul Tiras. The purple robes of the Kirin Tor. And those who were not human, yet who had come to pay their respects—the elves, the dwarves, even small gnomish faces peered up at her with sadness in their eyes.

Taria had prepared no speech. She would speak from her heart, as Llane always had. Looking at the sea of faces, she abruptly decided what she wanted to say. What Llane would have wanted.

"There is no greater blessing a city can have than a king who would sacrifice himself for his people," she began. There were a few sobs from the crowd, and her own throat was tight. She continued. "But such a sacrifice must be earned. We must deserve it! You are all here today, united in a single purpose. To honor a great man's memory. But if we only show our unity to mourn a good man's death, what does that say about us?"

This was not expected, and some of the mourners looked decidedly uncomfortable. *Good,* Taria thought. *War should make us uncomfortable. Refugees, violence, fear—all this should make us uncomfortable.*

She pressed on. "Was King Llane wrong to believe in you?"

The answer was swift—one lone voice shouting, "No!" That single word was echoed by others. More and more joined in, passion and tears on the faces she beheld. *No*, these people reassured her. *Your Llane was not wrong.*

Tears sprang to her own eyes, but they were tears of pride and happiness.

The cheers were coming now. They were ready. Khadgar, who had well earned the honor of a place here beside royalty and commanders, went to Llane's pyre. Respectfully, he picked up the great blade, carrying it laid out across the palm of his hands. He strode to where Anduin Lothar stood, one arm around each of her fatherless children—his neice and nephew—and held the blade out to the Lion of Azeroth. Her brother, and her husband's best friend. She knew he had taken it when it had fallen from Llane's hands, and used it to slay the Horde's warchief. It was fitting that the weapon now belong to him. Of all assembled here today, only his grief had come close to equaling her own. He was the only one left out of a brotherhood of three. One had sacrificed himself, the other had fallen to darkness, but had recovered. Only… not quite in time.

"We will avenge him, my lady!" came a shout.

"Lead us against the orcs, Lothar!" Others echoed this cry, their voices strong. The shouts became uniform, a chant of one single word:

"Lothar! Lothar! Lothar!"

Lothar stared at the sword for a long moment, so long that Taria thought he might refuse and turn away from the duty of serving his old friend's kingdom. She needn't have worried. Lothar gripped the hilt and strode toward her, ready to stand by her side now and during whatever might come. There, he looked out at the crowd and raised the sword, as if he would cleave the very sky in twain to protect Stormwind.

No. Not just Stormwind. Not anymore.

"For Azeroth!" shouted Anduin Lothar. "For Azeroth—and the Alliance!"

The crowd took up the cheer, and as all the soldiers present lifted their swords in salute to their commander, the stones themselves seemed to echo the words: *For Azeroth, and the Alliance!*

Had it only been a few days ago, Varian Wrynn thought as he stared at his scattered toy soldiers, since he had sneaked into the throne room to play with them? It felt like forever. How had toy battles seemed important, ever, now that his life had been so irrevocably altered by real ones? His dark-eyed gaze fell to one in particular, knocked over on its side: A tiny, carved king atop his steed, with a lion's head for a helm, brandishing a beautiful, hand-painted metal sword.

Hands slipped beneath his arms and lifted him up, onto the throne of Stormwind, onto the soft, white fur that blocked the chill of cold marble. Even so, Varian shivered. The grief was new, and he had never felt anything so suffocating, so overwhelming, so powerful, in his whole brief life. His small chest shuddered with each inhalation. Earlier, he had wept, a great deal. No one had told him he should not.

He looked at Khadgar with vision that swam. The young mage smiled, sadly but sincerely. "One day, you will be king," he said. "This will be your seat, when you come of age. But never think you are alone. You have your uncle Lothar, your mother, me, and the entire Alliance at your side." The mage paused, then added, "Your father did that for you."

Varian swallowed hard. The grief was still there, but the mage's words had somehow eased it. His legs dangled. He thought of how often his father had sat here, dispensing justice, arguing strategy. Tears threatened again.

Khadgar saw it, and stepped back, extending his hand. "Come," he said. "It's late, and your mother must be wondering where you are."

Varian took Khadgar's hand, slipping off the too-big seat and stepping past the crouching gold lions. He was partway to the door when he paused and looked back. Abruptly, he ran back to the pile of toy soldiers and searched through them, finding the one he wanted.

Gently, respectfully, Prince Varian Wrynn, future king of Stormwind, picked up the carved King Llane, and set it back down carefully—this time, not fallen, but upright and noble.

As his father ever was.

* * *

War.

Not a battle, or series of skirmishes; not a single mission or campaign. War, gritty, long, brutal, and cruel.

But this time, the humans of Stormwind did not stand alone. They were not a handful of legions, but an army, anointed with the blood of a hero's sacrifice, bound by the tales those who survived told of the horrors they had witnessed. The human kingdoms—the beleaguered Stormwind, Kul Tiras, and Lordaeron—might wear different uniforms, but they marched beneath the same banner. There were nobles and raw recruits, elders and some barely of age to fight. Men marched beside women. Alongside the humans were the dwarves, grim-faced and determined, bringing their weapons and their stubbornness to the fray. Other faces were small and childlike; still others, eerily fair and sculpted.

But all the faces were dusty, sweaty, and bearing expressions of commitment.

The army halted.

Before them was a fortress. It had no clean, strong lines, as in human construction, nor was it serviceable and stable as a dwarf's; it bore no elegant swirls or false delicacy disguising masterful construction, such as an elven fortress would display. This was all bone and iron, steel and ugly angles that served a purpose, and reflected those who built it.

This was an orc fortress.

The one known as Gul'dan oversaw everything. Monstrous, green, he leaned on his staff. Below him was a sea of brown and green skins, of weapons, of simmering anger and bloodlust.

Beside the orc who was her leader, if no longer her master, stood Garona Halforcen. Although she wore armor and carried a spear, she alone among the Horde did not shout for blood, nor spit toward her enemy, and her eyes were not on the approaching army. Instead, she looked away, her gaze distant, her thoughts not on the present moment, but the past… and a future that might one day be.

EPILOGUE

The river flowed, gently, steadily. Many things had been borne along by its current over the ages. Flower petals cast by young lovers. Leaves wept by trees as they mourned the fading of summer. Twigs, and cloth, and blood, and bodies. All had been ferried by the river's detached motion.

And on this day, this hour, this minute, a basket. Such the river had carried before, but never with such contents.

The wind sighed, helping to propel the strange little ship, and it might have whispered, had there been anyone who had the ears—and the wisdom—to hear it.

You will travel far, my little Go'el, sighed the wind that was not the wind. *My world may be lost, but this is your world now. Take what you need from it. Make a home for the orcs, and let no one stand in your way. You are the son of Durotan and Draka— an unbroken line of chieftains.*

And our people need a leader now... more than ever.

The child nestled within, green-skinned and wrapped in a blue and white cloth, was unique in this world. In any world. It was tiny, and small, and helpless, like all infants, and it had needs and wants that the river, carefully though it bore him, could not meet.

And so, the river, having kept its promise, surrendered the tiny marvel. The current swept the basket into the path of fishing lines, which rang with sweet notes to announce its presence. Footsteps approached, crunching on stones as they drew near to the bank.

"Commander!" came a voice. "You need to see this!"

The basket was lifted and brought up to a face, which peered at it intently. The baby was confused. This was not a face he knew, or even similar to such a face. And so, he did what came to him as instinctively as breathing.

He scowled, took a deep breath, and voiced his challenge.

ACKNOWLEDGMENTS

What a journey this has been! Thanks must go to so many I hardly know where to begin.

First and always, to Chris Metzen, who trusted me with previous incarnations of the heroic Durotan and Draka, and many books since; to the actors, who brought them and so many other wonderful characters to vibrant life; to director Duncan Jones, who is as much a fan as any of us, and finally, to everyone who has ever taken the time to let me know how much they have appreciated my work in this world.

Thank you all for your faith in me. May your blades never dull!

For Azeroth!

ABOUT THE AUTHOR

Award-winning and eight-time *New York Times* bestselling author Christie Golden has written over forty novels and several short stories in the fields of science fiction, fantasy and horror. Among her many projects are over a dozen *Star Trek* novels, nearly a dozen for gaming giant Blizzard's *World of Warcraft* and *StarCraft* novels, and three books in the nine-book *Star Wars* series, Fate of the Jedi, which she co-wrote with authors Aaron Allston and Troy Denning.

Born in Georgia with stints in Michigan, Virginia and Colorado, Golden has returned South for a spell and currently resides in Tennessee.

Follow Christie on Twitter @ChristieGolden or visit her website: www.christiegolden.com.

For more fantastic fiction, author events,
competitions, limited editions and more

VISIT OUR WEBSITE
titanbooks.com

LIKE US ON FACEBOOK
facebook.com/titanbooks

FOLLOW US ON TWITTER
@TitanBooks

EMAIL US
readerfeedback@titanemail.com